THE CHAPERON'S SEDUCTION

Sarah Mallory

Published in Great Britain 2015
by Mills & Boon, an imprint of Harlequin (UK) Limited,
Eton House, 18-24 Paradise Road, Richmond, Surrey, TW9 1SR

© 2015 Sarah Mallory

ISBN: 978-0-263-24784-8

Sarah Mallory was born in the West Country and now lives on the beautiful Yorkshire moors. She has been writing for more than three decades—mainly historical romances set in the Georgian and Regency period. She has won several awards for her writing, most recently the Romantic Novelists' Association RoNA Rose Award in 2012 (*The Dangerous Lord Darrington*) and 2013 (*Beneath the Major's Scars*).

**Visit the author profile page
at millsandboon.co.uk for more titles**

To my wonderful family, who make life so much fun.

Chapter One

Richard Arrandale had been in Bath for less than two weeks and was already regretting his promise to stay. It was not just that Bath in August was hot and dusty, it was exceedingly dull for one used to a hectic social round. He thought of the numerous invitations lining the mantelshelf of his rooms in London, including one from a dashing matron who had been putting out lures for some time. She wanted him to spend September with her at a house party in Leicestershire, where she promised him the hunting would be excellent and the evening entertainments more to his taste than anything he would find in staid and respectable Bath.

He did not doubt it, but he had given his word to his great-aunt Sophia, the Dowager Marchioness Hune, that he would remain in Bath until she was feeling better, even if that took him into the autumn, and he would not break his promise. Sophia had been the only one to support him in his darkest hour, when the rest of the world had seemed to be against him, and now that she needed him he would not walk away.

And it was not as if she expected him to dance attendance upon her at all times; she was quite content to see him every morning before she went off to the hot baths with her nurse, and for the occasional dinner at Royal Crescent. Apart from that he was free to amuse himself. Which was why he was now whiling away the evening playing hazard in a small and select gaming hell. From the outside, there was nothing to distinguish the narrow house in Union Street from its fellows. The ground floor was a tobacconist's shop but the curtains on the upper floors were rarely drawn back, the proprietor, one Mr Elias Burton, being determined not to distract his clientele by giving them any clue of the time of day.

Richard finished his wine before casting the dice on to the green baize.

'Seven,' called Henry Fullingham, leaning closer to peer short-sightedly at the ivory cubes. 'Trust Arrandale to cast a main with his first throw.'

'Well, I am not going to wager against him matching it,' laughed George Cromby. 'His luck's in tonight.'

Richard said nothing, merely picked up his

glass, which had been replenished by a hovering waiter the moment he had put it down.

'I won't bet against him either,' grumbled a thin, sour-faced gentleman in a green coat. 'Luck, d'ye call it? His throwing is too consistent by half.'

At his words a tense silence fell over the table. Richard scooped up the dice and weighed them in his hand, fixing his gaze upon the speaker.

'What are you trying to say, Tesford?' he asked, his voice dangerously quiet.

Fullingham gave a nervous laugh. 'Oh, he doesn't mean anything, Arrandale. It's just the drink talking.'

Richard glanced around. They had been playing for some hours with the wine flowing freely. Tesford's face was flushed and his eyes fever-bright. He was glaring belligerently across the table and for a moment Richard considered pressing the man, forcing a confrontation. After all, the fellow was questioning his honour. And a duel might alleviate his current *ennui*.

'Well, I ain't afraid to place a bet,' declared Fullingham cheerfully. 'Come along, Arrandale, throw again, we're all waiting!'

The murmur of assent went around the table. Wagers were being placed and Richard shrugged. Everyone was drinking heavily and it would be bad form to call out Tesford when it was clear he was in his cups. He cast the dice again.

'Deuce!' Fullingham laughed, a measure of relief in his voice. 'He's thrown out.'

Richard smiled and signalled to the hovering servant to fill his glass once more. Hazard was a game for those who could calculate the odds and he was good at that, but it was inevitable that sometimes the dice would fall against him. He did not like losing, but he was philosophical about it.

However, after another hour's play he was considerably richer than when he had arrived.

He was a gambler, but he knew when to stop and he was just gathering up his winnings when a noisy group of young bucks burst into the room. At their centre was a fashionably dressed gentleman, slightly older than his companions, whom Richard recognised as Sir Charles Urmston.

'They'll have come from the Assembly Rooms,' observed Cromby, looking round. He raised his hand and hailed the party. 'What news, my lads? I see young Peterson isn't with you, has he breached the defences of the fair Lady Heston?'

'Aye,' replied Sir Charles. 'He is escorting her home.'

'We won't be seeing him again before dawn then.' Cromby chuckled.

'And there's more news,' declared a red-faced young man coming closer to the table. 'A new heiress is coming to Bath!'

'And are you looking to this heiress to restore your fortunes, Naismith?' drawled Sir Charles. 'I doubt she would even look at you.'

Young Mr Naismith's face flushed an even deeper crimson.

'At least I'd make her an honest husband, Urmston,' he retorted. 'Everyone knows you played your late wife false.'

There was general laughter at that, but Richard saw the shadow of annoyance flicker across the older man's face.

'So who is this new heiress?' demanded Fullingham. 'Is she young, old, a beauty?'

'Young, definitely, but as for looks no one knows,' responded Mr Naismith. 'She is the daughter of the late Sir Evelyn Tatham and she is coming to live with her stepmama, Lady Phyllida Tatham, until her come-out next year.'

'A virgin, fresh from the schoolroom,' murmured Sir Charles. 'A plum, ripe for the plucking.'

Cromby frowned, drumming his fingers on the table. 'I remember old Tatham,' he said. 'He was a nabob, bought his knighthood after he made his fortune in India.'

Mr Naismith waved one hand dismissively. 'No one cares about that now. The thing is, Miss

Tatham is his only child and she inherits every-thing!'

'Then she may look like old Tom's prize sow and she would still attract suitors,' put in Tesford, draining his glass.

Sir Charles called to the waiter to bring them more wine.

'It seems a pity to have such a prize in Bath without making some attempt to win it,' he drawled.

Cromby grinned. 'Aye, by Gad. If I were not a married man I think I'd be making a push myself.'

'If the girl is so rich she will be well protected,' said Fullingham. 'Her guardians will be looking out for fortune-hunters.'

'There are ways to persuade a guardian,' put in Sir Charles, polishing his eyeglass. 'If the heiress was to lose her virtue, for example…'

'Of course,' exclaimed young Naismith. 'They'd want her married with all speed if that were to happen.'

'So shall we have a little wager as to which one of us will marry the heiress?'

Cromby banged on the table, looking up with a bleary eye. 'No, no, Urmston, that is unfair on those of us who are already leg-shackled.'

Sir Charles spread his hands.

'Very well, if you all want to have a touch, let us say instead, who will be first to *seduce* her.'

'Much better,' agreed Cromby, laughing immoderately. 'Then we can all have a pop at the heiress.'

Fullingham raised his hand. 'There must be witnesses, mind—a trustworthy servant or some such to confirm the prize is won.'

'Naturally.' Urmston smiled. 'Waiter, tell Burton to bring the betting book and we will write this down.' His hooded eyes surveyed the company. 'But there is one here who has not yet agreed to join us, one whose reputation as a devil with the ladies is well known in London. What say you, Arrandale? I should have thought you eager for this little adventure.'

Richard did not allow his distaste to show.

'Seducing innocents has never appealed to me. I prefer women of experience.'

'Ha, other men's wives.'

'Not necessarily, just as long as they don't expect me to marry 'em.'

There was general laughter at his careless response.

'What, man?' exclaimed George Cromby. 'Do you mean you have not left a string of broken hearts behind you in London?'

'Not to my knowledge.'

'Best leave him out of it,' cried Fullingham gaily. 'He is such a handsome dog the ladies can't resist him. The rest of us would stand no chance!'

'Certainly I have not heard of Arrandale being involved in any liaisons since he has been in Bath,' murmured Sir Charles, swinging his eyeglass back and forth. 'Mayhap you are a reformed character, Arrandale,'

'Mayhap I am,' returned Richard, unperturbed.

'Or perhaps, in this instance, you are afraid of losing out to the better man.'

Richard's lip curled. 'Hardly that.'

'So why won't you join us?' demanded Fullingham. 'You are single, if the chit took a fancy to you there is no reason why you shouldn't marry her. Don't tell me a rich bride wouldn't be an advantage to you.'

Richard sat back in his chair, saying nothing. As a second son he had been expected to find a rich bride, but his brother's disastrous marriage had made him shy away from wedlock and he was determined to remain a bachelor as long as possible.

He was fortunate to have inherited Brookthorn Manor from his godfather. It was a neat property in Hampshire that included a home farm and substantial estate. Without its income he would have been obliged to seek some form of employment by now. As it was, Brookthorn gave him independence, but he knew it could not support his lifestyle for much longer. It needed careful management, but when had the Arrandales ever been good at that? Their name was synonymous with scandal and disaster.

Sir Charles was standing over Richard, a faint, sneering smile on his face. He said quietly, 'A thousand pounds says I can secure the heiress before you, Arrandale.'

Surprised, Richard looked up. 'A private wager, Urmston? I think not.'

'Very well.' Sir Charles looked at the men gathered around the table. 'There are eleven of us here.' He gestured to the hovering proprietor to put the betting book, pen and ink down on the table. 'How much shall we say? A monkey from each of us?'

'What had you in mind, Urmston?' demanded Tesford.

'We will each stake five hundred pounds that we will be the first to seduce Miss Tatham. Burton shall hold the money until one of us is successful.'

'Capital! But we should set a date on it, Urmston,' cried Henry Fullingham, his words slurring a little. 'Can't have this going on indef—indefinitely.'

'Very well,' Urmston looked around the room. 'Shall we say the next Quarter Day?'

'Michaelmas,' nodded George Cromby. 'Just over a month. That should be sufficient time for one of us to succeed.'

'Very well. Five thousand pounds to whoever can seduce the heiress by September the twenty-ninth. And of course the added prize, the possibility of marriage for those of us who are single.'

Cromby laughed. 'And if I should be successful...'

'The way would be open for one of us bachelors to snap her up,' Tesford finished for him. 'And her family would be grateful for it, too. By Jove that is an excellent suggestion. I'm not averse to spoiled goods, if they come with a fortune.'

'Quite.' Urmston placed the book upon the table and quickly wrote down the terms.

'Well, Arrandale, what do you say, does five thousand pounds hold no appeal? Or perhaps you prefer to run away, like your brother.'

A sudden hush fell over the table. Not by the flicker of an eyelid did Richard show how that remark angered him. There was a mocking smile around Urmston's mouth, challenging him to refuse. Richard looked at the pile of coins before him on the table. A thousand pounds. He had been planning to use some of it for vital maintenance on Brookthorn Manor, but now, dash it, he would show Urmston who was the better man! He pushed his winnings back to the centre of the table.

'Let's double it.'

The tense silence was broken by gasps and

smothered exclamations. One or two men shook their heads, but no one walked away.

'Very well, a thousand pounds each.' Urmston corrected the terms and held the pen out to Richard. 'That's a prize of ten thousand pounds, Arrandale.'

Richard took the pen, dipped it in the ink and added his name to the others.

'Ten thousand,' he repeated. 'Winner takes it all.'

'There.'

Lady Phyllida Tatham placed the little vase of flowers on the mantelshelf and stepped back to look around the room. She had only signed the lease on the house at the beginning of the month and had been busy decorating it to her liking ever since, finally ending with this bedroom overlooking the street. Despite the open window there was still a faint smell of paint in the air but she hoped it would not be too noticeable. The room had been transformed from a rather austere chamber to a very pretty apartment by using cream paint on the panelling and ceiling and adding fresh hangings in a yellow floral chintz around the bed and the window. The dressing table and its mirror had been draped with cream muslin and new rugs covered the floor. Phyllida dusted her hands and smiled, pleased with the results of her handiwork.

It was just such a room as she would have liked when she had been on the verge of her come-out, and she hoped it would appeal in the same way to her stepdaughter. Ellen was even now on her way from the exclusive seminary in Kent to live in Bath with Phyllida. Doubts on the wisdom of this arrangement had been expressed by relatives on both sides of the family. Phyllida's sister had merely mentioned her concern in a letter, questioning if Phyllida had considered fully the work involved in being chaperon to a lively girl only seven years her junior. Her late husband's brother, Walter, was much more forthright and had even posted to Bath to remonstrate with Phyllida.

'My dear sister, you have no idea what you are taking on,' he had told her in his pompous way. 'My niece has always been flighty, but now at seventeen she is far too hot at hand. The tales Bridget and I have heard of her behaviour at the seminary are quite shocking!'

'She is spirited, certainly—'

'Spirited!' he interrupted her, his thin face almost contorting with disapproval. 'She even ran away!'

'No, no, you have been misinformed,' she corrected him soothingly. 'Ellen and her friends slipped off to see the May fair and they were back before midnight.'

'But it is well known who instigated the adventure! Surely you do not condone her gallivanting around town in the middle of the night?'

'Not at all, but thankfully she came to no harm, as Mrs Ackroyd was quick to point out.'

'She was also quick to inform you that she could no longer allow Ellen to remain in her establishment.'

'Only because the squire had developed an... an unquenchable passion for Ellen and had taken to calling at the most unreasonable hours.'

'And Ellen encouraged him!'

'No, she wrote to assure me she had done no more than allow him to escort her back from church.'

'From Evensong. At dusk, without even a servant in attendance.'

Phyllida frowned. 'How on earth can you know all this? Ah, of course,' she said, her brow clearing. 'Bridget's bosom bow, Lady Lingford, has a daughter at Mrs Ackroyd's Academy, does she not? Bernice.' She nodded. 'I recall Ellen telling me about her when she came home to Tatham Park for Christmas. An odious tale-bearer, she called her.'

'How I came by the information is neither here nor there,' replied Walter stiffly. 'The truth is that if Mrs Ackroyd, an experienced schoolmistress, cannot keep the girl safely contained then what chance do you have? I am sorry to speak bluntly,

my dear sister, but my brother kept you too protected from the real world. You are far too innocent and naïve to be my niece's guardian.'

'I am very sorry you think that, Walter, but Sir
Evelyn left Ellen in my sole charge and I am going
to have her live with me until next year, when she
will make her come-out under my sister's aegis.
You need not worry, I am quite capable of looking after her.'

When she had spoken those words to her
brother-in-law Phyllida had felt quite confident
but now, with Ellen's arrival so imminent, she
felt a moment's doubt. Had she been foolish in
bringing Ellen to live with her? Since Sir Evelyn's
death a year ago Phyllida had been very lonely,
living retired and out of the way with only an
aged relative for company. More than that, she
had been bored. She had not realised how much
she would miss the life she had enjoyed as the
wife of Sir Evelyn Tatham. She had entered the
marriage with some trepidation and few expectations, but Sir Evelyn had shown her a kindness
and consideration she had never known at home.
She had enjoyed running his household and there
was even some comfort to be found in his bed,
although there was never the heart-searing elation she had read about in novels or poetry. That,
she knew, needed love and she had come to think
that such love, the sort that sent one into ecstasy

or deep despair, must be very rare indeed. But it did not matter, she filled her days with her new family and friends. It had been enough, and she had felt its lack during those twelve long months of mourning. She also knew from her stepdaughter's letters that Ellen was growing increasingly frustrated at her school. She wanted to be out in the world, to try her wings. When Mrs Ackroyd had written, saying that it was with the utmost reluctance she must request Lady Phyllida to remove her stepdaughter from her establishment, hiring a house in Bath for herself and Ellen had seemed the perfect solution.

The sounds of a carriage below the window recalled her wandering attention. She looked out to see her own elegant travelling chaise at the door and her smile widened. She said to the empty room, 'She's here!'

Phyllida hurried down the stairs, removing her linen apron as she went. By the time she reached the hall it was bustling with activity as the footmen carried in trunks and portmanteaux under the direction of a stern-faced woman in an iron-grey pelisse and matching bonnet. Her appearance was in stark contrast to the other female in the hall, a lively young lady of seventeen with an excellent figure displayed to advantage by a walking dress of the palest-blue velvet and with a frivolous cap upon her fair head. Phyllida's heart swelled with pride and affection as she regarded her pretty stepdaughter. Ellen was chatting merrily to Hirst, the elderly butler whom Phyllida had brought with her to Bath, but when she saw Phyllida she broke off and rushed across to throw herself into her stepmother's open arms.

'Philly! At last.' Ellen hugged her ruthlessly. 'I am so pleased to be with you!'

'And I am pleased to have you here, my love. Goodness, how you have grown, I would hardly have recognised you,' declared Phyllida, laughing as she returned the girl's eager embrace. 'Was it a horrid journey?'

'Not at all, your carriage is so comfortable and everyone we met on the journey was very kind. When we stopped for the night at the Stag we thought we should have to eat in the coffee room because a large party had taken over most of the inn, but when they heard of our predicament they were generous enough to vacate one of their parlours for us, and then last night, at the Red Lion, a very kind gentleman gave up his room to us, because ours overlooked the main highway and was terribly noisy.'

'Thank goodness you were only two nights on the road, then, or heaven knows what might have happened next,' exclaimed Phyllida. 'Perhaps I should have come to fetch you, only I wanted to make sure the house was ready.'

'And you knew I would be perfectly safe with dear Matty to look after me.'

Hearing her name, the woman in the grey pelisse looked up.

'Aye, but who has looked after my lady while I've been away?' she demanded.

'The new girl we hired, Jane, has done very well,' responded Phyllida calmly. 'I think she will suit me perfectly.'

'Do you mean Matty will no longer be your maid?' asked Ellen, wide-eyed.

'No, love, Miss Matlock would much prefer to look after you. After all, she was your nurse until you went off to school.'

'What my lady means is that I am aware of all your hoydenish tricks, Miss Ellen,' put in Matlock, not mincing matters.

'I have no hoydenish tricks,' exclaimed Ellen indignantly.

'No of course not,' Phyllida replied, hiding a smile and recognising a little of the old Ellen beneath that new and stylish exterior. 'Now let us leave Matlock to see to all your bags and we will go into the morning room. I have lemonade and cakes waiting for you.'

Thus distracted, Ellen followed Phyllida across the hall.

'Oh, it is so *good* to be with you again, Philly,' she said as soon as they were alone. 'Apart from those two weeks at Christmas I have not seen you for a whole year.'

'You know we agreed it was important that you finish your schooling, and you would have found it very dull at Tatham Park this past twelve months.'

'I suppose you are right. But I was afraid, with Papa gone, I should have to live with Uncle Walter and his family until my come-out.'

'Now why should you think that, when you know your father made me your guardian?'

'Because I know how much you dislike fuss, and with everyone saying you were far too young to be my stepmama—'

'When I first married your father, perhaps, but I am four-and-twenty now!' protested Phyllida, laughing.

'*I* know that, but you look far younger and I thought they would bully you into submission.'

Phyllida put her hands on Ellen's shoulders and looked into her face.

'I know I was very shy and, and *compliant* when I married your papa,' she said seriously, 'But I have changed a great deal since then, my love. I made my come-out fresh from the school-room and I knew nothing of society, which is a great disadvantage. I was determined you should not suffer the same way, which is why I thought a few months in Bath would be most beneficial to you.'

'And so it will be.' Ellen enveloped Phyllida in another embrace. 'We shall have such *fun* together, you and I.'

'Well, yes, I hope so,' said Phyllida. 'The past year, living on my own, has made me heartily sick of my own company. Now,' she said, leading Ellen to the table. 'Come and try some of the lemonade Mrs Hirst has made especially for you.'

The evening passed in non-stop chatter and by the time she went to bed Phyllida realised how much she had missed her stepdaughter's company. Phyllida had been just eighteen when she had married Sir Evelyn and she had made great efforts to befriend his eleven-year-old daughter. Even though Ellen had been packed off to school soon after the marriage they had remained close, much more like sisters than mother and daughter. Phyllida had always felt that to be an advantage, but as she blew out her candle she was aware that the tiny worm of anxiety was still gnawing away at her comfort.

At seventeen Phyllida had been painfully shy. She had been educated at home with her sister and had experienced nothing beyond the confines of the small village where they lived. Ellen was not shy. The select seminary in Kent where she had spent the past five years might have given her an excellent education but from her artless conversation it was clear that she had enjoyed far more licence than Phyllida had known at her age. It was doubtful she would feel any of the mortification Phyllida had experienced during her one London Season.

Phyllida had stood firm against every argument the family had put forward but now she wondered if she had been selfish to insist upon bringing Ellen to Bath. The recent elopement of the late Marquess of Hune's daughter with a penniless adventurer showed that danger lurked, even in Bath. What did she, Phyllida, know about playing chaperon to a young girl, and an heiress at that? With a sigh of exasperation she punched her pillow to make it more comfortable.

'Ellen will have me and Matty to look after her, she cannot possibly come to any harm,' she told herself as she settled down again. 'I shall not let doubts and anxieties spoil my pleasure at having Ellen with me. We shall have a wonderful time!'

Chapter Two

'Good morning, sir. Her ladyship's compliments, she hopes you will be able to break your fast with her this morning.'

Richard groaned at his valet's determinedly cheerful greeting. It was not that Fritt had woken him, nor a sore head that caused him to mutter an invective as he sat up in bed, but the memory of last night's events. Had he really signed his name to that foolish wager? He had obviously been more drunk than he realised because he had allowed his dislike of Sir Charles Urmston to get the better of him. It was too late to cry off now, it was against his code of honour to renege on a bet. Damn the man, even the memory of Urmston's self-satisfied smile had Richard fuming. The valet gave a little cough.

'As time is pressing, sir, I have brought your shaving water. I thought we might make a start…'

'Surely it can't be that pressing,' retorted Richard. 'Where is my coffee?'

'Beside your bed, sir, but her ladyship is always in the breakfast room by nine and it is nearly eight o'clock now…'

'For Gad this is an unholy hour,' grumbled Richard. 'What time did I get to bed?'

'I think it must have been about four, sir. Would you like me to inform her ladyship that you are indisposed?'

'You know that's impossible. She doesn't ask much of me, so I must do this for her.' Richard swallowed his coffee in one gulp. 'Very well, let us get on with it.'

He jumped out of bed, yawning but determined. He owed this much to Sophia. She had stood by him when the rest of the family had wanted him to disown his brother and he would never forget it.

'Hypocrites, the lot of 'em,' she had told him when the scandal broke. 'The Arrandales have always had skeletons in their cupboards. Why should they object so much to yours? My door is always open to you Richard. Remember that.'

He had been just seventeen at the time and grateful for her support. She had neither judged nor censured his conduct, even when he left Oxford and took London by storm, embarking upon a frantic round of drinking, gambling and

women. No, she had not tried to stem his outrageous behaviour; it was in his blood, his father had told him as much. Everyone knew the
Arrandales spread scandal and mayhem wherever
they went. He plunged his head into the bowl of
warm water on the washstand. He would stay in
Bath just as long as Sophia needed him.

An hour later Richard walked into the breakfast room, washed, shaved and dressed in his
morning coat of blue superfine. His great-aunt
was already sitting at the table.

'Good morning, Sophia.' He kissed her cheek.
'You are looking very well this morning.'

'Which is more than can be said for you,' she
retorted. 'I'm surprised that man of yours let you
out of your room dressed in that fashion.'

Richard laughed.

'Are my shirt points not high enough for you?'

The Dowager Marchioness of Hune gave an
unladylike snort.

'They are more than high enough. I can't abide
the fashion for collars so high and stiff men can't
move their heads, they look like blinkered horses!
No, 'tis your neckcloth. Too plain. Not a scrap
of lace. Your father wore nothing but the finest
Mechlin at his neck and wrists.'

Richard sat down at the table.

'Well, you will have to put up with me as I

am,' he replied, unperturbed by her strictures. 'It shows my affection for you that I am out of bed at this dashed unfashionable hour.'

'If you did not stay up so late you would find this a very reasonable hour to be up and about.'

'If you say so, ma'am.'

She gave him a darkling look. 'Don't think I don't know how you spend your evenings.'

'Gambling, I admit it.' He grinned. 'It could be worse. I am avoiding the muslin company.'

'I should think so, after that latest scandal in town. From what I hear you were not only involved with the wife of a government minister, but with his mistress, too.'

'Yes, that was a little complicated, I admit. So, in Bath I will stick to the gaming tables. But you may be easy, ma'am, I never gamble more than I can afford.'

He decided not to mention last night's little wager. A mistake, that. He had no intention of joining the pack; they would be sniffing around the heiress like dogs around a bitch on heat. He hid a little grimace of distaste. He would rather lose his thousand pounds, write it off to experience. An expensive lesson and one he could ill afford, but he would not sink to that level.

'And what are your plans for today?'

Lady Hune's question surprised him. Generally she left him to his own devices until dinner time.

'Why, I have none.'

'Good. Duffy has the toothache and I am packing her off to the dentist this morning. I shall forgo my visit to the hot baths but I hoped you would accompany me to the Pump Room.'

'With pleasure, ma'am. Shall you take the carriage?'

'Damn your eyes, boy, I am not an invalid yet! If you give me your arm I shall manage, thank you.'

Richard quickly begged pardon, pleased that his great-aunt had recovered much of her old spirit in the two weeks he had been staying with her. When she had sent for him the tone of her letter had caused him concern and he had set out for Bath immediately. He had found the dowager marchioness prostrate on a day-bed, smelling salts clutched in one hand, but his arrival had greatly relieved her distress and she had soon been able to explain to him the cause of it. She had handed him a letter.

'Read this,' she commanded him. 'It is from that ungrateful baggage, my granddaughter.'

'Cassandra?'

'The very same. She has turned out to be a viper in my bosom. I took her in when her parents died, gave her the best education, petted and spoiled her and this is how she repays me, by running away with a nobody.'

Richard scanned the letter quickly.

'The signature is blotched,' he observed, 'As if tears were shed in the writing. Oh, damn the girl, I never thought Cassie would treat you in this way.'

'She thinks she is in love.'

He looked up. 'This is dated the end of July. Two weeks since!'

'I thought at first Cassie might think better of it and come back. When she did not and my health deteriorated, Dr Whingate suggested I should have someone to bear me company, which is why I wrote to you.' She gave a sharp crack of laughter. 'Whingate expected me to summon poor Cousin Julia, but she is such a lachrymose female I couldn't face the thought of having her with me.'

'I can think of nothing worse,' he agreed, with feeling. 'Well, Sophia, what do you want me to do?' he asked her. 'Shall I go after them? I drove to Bath in my curricle but doubtless you have a travelling chaise I might use.'

The old lady shook her head.

'No, they fled to the border, you know, and were married there. She is now Mrs Gerald Witney.'

His breath hissed out. 'If you had sent for me immediately I might have caught up with them.' He lifted one brow. 'I could still find them, if you wish it, and bring her back a widow.'

'And have her hate me for ever more? Not to mention the additional scandal. No, no, if she loves him let her go. Witney is a fool but I do not believe there is any harm in him. To bring her back would only cause more gossip. It was a seven-day wonder here in Bath of course, everyone was talking of it at first, but that has died down now.' She sighed. 'Her last letter said they were taking advantage of the peace to go to Paris. Cassie always wanted to travel, so I hope she is happy with her nobody.'

'I take it you forbade the banns?'

'Of course I did. As soon as I saw which way the wind was blowing I made enquiries, told her Witney was a penniless wastrel but she would not listen, she had already lost her heart. I did my best to confound them, with Duffy's help, but she slipped away in the night. Laid a false trail, too, sent us careering in the wrong direction. By the time we discovered the truth they had already reached Gretna and were married.' She scowled. 'I have no doubt that was all Cassie's idea, too. She is by far the more intelligent of the pair and not afraid to cause outrage!'

'She is a true Arrandale, then.' Richard gave a wry smile. 'It's in the blood, ma'am. There ain't one of us that hasn't caused a scandal of some sort. Why, if what they say is true, you yourself ran off with Hune.'

'But at least he was a marquess, and rich, to boot! No, I told Cassie I would not countenance her marriage to Witney. His birth is acceptable but he has no fortune, no expectations. Not that that bothered Cassie, she fell for his handsome face. Oh, he is pretty enough, I'll grant you, and amiable, too, but he has not a feather to fly with.'

'Then how will they manage?'

'She took all her jewels. She must sell them and live on that until she gains her majority next year. Then she will have a pretty penny to her name, enough to dispel any lingering gossip. They will be rich enough to be accepted everywhere. 'Tis the way of the world.'

The dowager had shed a few uncharacteristic tears then, and Richard had made his promise to stay.

Cassandra's elopement had not been mentioned since, but it was clear that Sophia had been badly shaken by the incident and Richard was too fond of his great-aunt to abandon her until her health and spirits were fully returned. Thus it was that shortly after noon on a sunny day in late August Richard escorted Lady Hune to the famous Pump Room.

Their progress was slow, for Lady Hune was well known in Bath and they encountered many of her acquaintances, all of whom wished to stop and enquire after her health. They were distantly polite to Richard, making it very clear that he was only tolerated because of his connection to the dowager marchioness. He expected nothing else, given his reputation. After all, he was an Arrandale: they lived hard, played hard and devil take the hindmost.

The Pump Room was busy and noisy, echoing with chattering voices.

'I know now why I have not been here since I arrived in Bath,' muttered Richard as he led his great-aunt through the crowd. 'The great and the good—and the not so good—gather here to gossip about and pass judgement upon their acquaintances. By George how they stare!'

'Most likely they are wondering who my handsome escort can be.' Sophia chuckled.

'Oh, I know most of 'em,' he replied bitterly. 'It is more likely they think no son of the shamed house of Arrandale should be allowed to sully these hallowed portals, especially one whose brother was branded a murderer.'

Sophia tapped his arm with her fan. 'Enough of that nonsense, Richard. You forget that I, too, am an Arrandale.'

'But you married your wealthy marquess, ma'am. That lifts you out of the mire surrounding the family's name. Look at them all. They smile now, but when trouble descends they will not hesitate to tear one apart, like hounds scenting blood, as I know only too well.'

'Not all of them. The Wakefields, for example, are charming people. I see Lady Wakefield is here today, would you like me to introduce you?'

'No need, I am acquainted with the son and I agree, they set no store by my wicked reputation. But they are the exception. The rest live for gossip. You told me how they all gloated over Cassie's elopement, how can you bear to be polite to them now?'

'Easily,' she replied. 'We nod and smile and return each other's greetings with equal insincerity. Hush now, Lady Catespin is approaching.'

'My dear Lady Hune!' A gushing matron bore down upon them, her generous proportions swathed in yellow sarcenet and a feathered bonnet perched on her improbably black curls. Richard was forcibly reminded of a galleon in full sail and was obliged to hide a grin as his great-aunt responded to the lady's fulsome greeting.

'And Mr Arrandale, too, what a pleasure to see you here, sir. I heard you were in Bath, but our paths have not crossed since we met in town—when was it—Lady Whitton's rout, I believe?'

He bowed. 'I believe you are right, ma'am.'

The matron turned back to Lady Hune, saying with blatant insincerity, 'It must be such a comfort to you, ma'am, to have Mr Arrandale staying with you in Royal Crescent. The house must feel so empty with poor Lady Cassandra gone.'

Sophia's claw-like fingers dug into Richard's arm and he covered her hand with his own, giving it a little squeeze of support.

'Yes, Lady Cassandra has married her beau,' he said easily. 'We received a letter from her only the other day, did we not, Aunt? She is ecstatically happy.'

Lady Catespin blinked, her look of spurious sympathy replaced by one of surprise.

'Oh. You…you *approve* of the match?'

'We do not challenge it,' put in Lady Hune, every inch a marchioness. 'I might have preferred a different husband for her, but one cannot always regulate one's affections. My granddaughter is lawfully married now, there is nothing more to be said.'

'Ah, of course. I see.' The wind might have been taken out of Lady Catespin's sails, but she was not yet becalmed. 'And you are here to support your great-aunt, Mr Arrandale. Your family is no stranger to tribulation, is it, sir, what with your brother…?' She gave a gusty sigh and turned her eyes back to Lady Hune. 'I am sure your great-nephew will know just how best to comfort you, my lady.'

'He would, if I needed comfort,' retorted Sophia, losing patience. 'What I *do* need is his arm to push through the crush of gossiping busybodies one finds in the Pump Room these days!'

Lady Catespin drew back at that, flushing beetroot.

'That's spiked her guns,' murmured Richard as they walked away from the speechless matron. 'I thought you said we should merely smile and ignore their barbs?'

'I forgot myself. Bad enough that she should goad me about Cassie, but to bring up something that happened years ago was more than flesh and blood can bear!'

Richard shrugged. 'You have no need to rush to my defence. I have grown used to the censure, even from my own family. Everyone except you thought I was wrong to stand by my brother, ma'am.'

'I really do not know why they were all so quick to condemn Wolfgang. Nothing was ever proved.'

'But Father was convinced he murdered his wife. Convinced enough to try to break the entail.'

Lady Hune waved one dismissive hand. 'Whatever Wolfgang has done he is still your brother. The world is too quick to censure, in my opinion, and in Bath they are more self-righteous than anywhere else.'

'Dash it, Sophia, if that is the case why do you stay?'

'For my health.' She added with a wicked glance, 'And the fact that I enjoy gossip as much as anyone. There is very little else to do when one is my age!'

They had reached the pump and waited silently while a bewigged-and-liveried footman dispensed a beaker of the warm water to Lady Sophia. She sipped it with obvious distaste while Richard stood patiently beside her. Glancing around the crowded room, he nodded to a few acquaintances, including a couple of gentlemen from the gambling hell. He was just wondering how much longer his great-aunt would want to remain when he heard her exclaim.

'Ah, I was wondering if she would make an appearance today.'

'Who, ma'am?' He was at that moment observing a rather handsome brunette who was casting roguish looks in his direction and so did not look round.

'Phyllida Tatham. And she has brought her stepdaughter with her.'

The heiress. Richard's interest sharpened immediately. The dashing brunette was forgotten and his eyes moved to the door, where two ladies were hesitating on the threshold. They were both fashionably attired but his eyes were immediately drawn to the dainty blonde dressed in a cream-muslin gown with a blue spencer fastened over it. A straw bonnet rested on her golden curls, held in place by a blue ribbon, tied at a jaunty angle beneath one ear. This enhanced the startling perfection of her heart-shaped face with its straight little nose and huge, cornflower-blue eyes. Her companion was slightly taller and far less striking in a simple walking dress the colour of rose leaves with a matching cap pinned to her neat brown hair. At least, he considered her less striking until she spotted Lady Hune and a sudden, wide smile transformed her countenance. He was reminded of the sun breaking through on a cloudy day.

'Ah, good. She's seen me and is coming over.'

Richard stifled an exclamation. '*That* is Lady Phyllida? Why, she is scarcely older than her stepdaughter.'

'Tatham married her almost out of the schoolroom,' Sophia told him. 'Nice gel, never a hint of scandal to *her* name, although there was no end of talk at first, because Sir Evelyn was almost in his dotage.'

'Lady Hune.' The widow came up and sank into a graceful curtsy before the marchioness. 'I am very glad to find you here, for I would like to present my stepdaughter to you.'

So this was the heiress. Richard surveyed Miss Ellen Tatham with a coolly professional eye. She was certainly a beauty, from her guinea-gold curls to the dainty feet peeping out beneath the hem of her embroidered muslin. Her figure was good, her tone lively without being strident and she bore herself well, greeting Sophia with a pretty deference that he knew would please. Great heaven, even without a fortune every red-blooded male in Bath would be falling over themselves to court her!

'…my great-nephew, Richard Arrandale.'

Sophia was presenting him to Lady Phyllida. He dragged his attention back, summoning up a careless smile as he reached for the lady's hand. Her eyes widened, dilating as he grasped her fingers. What the devil? Richard concealed his surprise: he had not said or done anything to frighten her. She must know of his reputation, he thought as he kissed her hand and felt it tremble, but she replied calmly enough to him and stepped back to introduce her stepdaughter.

Surely the young widow could not have sole responsibility for this piece of perfection? But it appeared to be so, for even as he addressed Miss Tatham, Lady Phyllida was explaining as much to Sophia.

'Ellen is going to live with me in Bath until the spring,' she was saying in her soft, musical voice. 'Then we go to London, to my sister, Lady Olivia Hapton, who is to bring Ellen out.'

'And will you return to Bath afterwards, Lady Phyllida?' asked Sophia.

'Perhaps, I have not considered. I moved here so that I might have Ellen with me. I thought we could enjoy a little society while she continued her education through the winter.'

'Philly—that is,' Ellen corrected herself with a mischievous look, '*Stepmama* has kindly organised lessons for me in singing, dancing and Italian. Of course I learned all those things at school, but one can always improve.'

'Indeed, it is never too late to improve oneself,' agreed Sophia. Richard felt rather than saw the look she cast at him. 'No doubt you will be attending the balls and concerts, too?'

'Oh, yes, ma'am. That is all part of my education, ready for my come-out in London next year.'

'A very pretty-behaved child,' opined Sophia when Lady Phyllida led her stepdaughter away a short while later. 'Pretty face, too.'

'Exceptional,' agreed Richard. 'A veritable diamond.'

'She has everything,' continued Sophia slowly. 'She is handsome, of good birth and has a considerable fortune, just like—'

She broke off as an elderly gentleman approached and Richard stood back, lost in thought as they conversed. He guessed what she had been about to say.

Just like Cassandra.

Sophia was clearly on good terms with the widow and inclined to approve of her stepdaughter. Thank heaven she did not know about the wager!

'So you have stolen the march on us already with the heiress.'

A soft, drawling voice intruded upon Richard's reverie and he turned to find Sir Charles Urmston at his shoulder.

'Quite a piece of perfection, isn't she?' Urmston continued, raising his glass to study Miss Tatham, who was now on the far side of the room talking with the Wakefields. 'I had thought Miss Julia Wakefield the most attractive girl in the room, but her prettiness is quite eclipsed by Miss Tatham's golden beauty. A fortune is always worth pursuing, but when it comes so deliciously packaged, how can one resist?'

Richard frowned. The idea of Urmston pursuing Ellen Tatham did not please him. Sir Charles was a cousin of Richard's late sister-in-law and they had met upon occasion, but Richard had not felt any inclination to pursue the acquaintance following his sister-in-law's premature demise eight years ago. Richard sensed a cruel and predatory nature behind Urmston's ready smile and urbane manners. He had met his sort before, a charming man about town, befriending eager young bucks and helping them to spend their—or rather their family's—fortune. He did not condemn Urmston for his way of life, after all a man must live.

It was no secret Urmston had bullied his wife, who had died in childbirth a year ago, along with their unborn baby. The idea of any innocent young girl being cruelly tricked into marriage and treated badly was not something Richard could condone, yet he had signed up to the wager, along with the others. His frown deepened as he considered the men who had put their signatures in the book. There was no doubt that any one of them would cold-bloodedly ruin the girl in order to win the prize money. That thought proved equally distasteful, though he knew seductions such as this were common practice. And it was not only Ellen Tatham who would suffer. A sudden vision of Lady Phyllida's distress disturbed him and he quickly pushed it away. Good God, when had he become so fastidious? He must be getting old.

Suddenly the idea of making a play for the heiress himself seemed almost sensible. He would be doing the girl a kindness if he married her, not to mention the fact that her fortune would prove very useful. If reports were true it was sufficient for him to maintain Arrandale and still keep his own family in luxury. He had not come to Bath looking for a wife but it was expected that he would settle down one day, and if Wolf should not return it would clearly be his duty to carry on the line. Perhaps he should not let this chance slip by. He glanced across the room to where Lady Phyllida was presenting her stepdaughter to Lady Wakefield. From this distance they might have been sisters.

It would be an easy seduction. The stepmother was no dragon and he had no doubt he would easily gain her approval. After that, it would be a simple matter to win the hand and the heart of the beautiful Miss Tatham. It was of little consequence whether *his* heart was engaged. He would treat her well and she would be better off with him than any of the other men who would be vying for her attentions. He had no doubt he would win, by fair means or foul. After all he was a rake, wasn't he? One of the infamous Arrandale family. And rake hell was what they did.

So now he smiled at Urmston. 'As you say, Sir Charles, how can one resist such a beauty? I give you fair warning, this is one wager I mean to win!'

Phyllida kept her smile in place as she progressed around the Pump Room, making Ellen known to her many acquaintances, but inside her heart was racing, as were the chaotic thoughts that flew around her head until she felt quite giddy. Richard Arrandale was the last man she had expected to meet in Bath. Since marrying Sir Evelyn their paths had not crossed, but seeing him again had brought it all back, that night at Almack's, seven years ago, when he had danced with her.

She remembered it all so clearly. He had been the most handsome young man she had ever seen, with his brown hair gleaming in the candlelight, and that laughing twinkle in his blue eyes. He was only a year or so older than Phyllida but already he had been a confident man about town, whereas she had been a tongue-tied young girl, fresh from the schoolroom and dressed in an unbecoming pink gown that her mother had thought the appropriate colour for a débutante. Her first and only Season had been a tortuous round of parties and dances, where she had been too shy and plain to attract the attention of any young man. She had spent long evenings sitting at the side of the room while the other young girls danced and laughed and enchanted their partners. Even those gentlemen who were persuaded to stand up with her quickly made their exit when they found that she was too shy to do more than blush and return monosyllabic answers to their attempts at conversation. She had told herself it did not matter, that she cared for none of them, and that was true, until she had danced with Richard Arrandale.

Phyllida had known his reputation—everyone in London was aware of it—but in her silly schoolgirl mind she had thought that she could tame him, that if only he could see past her rather plain looks he would be captivated by her goodness and would repent his wild ways.

How he must have despised her for her awkwardness, even though he had laughed and made light of it when she had moved the wrong way in the dance and collided with him. He had responded to her mistake by giving her his whole attention, smiling at her, putting her at her ease. He had looked at her, really *looked*, as if she was the only lady in the room. As if she mattered. At that point she had lost her heart completely. In her foolishness she had dreamed of him making her an offer, going down on one knee and declaring that he was reformed, for her sake.

All nonsense, of course. A handsome gentleman like Richard Arrandale would never be interested in a gauche schoolroom miss with mousy hair and nondescript grey-green eyes. As her newly married sister had said, when Phyllida had returned starry-eyed from Almack's that night; 'Men like Arrandale can turn on the charm whenever they wish. He will not even remember you tomorrow.'

And Olivia had been right. The next time Phyllida had seen Richard Arrandale in Bond Street he had not even noticed her. It had been a salutary lesson and when, a few days later Papa had told her she was to wed Sir Evelyn Tatham, she had buried her girlish dreams for ever.

Phyllida knew she had been right to do so. While she had concentrated on being a good wife to Sir Evelyn, Richard Arrandale had blazed a trail through London society like a shooting star, his outrageous behaviour discussed, condemned and dissected in the society pages of the newspapers. His name was linked with all the most dashing matrons, he attended the most riotous house parties and was thought to have lost more than one fortune at the gaming tables.

Everyone said it was only to be expected, for it was well known that his older brother had killed his wife and run away with the family jewels. Nothing had been proven, the matter had been hushed up as was the way with rich, powerful families, but everyone knew it all the same. Bad blood, they said, and Phyllida knew she should be grateful not to have attracted the notice of such a notorious rake as Richard Arrandale. But sometimes as she lay in her bed with her kind, worthy husband snoring beside her, Richard's image would return and she could not help sighing for what might have been.

* * *

Too late had Phyllida recognised the tall figure standing beside Lady Hune in the Pump Room and recalled that the dowager marchioness was an Arrandale by birth. She was already committed to approaching, but when Richard had taken her hand and kissed it the years had fallen away and she was once again the awkward girl in her first Season, being saluted by a man who was the embodiment of her dreams.

Only, Richard Arrandale was not the heroic figure of her girlhood fantasies. She knew that only too well and looking up into his face she had seen the faint lines of dissipation about his mouth and eyes. There hung about him a world-weariness that made him seem older than his years, for he could not possibly be more than five- or six-and-twenty. Richard Arrandale was a rake and it was only his connection with Sophia, Dowager Marchioness of Hune, that made her acknowledge him and introduce him to her stepdaughter.

Phyllida took Ellen on a full circuit of the room but afterwards she could never recall just whom they had met, nor what was said. All she could remember was Richard Arrandale's laughing eyes and the touch of his lips against her gloved hand. As she and Ellen left the Pump Room arm in arm she risked a last look back. He was still watching them, or, more correctly, he was watching Ellen.

'What is wrong, Philly?' Ellen stopped in the doorway and turned an anxious gaze upon her. 'You are shivering, but it is not at all cold. Are you unwell?'

'What? Oh, no, my love, no, not at all.' She shook off her uneasy thoughts and summoned up a smile. 'We elderly ladies are prone to sudden chills, you know.'

Ellen gave a little trill of laughter.

'Very well, my aged Stepmama! I shall take you home, tuck you up in a shawl and feed you gruel.'

'That will certainly do the trick.'

'I hope so, because you promised we could go shopping today.'

'Very well, let us do so immediately. It will be infinitely preferable to eating gruel,' said Phyllida, laughing.

The sun came out at the moment and her spirits lifted. She was foolish to allow an old memory to make her so fanciful. She squeezed Ellen's arm, quickened her step and set off for Milsom Street to indulge in a few hours of frivolous expenditure.

Chapter Three

Having decided to pursue the heiress, Richard lost no time in making his plans. The Bath season did not start until October, but he was determined not to wait until then to advance his acquaintance with Miss Ellen Tatham. At breakfast the following morning he made his first move.

'Do you wish me to come to the Pump Room with you again today, Sophia?'

'Thank you, no. Duffy had the offending tooth removed yesterday and is quite recovered now. You must have more entertaining things to do than attend an old lady.'

'It is always a pleasure to escort you, ma'am. And I was heartened to find that not all those attending the Pump Room are valetudinarians. Lady Phyllida, for example.'

'Yes. She's a quiet gel, but very sensible, and makes a good partner at whist. I have always liked her.'

This was very encouraging. He said, 'You knew her before she came to Bath?'

'We have mutual acquaintances in Derbyshire, near Tatham Park. I met her there often when Sir Evelyn was alive. Glad to see she is out of mourning now and back in the world where she belongs.'

'What's her background?' Lady Hune shot him a swift, suspicious glance and he added quickly, 'Lady Phyllida looks familiar, and I would judge her age to be similar to my own. I thought perhaps I might know her.'

'She is possibly twelve months your junior. One of the Earl of Swanleigh's two girls. The elder married Lord Hapton and Swanleigh wanted a similar success for Phyllida. She was presented in…let me see…'ninety-six and caught the eye of Sir Evelyn, who was then a widower and looking for a new wife to give him an heir. They were married within the year. Of course there was a lot of talk, but those who prophesied disaster were only half right. The hoped-for heir never materialised but the marriage seemed happy enough. When Tatham died last year it was assumed Lady Phyllida would go to live with her sister or with Tatham's brother and dwindle into mediocrity as some sort of live-in companion, little more than a glorified servant. But give the girl her due, she refused to relinquish her independence. She retired to her house in Derbyshire for her period of mourning.'

'And now she is in Bath.'

'Yes. She has taken a house in Charles Street for herself and her stepdaughter.' Sophia shook her head, adding darkly, 'How *that* will work out I don't know.'

'Ninety-six.' Richard's brow creased in thought. 'Hmm, seven years ago. I had left Oxford and was in town then.'

'Aye, you were, and already kicking up a dust!'

'I must have danced with her. Trouble is, ma'am, I danced with a deuced lot of young ladies in those days.'

'It's no wonder if you don't remember her. Her looks were never out of the ordinary, nothing to attract you. Tatham, however, was desperate for an heir. I think he would have taken anyone.' She looked up, saying sternly, 'She is a fine young woman, Richard, and I count her a friend. I would not have you doing anything to upset her.'

He looked pained.

'I promise you I have no intention of upsetting her.'

No, he had no intention of upsetting anyone, he thought, as he presented himself at the freshly painted front door in Charles Street later that day.

He was shown into the drawing room, where Lady Phyllida received him with cool politeness.

He bowed. 'I was pleased, yesterday, to renew my acquaintance with you, my lady.' Her brows went up and he continued smoothly, 'We met in town did we not, at your come-out. We danced together at Almack's.'

This was a chance shot but he thought it had hit its mark. An added flush of colour painted her cheeks, but she spread her hands and gave him an apologetic smile.

'I vow I cannot recall. I know my mother bullied every gentleman present to stand up with me, however reluctantly.'

'There was no reluctance upon my part, ma'am, I assure you.'

'But after, what is it…five years, six?...I am flattered that you should remember.'

She doesn't believe me.

Richard kept his smile in place as he met her gaze. He had thought yesterday her eyes were grey but he saw now that they were flecked with green and her look was surprisingly direct. He had a sudden urge to tell the truth and confess that he didn't remember her at all. Impossible, of course. He must hold his nerve.

She invited him to sit down.

'How are you enjoying Bath?' he asked her as he lowered himself into a chair opposite her own.

'Very much. After the isolation of Tatham Park, Bath seems very busy.'

'And will you put your name down in the book when the subscription opens later this month? That is necessary, I believe, if you wish to attend balls in the Upper Rooms?'

'I shall indeed.'

'But there is still dancing to be had, even now,' he persisted. 'There is a ridotto on Monday night, did you know of it?'

'Yes, I am taking Ellen.'

'Then we will be able to dance together again.'

The tell-tale rosiness deepened on her cheek.

'I am going as Ellen's chaperon, Mr Arrandale. I shall not dance.'

There was a wistful note in her voice. Faint, but he detected it.

'Is it in the rules that widows are prohibited from dancing? I have never heard of it.'

Now why the devil had he said that? It was not the widow he wanted to dance with.

Phyllida's nerves fluttered. Had she been mistaken? Had he really remembered standing up with her at Almack's? She stole another look at him. He was being perfectly charming. Perhaps the lines that creased his lean cheeks might be caused by laughter rather than dissipation and wild living, despite the gossip. She did not think they detracted from his charm, either. If anything she thought him more attractive than ever, especially when he smiled at one in just that way...

She started guiltily when the door opened and Ellen came in, chattering even as she untied the ribbons of her bonnet.

'There you are, Philly! *Such* fun we have had, I wish you had been there to share—oh, I beg your pardon. Hirst did not tell me you had company, but then, I did not give him time!' She came forward, greeting their guest with her sunny smile and no hint of shyness. 'Mr Arrandale, good day to you.'

He had jumped up when Ellen appeared and Phyllida watched him greet her, his charming smile and nicely judged bow perfectly civil. Too perfect, she thought, her earlier suspicions rising again.

'How do you do, Miss Tatham. Have you been shopping, perhaps?'

'No, sir, I have been to Sydney Gardens with Miss Desborough and her mama. Do you know the Desboroughs, Mr Arrandale?'

'I'm afraid not, I have not been in Bath that long myself.'

'Oh, I see. Well, we were introduced yesterday and Penelope and I found ourselves in such accord that Mrs Desborough invited me to join them in a walk to Sydney Gardens today. Oh, I wish you had come with us, Philly, it was quite delightful. The Ride that runs around the perimeter of the gardens is very well laid, so one can keep one's shoes and feet dry even if the weather has been very inclement. And there is a labyrinth, too, but there was no time to go in and Mrs Desborough says we should buy a plan before we attempt it.'

'Then we shall do so, when we visit.' Phyllida smiled.

'Perhaps I might escort you.'

Phyllida acknowledged Richard's offer with a slight inclination of her head but she did not encourage him. Unperturbed he returned his attention to Ellen.

'I understand you are attending the ridotto on Monday, Miss Tatham. I hope you will stand up with me. If your stepmama allows it, of course.'

'I should be delighted, sir—and you will consent, will you not, Philly?'

Phyllida was tempted to refuse, but Ellen would be sure to demand the reason and she was not at all sure of the answer.

'Of course,' she said at last. 'There can be no harm in you dancing with a gentleman.' Would he notice the slight stress she put on the last word? 'After all, the reason for bringing you to Bath was to accustom you to a larger society.'

'And I have any number of acquaintances in Bath now,' declared Ellen happily. 'Not just

Penelope Desborough and Julia Wakefield, who are my especial friends. Mrs Desborough was good enough to present *several* gentlemen to me today when we were in the gardens.'

'Did she?' murmured Phyllida, slightly startled by this revelation.

Ellen threw her a mischievous glance. 'I have no doubt some of them will be seeking you out soon, Philly, for they, too, mentioned the ridotto. However I made it very clear I could not dance with any of them unless they had your approval.'

'I am glad to hear it.'

'And you *will* approve them, will you not, *dearest* Stepmama?'

For once Phyllida did not feel any inclination to laugh at Ellen's sauciness. She was aware of Richard watching her and, disconcerted, she responded rather more tartly that she had intended.

'Since I have approved Mr Arrandale, I doubt I will have any choice with the rest!'

'But they are all very respectable, Philly, or Mrs Desborough would not have introduced them to me.'

Ellen was gazing at her, puzzled, and Phyllida pulled herself together.

'No, of course she would not. I am sure they are all pillars of Bath society.'

A scratching at the door diverted her attention and she looked up as Matlock entered the room.

'Signor Piangi has arrived, my lady. I have put him in the morning room.'

'Oh, is it time for my Italian lesson already?' cried Ellen. 'I will come with you directly, Matty. If you will excuse me, Mr Arrandale.'

He bowed.

'Until Monday, Miss Tatham.'

Phyllida watched Ellen skip out of the room. Matlock hovered by the door, as if unwilling to leave them alone, but Phyllida waved her away.

'Go with her, Matty. You will remain in the morning room until the *signor* leaves.' Richard was watching her and she added, as the door closed upon them, 'It is important to me that no hint of impropriety should touch my stepdaughter while she is in Bath.'

He inclined his head. She thought for a moment he would resume his seat but instead he picked up his hat and gloves from the table.

'I have an appointment I must keep.' He hesitated. 'If you and Miss Tatham would like to visit Sydney Gardens on Sunday, I should be very happy to escort you there.'

'Thank you, sir, but, no. We are, um, otherwise engaged.'

It was not true, and she prayed he would not ask what that engagement might be.

'Of course. Until Monday, then.'

He bowed and was gone.

Phyllida sank back into her chair, her spirits strangely depressed. She would like to believe that Richard Arrandale had merely come to pay his respects to her, that he had truly remembered dancing with her all those years ago, but she doubted it. After all, she had never been rich enough or pretty enough to attract much attention in her one and only Season. Who wanted a soft well-modulated voice when they could enjoy Miss Anston's trilling laugh, or Miss Rollinson's lively tones? The more direct of the mothers with daughters to wed had called her thin and unattractive.

Phyllida gave herself a little shake. That was all in the past. She had lost her girlish ranginess, her glass told her that her willowy form and firm, full breasts showed to advantage in the high-waisted, low-cut gowns that were so fashionable. Yet, for all that, she paled to insignificance when compared to her lovely stepdaughter and she would be a fool to think otherwise.

Richard Arrandale had clearly set his sights upon Ellen. She remembered how he had been watching her in the Pump Room. She might ask Lady Hune to warn him off, but although she was very fond of the indomitable marchioness she could not imagine that Sophia would have much influence over her rakish great-nephew.

No. Phyllida knew it would be up to her to keep Ellen safe.

* * *

Richard strode away down Charles Street, well pleased with his first day's work. The widow was cautious, which was as it should be, but Ellen was friendly enough. Very young, of course, but a taking little thing. He frowned when he recalled how she had spoken of the fellows in Sydney Gardens clamouring for an introduction. He had no doubt that some—if not all—of them were involved in the wager, but he had the advantage and he intended that it should stay that way. However, he knew better than to rush his fences. He would dance with the chit on Monday night. None of the others were likely to steal her heart before then.

By the time Phyllida went to bed that night she had made a decision. Jane was waiting to braid her hair and help her to undress, but as soon as she had donned her nightgown Phyllida threw on her silk wrap and went to Ellen's room.

'May I come in?'

She peeped around the door. Ellen was already in her bed, propped up against a billowing mass of pillows, reading by the light of a branched candlestick that was burning perilously close to the bed-hangings. As the door opened she jumped and attempted to hide the book under the bedcovers, but when she saw it was Phyllida she heaved a sigh of relief.

'Oh, it is you. I thought it was Matty.'

'What are you reading? Is it so very bad?'

Ellen nodded, her eyes shining.

'Ambrosia, or the Monk,' she announced with relish. 'It is quite shocking. When I told Matty she promised to burn it if she found it.'

'I am not at all surprised. How did you get a copy?

'Oh, it has been circulating at school for months, but I did not have the opportunity to read it so I brought it with me. You need not worry, Philly, it is the later version, where Mr Lewis has removed the most salacious passages. Although I would dearly like to know what they were, because the story is still quite horrid in places!'

'Then you should not be reading it.'

Phyllida lunged for the book but Ellen was too quick and thrust it under her pillows, saying loftily, 'You know Papa decreed that ignorance was the worst of all sins. He always said I could read whatever I wished, as long as I discussed with him or you anything I did not understand.'

With a sigh Phyllida curled up on the end of the bed, unequal to the task of physically struggling with Ellen.

'Unfortunately I have a lowering suspicion that there is much in Mr Lewis's Gothic tale that I would not understand,' she admitted. 'I am wondering if I have done you a grave disservice in bringing you to Bath, Ellen.'

'No, how could that be?' Ellen frowned suddenly. 'Has Uncle Walter been complaining to you again? Aunt Bridget wrote and invited me to go and stay with them, but I know the only reason she did so is because they do not approve of my coming to live with you.'

'No, it is nothing like that, but—' Phyllida stopped, considering her words carefully. 'There are…dangers in society, Ellen.'

'What sort of dangers?'

'Gentlemen will sometimes prey upon innocent young women, especially if they are…'

'If they are rich,' finished Ellen, nodding sagely. 'I am well aware of that. Mrs Ackroyd was at pains to make sure we all knew the risks that gentlemen posed.' Again that mischievous light twinkled in her blue eyes. 'She prepared us very well, I think. I may even know more than you, Philly.'

'That is very possible,' replied Phyllida, sighing. 'You have had a very good education and I am sure the teachers told you much about the world, but it is very easy to have one's head turned and succumb to the attentions of a personable gentleman.' Phyllida saw the speculative look in Ellen's eye and added quickly, 'At least

I believe it is so, although I have never experienced it myself.'

'Poor Philly. Did Papa snabble you up before you could fall in love with anyone?'

'Yes—no! Ellen, that is not the point.'

Ellen laughed.

'I think it is very much the point, my love. You were very young and innocent when you became my stepmama, were you not? Seventeen, in fact. As I am now.'

'Quite. And I was very shy and retiring.'

'Which I am not, so you may rest easy, my love.'

Phyllida shook her head at her. 'You may think you know the ways of the world, Ellen, but there are gentlemen in Bath who may seem very pleasant and respectable, yet they are not to be trusted.'

'Do you mean rakes?' asked Ellen. 'There were several residing near the school, hoping one of us would be foolish enough to run off with them. Mrs Ackroyd pointed them out to us.'

'Heavens, I knew nothing of this!'

'No, well, I could hardly write and tell you about it, you would have wanted to fetch me away immediately. In fact we had to sit on that sneak Bernice Lingford to stop her from gabbing about the whole. It's a pity she doesn't have a fortune, because without some incentive no one will ever want to run off with her.'

'Ellen!'

'Well, it is true,' replied Ellen. 'She is a spite-ful, greedy cat, so no man could like her, even if she wasn't buck-toothed and fusby-faced.'

'Let us hope she will grow out of it,' replied Phyllida, trying to be charitable. 'However, we are straying from the point—'

'The point is, Stepmother dear, that we were all perfectly safe at school. That was why Papa chose Mrs Ackroyd's institution for me, because she is accustomed to having the daughters of the very rich in her care.' Ellen drew up her knees and wrapped her arms about them. 'She is very progressive, though, and thinks that education is the best preparation for any young lady making her come-out. She taught us what to expect from a husband, too, because she says mothers invari-ably make a hash of it. '

Phyllida blinked, momentarily silenced by her stepdaughter's matter-of-fact statement.

'I am very glad of it,' she said at last. 'But I would still urge you to be cautious. It is very easy for a young lady to lose her heart to a rake.'

'But you said *you* never had done so,' objected Ellen.

Phyllida was about to correct her but thought better of it.

Ellen continued thoughtfully, 'It is not too

late, though. We might well find you a husband in Bath.'

'I do not want a husband! That is not why I came here.'

'But you said yourself you were lonely at Tatham Park.'

'That is true, Ellen, but only because I was missing your father. And you. I am very much looking forward to our time here together.'

'But once I have made my come-out, what then? I have no intention of settling upon a husband too soon but I suppose I must marry at some point and then you will be alone again.'

Phyllida felt the conversation was getting away from her. She said crisply, 'I am glad you do not intend to rush into marriage with the first young man who takes your fancy, so I need not contemplate my future for a long time yet.' She slid off the bed. 'Now, I have said what I wanted to say, although it would seem Mrs Ackroyd has already prepared you for the perils of the world, so I shall leave you to sleep.' She leaned close to kiss Ellen's cheek and felt the girl's arms wind about her neck.

'Goodnight, my darling stepmama. We shall have such fun in Bath together.'

Phyllida gave Ellen a final hug and made her way back to her own room. The discussion had not gone quite as she had imagined and she was beginning to suspect that looking after Ellen would be far more challenging that she had anticipated.

The next few days were filled with shopping and visitors. None of the gentlemen Ellen had met in the park were brave enough to call at Charles Street uninvited but when Phyllida took her step-daughter to the morning service at the Abbey on Sunday it seemed that every one of her acquaintances wished to perform an introduction to Mr This or Sir That. Ellen behaved impeccably, but Phyllida found herself scrutinising every gentleman who came up to her, watching for signs that they might be trying to fix their interest with Ellen. There were several married gentlemen amongst their number, such as Mr Cromby whose jovial, avuncular style was not to her taste. Neither did she warm to the fashionably dressed widower, Sir Charles Urmston, although he appeared to be a favourite of Mrs Desborough, who made the introduction.

Phyllida noticed Lady Hune coming out of the Abbey on the arm of her great-nephew. The dowager looked magnificent, as always, in black and silver but Phyllida's eyes were drawn to Richard's lean upright figure. She thought how well the simple lines of the dark coat and light-coloured pantaloons suited him. When he removed his hat to bow to an acquaintance, his short brown hair glinted with gold in the sunlight. He looked like the epitome of a gentleman and she stifled a sigh. How deceptive appearances could be. The marchioness was moving through the crowd towards her carriage, but when she saw Phyllida she stopped and beckoned to her. Ellen was deep in conversation with Julia Wakefield and Phyllida did not call her away, preferring not to bring her into Mr Arrandale's orbit more than necessary.

Lady Hune greeted Phyllida cordially and invited her to take tea with her later, a singular honour that Phyllida had no hesitation in accepting on behalf of herself and her stepdaughter. Too late did she recall that she had told Richard they were not free. She saw the laughter in his eyes and felt the heat rising to her face.

'Your previous engagement today has been cancelled, perhaps?' he murmured.

'You are promised elsewhere?' said Lady Hune, overhearing. 'My dear, you must not break your engagement on my account.'

Phyllida shook her head, saying hastily, 'I had mistaken the day. We should be delighted to join you, ma'am.'

Richard Arrandale was in no wise discomposed by the fulminating glance she threw at him, merely casting a grin in her direction before he turned aside to greet another acquaintance.

'I am glad you can come.' Lady Hune nodded.

'You will be able to tell me how your charming stepdaughter goes on in Bath. Very well, if appearances are anything to go by.'

Phyllida followed the dowager's eyes to where Ellen was now part of a lively crowd of young people.

'She has already made new friends of her own age, Lady Hune.'

'Which is as it should be—' The dowager broke off as Ellen and Julia Wakefield ran up, their faces alight with excitement that could barely be contained while they made their curtsies. The old lady's eyes gleamed with amusement.

'You are clearly big with news,' she observed solemnly. 'You had best get it out before you burst.'

Julia giggled and Ellen, after a blushing smile towards Lady Hune, turned her expressive eyes towards Phyllida.

'Lady Wakefield says there are the most romantic Gothic ruins just a few miles from Bath at Farleigh Castle. We are on fire to see them and Lady Wakefield says she will set up a riding party, if only you will give your permission, Philly. Dearest, do say I may go. Lord and Lady Wakefield will be accompanying us and Julia has a spare pony that I may ride—'

Laughing, Phyllida put up a hand to stop her.

'Of course you may go, and there is no need

to borrow a horse, for Parfett is even now bringing our own horses from Tatham Park. I thought
we might like to ride out occasionally before the
weather closes in.'

'Will you come, too, Lady Phyllida?' asked
Julia in a breathless whisper, 'It will be delightful
if you can, I am sure—' She broke off, blushing
scarlet when she realised her company. 'And Lady
Hune, of course,' she added hurriedly.

'My riding days are over,' replied the dowager, choosing to be amused by Julia's artlessness.

'If Lady Wakefield is going with you then you
do not need me to come,' said Phyllida, not wishing to put herself forward. Besides, she had made
up her mind not to be a clinging chaperon. 'You
may go off and enjoy yourself with my goodwill.'

Lady Hune turned to Julia.

'Does your mama know the family at Farleigh
House?' When the girl shook her head the dowager continued. 'Tell her to write to the housekeeper there, mention my name and I have no
doubt she will receive you.'

'Th-thank you, ma'am,' stuttered Julia, wide-
eyed.

'Well, off you go and tell your mother to arrange the whole,' Lady Hune dismissed her impatiently.

Ellen looked to Phyllida and, receiving a nod,
she curtsied and ran off after her new friend.

Lady Hune tutted. 'She will keep you busy, Phyllida.'

'I think she will, ma'am, but I shall enjoy the distraction, after spending so long alone.'

'I am glad you are come to Bath. You were too young to be incarcerated at Tatham Park.' The dowager tapped Phyllida's arm with one be-ringed finger, saying urgently, 'Find yourself a husband, Phyllida. You are still young and Tatham left you well provided for, so you need not regard the money. This time you can marry to please yourself.'

Phyllida blushed hotly. 'I assure you, my lady, I was perfectly happy—'

'Aye, but no need to tell me it wasn't a love-match.'

'Perhaps not, but Sir Evelyn was a kind husband, and I have a duty to his daughter.'

'Of course, and I know you well enough to be sure you will do your best for the gel, but do not sacrifice your own happiness, Phyllida.' She looked up as her great-nephew came up.

'There is a chill wind getting up, ma'am. Shall I escort you to your carriage?'

'Very well, although I am not so frail that I cannot withstand a little breeze.' She looked back at Phyllida, a decided twinkle in her faded eyes. 'You see how I am bullied?'

'I dare anyone to try and bully you, ma'am.'

Phyllida laughed and without thinking she looked at Richard Arrandale, knowing he would share her amusement. The noise and bustle around them ceased to exist as he drew her in with a smile of genuine warmth. The moment felt special, as if they were the only two people in the world. Phyllida's heart leapt to her throat before settling back again, thudding so hard against her ribs that she found it difficult to breathe.

Lady Hune's sharp voice broke the spell. 'You can take me home now, Richard. I shall expect you later, Lady Phyllida!'

Phyllida did not move as they walked away. Suddenly the sun did not seem as bright and she became aware of the cold wind that Richard had mentioned. That was the trouble with the man, she thought, putting her hand up to make sure her spencer was buttoned up. He made her forget to be sensible. She supposed it must be so with all rakes, for how else could they wreak such havoc with ladies' hearts?

Her thoughts went back to the dowager's suggestion that she should find a husband. She did not know whether to be amused or indignant. Lady Hune meant well, she knew that, and perhaps she might consider marrying again at some stage, but for now her mind was fully occupied with looking after her stepdaughter and keeping her safe from men like Richard Arrandale.

* * *

Taking tea with the Dowager Marchioness of Hune was a protracted affair and full of ceremony. Richard decided he would make himself scarce until towards the end, when he would offer to escort Miss Tatham and her stepmother back to Charles Street. Sophia would approve of his civility and his absence for most of the afternoon might prevent her from guessing his intentions towards the heiress.

His plan worked perfectly. He walked in just as Sophia was refilling the tea pot. He accepted a cup from his great-aunt and since Lady Phyllida was sitting next to the dowager he took a seat beside Miss Tatham and engaged her in conversation. He had soon put her at her ease and she chatted away to him in the friendliest manner. Well aware that they were in company and every word could be overheard, Richard said nothing untoward and made no attempt to flirt with Ellen, but since she was well educated as well as quick-witted they were soon getting on famously, so much so that when Lady Phyllida rose to take her leave and he suggested he should escort them home, Ellen was quick to support him.

Lady Phyllida smiled and shook her head. 'I am obliged to you, sir, but I think not. You have only just come in. I am sure Lady Hune would like to have you to herself for a while.'

He laughed. 'But it is only a step. I shall be back again in a matter of minutes.'

'As you say, Mr Arrandale. It is only a step, so Ellen and I will manage perfectly well, but I am grateful for your offer.'

Lady Phyllida smiled but her grey-green eyes held a steely look. It surprised him, for he had thought her a meek, biddable creature. However, he said nothing, merely inclined his head in acquiescence as the visitors went on their way.

'Well, that was much more enjoyable than I anticipated,' declared Ellen as they turned into Chapel Row on their way to Charles Street. 'And *not* just because Mr Arrandale spent a good twenty minutes talking to me! I thought Lady Hune might treat me as a child but she was very pleasant, was she not?'

'That is because she likes you,' returned Phyllida. 'And she is accustomed to having young people about her. Until recently she had her granddaughter living with her.'

Ellen stopped and turned her wide-eyed gaze upon Phyllida. 'Of course. Lady Cassandra! It was in the newspapers that Lady C—had eloped from Bath, but I had not connected her with the marchioness.'

'Yes, that was her granddaughter. The elopement took place just before I came to Bath but I know Lady Hune was distraught, and not only did she have the worry of what had happened to Lady Cassandra, she had to endure Bath's gossipmongers. I believe it has taken a great deal of fortitude.'

'How dreadful for her,' said Ellen, shocked.

'It was,' agreed Phyllida as they began to walk on. 'The gossip has died down now in Bath but it is still mentioned occasionally, even though Lady Cassandra is married and gone out of the country.'

'I had not thought of it before,' said Ellen slowly, 'but as exciting as an elopement is for the couple involved, there must be a great deal of horrid scandal to be endured by the family left behind.'

'I am glad you realise that, my love.'

Ellen slipped her arm through Phyllida's and gave it a quick squeeze.

'Do not sound so serious, Philly, I have no intention of eloping.' She added, with a mischievous gurgle of laughter in her voice, 'And woe betide any man who tries to persuade me to it!'

Chapter Four

The dancing had already started when Richard arrived at the Upper Rooms on Monday night. Miss Tatham was going down the dance with Henry Fullingham and he had leisure to admire her golden beauty, which was in no way dimmed by the simplicity of her embroidered muslin. As he stood waiting for the music to end he wondered if he had been wise to leave his arrival so late. The other gentlemen present would not waste any time in securing a dance with such a diamond. But his doubt was only momentary, and when Ellen's partner escorted her back to Lady Phyllida, Richard made his way through the crowd towards them.

Ellen greeted him with a smile of unaffected delight and an assurance that she had saved a dance for him. The widow, he noted, had looked composed, even serene, until she saw him approaching and then a slight frown creased her brow. He must try to reassure her.

'I hope you do not object, my lady?'

'Not at all, Mr Arrandale.'

The frown was put to flight by a smile and he thought how well it became her, warming her eyes and turning them a soft green. Or perhaps that was merely the reflection from her gown of sage-coloured silk. It was fashioned in the Greek style, falling in soft folds from the high waistline. Her hair was piled up and held in place by bands of matching green ribbon with a single glossy ringlet allowed to fall to her shoulder. It attracted his gaze to the flawless skin exposed by the low neckline of her gown.

A single teardrop diamond was suspended on a gold chain around her neck, drawing his attention to the shadowed valley between the softly rounded breasts. His thoughts strayed. In his imagination he was slowly untying the ribbons of the gown and pushing it aside while he laid a trail of kisses down the slender column of her neck and into that same valley...

'Mr Arrandale?'

He started as Phyllida interrupted his reverie.

'The sets are forming for the next dance.'

'What? Oh, yes.'

His eyes searched her face. Could she have read his thoughts? The hint of a smile in her own and the direct way she met his gaze made him hopeful she had not.

'Ellen is waiting, Mr Arrandale.'

The gentle reproof in her voice finally recalled his wandering attention. He took Ellen's hand and led her to the dance floor, but for all the perfection of his dancing partner, Richard could not quite shake off the image of Lady Phyllida's softly twinkling eyes. She was not conventionally pretty, but there was something very striking about Lady Phyllida Tatham that made it impossible to forget her.

Phyllida retreated to the benches against the wall to watch the dancing. There was no denying that Ellen and Richard Arrandale made a handsome couple. She noted that Mr Fullingham was still hovering nearby, clearly hoping to secure another dance with Ellen, but there were several other young gentlemen who had not yet stood up with her, and Phyllida would not allow any man more than two dances with her stepdaughter.

By the time the music was suspended for the interval, Phyllida knew that Ellen was a success. Not that she had ever doubted it, for her stepdaughter had beauty, poise and elegance, not to mention the fortune she would inherit when she reached one-and-twenty. She had danced every dance and there were still gentlemen waiting for the opportunity to stand up with her. Ellen's present partner was Sir Charles Urmston, who accompanied them to the tea room, where supper was set out on sideboards. Phyllida was pleased to note that Ellen did not appear to favour the gentleman over any of her other admirers. She chatted away quite happily, but showed no sign of discontent when he left them.

'Are you enjoying yourself, my love?'

'Oh, immensely,' declared Ellen, her eyes shining. 'Everyone is so kind and the Upper Rooms are so grand, compared to the George, which is where we attended the assemblies with Mrs Ackroyd. And the company is superior, too. So many gentlemen, when we were used to dance mainly with the local farmers and their sons. But Mrs Ackroyd maintained that it was very good practice and she was right, for I was not at all nervous when I stepped on to the dance floor here tonight.'

'Did you expect to be?'

Ellen's brow wrinkled. 'I am not sure—yes, I suppose I did, for I had never attended a real grown-up ball before, but it is the most tremendous fun. Oh, Philly! How can you bear to sit and watch? I know you love to dance!'

Phyllida had indeed felt a little pang of envy as she had watched her stepdaughter skipping around the floor, but now she said lightly, 'I am your chaperon, Ellen. How can I look after you if I am enjoying myself on the dance floor?'

'Oh, I do not need looking after,' came the cheerful reply. 'I am very well able to look after myself. So if we come again, Philly, promise me you will dance. I hate to see you sitting on the benches like an old lady.'

'As to that, my love, we shall see. I do not want the mortification of having no one ask me to stand up with them.'

'Oh, that won't happen,' replied Ellen. 'I shall refuse to stand up with any gentleman unless he has danced with you first!'

When the music started up again Ellen's hand was claimed by Mr Cromby. Phyllida watched the pair closely, not sure how Ellen would deal with the elderly roué. He was clearly paying her the most fulsome compliments whenever the movement of the dance allowed it, but her mind was greatly relieved when Ellen passed close by and threw her a look brimming with mischief.

It was not far from the Assembly Rooms to Charles Street, but Phyllida had arranged for her carriage to collect them. It was an extravagance, but she deemed it worthwhile, since they need not accept any of the numerous offers to escort them home. As they settled themselves into the carriage she asked Ellen how she had enjoyed her first ridotto.

'Oh, I liked it very much,' came the enthusiastic reply. 'I do not think I missed a single dance.'

'I can vouch for the fact!' declared Phyllida. She asked, trying not to show concern, 'And was there a favourite amongst your partners?'

Ellen was quiet for a moment as she considered the question.

'Everyone was most kind. Sir Charles Urmston was very charming, was he not? You will recall he was the gentleman who escorted us to tea. And Adrian Wakefield, Julia's brother.' Ellen laughed. 'The poor boy was so afraid of missing his steps he barely spoke two words to me.'

'It was most likely his first grown-up entertainment, too.'

'Yes, I think so. But, of all the gentlemen who were present tonight, I think I liked Mr Arrandale the best, do you not agree?'

Phyllida's heart sank. She replied with forced lightness, 'Why I hardly know, how can one tell from so short an acquaintance?'

'Unfair, Philly! After all, you asked me if I had a favourite.'

'So I did.' Hastily she begged pardon.

'Which of them do you think would make the best husband?'

'Why none of them. You are far too young to be thinking of such things.'

Ellen laughed. 'You are quite right, but I thought it a question that would never be far from a mother's mind. Even a stepmother.'

This was so true that Phyllida did not know how to respond and she was relieved that the carriage had arrived at their door, where she was spared the necessity of answering. She followed Ellen into the house and sent her upstairs with Matlock, who was waiting to hear all about her young mistress's success in the ballroom.

The following day saw several calling cards left at Charles Street as well as a couple of bouquets. There was nothing, however, from Richard Arrandale. Phyllida wondered if the omission was deliberate, intended to pique Ellen's interest, but perhaps she was becoming far too cynical. Putting aside such thoughts, Phyllida suggested they should walk to Sydney Gardens, and since Lord and Lady Wakefield lived in Laura Place, which was on their way, they might call and ask if Julia would like to go with them. Ellen agreed eagerly and as soon as they had breakfasted the pair set off.

By happy chance Lady Wakefield and her children were just preparing to walk to the gardens themselves and they were only too pleased to make up a party. The ridotto had cemented the young people's friendship and even Mr Adrian Wakefield had overcome his shyness enough to offer Ellen his arm as they set off along the Ride, the main route around the gardens. The three young people were soon chattering away together, leaving Phyllida to walk behind with Lady Wakefield. The two ladies were soon on friendly terms, but they had not gone far when Ellen's voice alerted Phyllida to danger.

'Oh, look. It is Mr Arrandale!'

Phyllida saw Richard's familiar figure approaching from one of the narrower side paths. His eyes were fixed upon Ellen and it was easy to envisage what would happen next. He would have no difficulty in separating Ellen from the others and once he had her on his arm she would feel the full force of his attraction. Quickly Phyllida stepped on to the path, blocking his way and holding out her hand to him.

'Mr Arrandale, good day to you, sir. Have you come to take pity upon us? You will see that the younger members of our party have left Lady Wakefield and me without an escort. We feel shamefully neglected.'

He stopped, looking faintly surprised but to his credit he covered it well.

'That is easily resolved,' he said with his ready smile. 'I shall escort you.'

Julia looked a little disappointed and Ellen intrigued, but Phyllida kept her smile in place as she laid her fingers on the gentleman's sleeve. She avoided the questioning look Lady Wakefield threw at her. She had never put herself forward in such a way before. She felt dreadfully *fast*.

'We are going to the labyrinth,' Ellen informed him. 'Have you been there, sir?'

'Why, yes, I have,' Richard replied. 'However I believe it is very crowded today. It must be an apprentices' holiday or some such thing.'

'Indeed?' uttered Lady Wakefield, dismay in her voice. 'It will be dreadfully noisy, then.'

'They can be a little boisterous, too,' he added. 'Especially if they have visited the ale house.'

'Then let us leave the labyrinth for another day,' suggested Julia, looking nervous.

'Yes, I think that might be best, especially since it is so hot,' agreed Phyllida, thinking of how easy it would be for Richard to be alone with Ellen in a maze. She raised her hand and pointed. 'That path winds through the trees. It looks very picturesque and has the advantage of being quiet *and* shady. But you have just come that way, Mr Arrandale. We must not ask you to retrace your steps.'

He was not so easily dismissed and replied with a bland smile, 'Not at all, ma'am. I am only too delighted to escort you.'

The party set off again, the younger ones leading the way, Lady Wakefield and Phyllida on either side of Mr Arrandale. Phyllida was still trying to recover from her own forwardness. She had never before accosted a gentleman so brazenly and for a while she was unable to make conversation. Thankfully Lady Wakefield was not similarly disabled. It was clear from their conversation that Mr Arrandale was on friendly terms with Adrian Wakefield and had thus earned the approval of that young man's fond mama and they were soon discussing the pleasures of Bath. Phyllida was happy to let them continue, until she heard Lady Wakefield mention the forthcoming ride to Farleigh Castle.

'My great-aunt is related to the owners of Farleigh House, you know,' he said.

'Yes, Lady Hune has kindly given us an introduction. The housekeeper is to provide refreshments for us at the house,' replied Lady Wakefield. 'I am very glad the family is not at home, for I should feel awkward imposing upon them, but now we can be easy. We are all looking forward to it. Julia has been reading about the castle in a book of local antiquities.'

'It sounds a delightful party, ma'am. I believe Farleigh Castle is well worth a visit. Indeed I should like to see it myself.'

'Then why do you not join us, Mr Arrandale?' Lady Wakefield gave a little laugh. 'We are planning to go a week on Monday. We should be pleased to have you with us in any case, but since you are related to Lady Hune that would make your presence even more welcome.'

Phyllida held her breath, hoping he would refuse. Hoping he might even be planning to leave Bath before then.

'How kind of you, Lady Wakefield. I can think of nothing I should like more.'

'Excellent. Do you hear that, Julia?' Lady Wakefield raised her voice and the three young people stopped obligingly. 'Mr Arrandale is joining us on our trip to Farleigh.'

'That is wonderful news,' cried Ellen.

Her obvious delight in this addition to the party dismayed Phyllida. It prompted her to say gaily, 'I must admit the idea of the Gothic ruin intrigues me. Would you object if I made one of your party, too, ma'am?'

'Not at all, my dear, I am very pleased that you have decided to join us.'

They had now reached a section of the gravel path that had become seriously overgrown and was only wide enough for them to pass one at a time. Phyllida stood back to allow Lady Wakefield to precede her, but as she picked her way along the narrow path her spine tingled with the knowledge that Richard Arrandale was at her back. She heard his voice close behind.

'So you did not originally intend to join the party to Farleigh Castle,' he said. 'What made you change your mind?'

'It sounds too delightful to be missed.'

'I wondered if you were having second thoughts about allowing Miss Tatham to go without you.'

'Oh, heavens, no. Ellen is very sensible. I would have no worries about her riding out with the Wakefields.'

At least, I would not if you were not one of the party.

Phyllida walked on quickly. Would there come a time when she would have to tell Richard that he must stay away from her stepdaughter? A quiet voice said she should hint him away now, before Ellen lost her heart, but she was very much afraid that hints would not work with Richard Arrandale, not if he had set his heart upon winning the heiress. She must be direct, then. Her mind shied away from such an action, it was not in her nature to confront anyone. She comforted herself by remembering Ellen's assurances that she had no intention of rushing into marriage, but hard upon the memory came the thought that falling in love was not something one could command.

Phyllida mentally braced herself. She would do whatever was necessary to protect Ellen.

The winding path widened and Richard resumed his place between the ladies. They came up with the younger members of their party at the park gates, where Julia and her brother were arguing about who was the best rider. They called upon their mother to adjudicate and the three of them walked ahead into Great Pulteney Street, deep in conversation.

Richard smiled. 'That leaves me to escort you, ladies. If you will permit?'

Ellen immediately took his proffered arm and Phyllida was obliged to fall in on the other side. She listened with growing unease as Ellen chattered away as if she had known Richard Arrandale for years. The man was so charming and attentive it would be no wonder if he turned Ellen's head. As soon as there was a break in the conversation Phyllida addressed him.

'How long are you planning to stay in Bath, Mr Arrandale?'

'That depends rather upon my great-aunt. She has not been well, you know.'

'I do know it, but when we took tea on Sunday she assured me she is much recovered now. And with the season here about to begin I feel sure there will be distractions enough to amuse her.

However I have no doubt you would find them a little tame, sir.'

'Why do you say that, Philly?' cried Ellen. 'It sounds almost as if you wish Mr Arrandale to leave Bath.'

'Not at all,' she replied coolly. 'I am merely saying that the coming season will provide Lady Hune with more diversions, and she has many friends here, too, so you must not think that she will be without company, Mr Arrandale.'

'I do not see that anyone would want to leave Bath,' remarked Ellen. 'Why, there are concerts and balls, and the shops—the finest outside London, I dare say!'

Richard laughed. 'When you put it like that, Miss Tatham, I am tempted to remain here all winter.'

No! The idea was intolerable.

Phyllida said quickly, 'But you have estates of your own, do you not, sir? They must require a great deal of your time.'

'I have Brookthorn Manor, in Hampshire, but there is nothing there that cannot wait.' Amusement rippled through his voice. 'Why, Lady Phyllida, is Miss Tatham correct, *are* you trying to get rid of me?'

She managed a lighthearted laugh. 'Not at all, sir.'

'No, of course she isn't,' declared Ellen. 'Why should she wish to do that?'

'Why indeed?' he murmured.

Phyllida risked glancing up and read such amusement in his eyes that she quickly looked away again, her face flaming. Angrily she told herself not to be so foolish. If he knew she was aware of his intentions then so much the better.

Richard's lips twitched. Really, Lady Phyllida looked quite delightful when she was blushing and the urge to tease her was almost irresistible. He also felt unusually protective. She was far too young and inexperienced in the ways of the world: how could she hope to protect her stepdaughter from the wolves that were hunting her, himself included? True, she had managed to keep him from having Ellen to himself on this occasion, but she would not always be able to keep him at bay.

The problem was, neither would she be able to keep the other fellows away. And knowing the prize at stake, some of them might prove much more unscrupulous than he. Today Richard had been fortunate. A few coins had elicited the information from her footman that Lady Phyllida was going to Sydney Gardens, and when he had seen Fullingham on his way to Charles Street he had been able to save him the trouble of calling by informing him that Lady Phyllida was not at home.

Remembering Ellen's wish to see the labyrinth, he had made his way directly to this popular spot only to find Tesford and Cromby were there before him. From their brief conversation he realised that they had also bribed Lady Phyllida's footman. Devil take it, the fellow would be able to retire from service at the end of the season if this continued! Luckily Richard had intercepted the ladies and persuaded them to take another route away from the labyrinth. Things had gone his way, but he would have to remain vigilant if he was to win the wager and the heiress for himself.

They had reached Laura Place, where the Wakefields stopped to take their leave. Richard turned to Phyllida.

'Perhaps, ma'am, you will allow me to escort you and Miss Tatham to Charles Street?'

'That is very kind of you, Mr Arrandale, but we are not going directly home. I promised Ellen that we would do a little shopping in Milsom Street. To buy ribbons.'

Richard was not surprised at the lady's response. She suspected his motives and it would be as well if he did not press his suit any further today. He was about to bow and take his leave when he noticed Sir Charles Urmston strolling towards them. He was coming from the direction of Pulteney Bridge but Richard did not doubt that he would turn back to escort the ladies to Milsom Street, given the chance. Richard had no intention of allowing him the opportunity, if he could help it.

He smiled. 'Then allow me to escort you there. I am very good at choosing ribbons.'

'Thank you.' Phyllida shook her head. 'However, we could not impose upon you any longer today.'

'Oh, I am sure it could not be an imposition,' put in Lady Wakefield, who overheard this exchange and had clearly fallen under Richard Arrandale's spell. 'I am old-fashioned enough to think it a good thing to have a gentleman's escort when one walks about town, even in Bath.'

'Oh, yes, pray do come with us, Mr Arrandale,' said Ellen, just as Phyllida was about to make a firm denial. 'I have seen a bonnet that I should like to buy. The milliner told me it is in the latest London fashion but I am not so sure, and I would value your opinion.'

'Then I shall be happy to give it,' he responded promptly.

'There you are then,' declared Lady Wakefield, smiling. 'We shall bid you good day, Lady Phyllida.'

Phyllida pressed her lips together, trying to hide her dismay as Lady Wakefield went off with Julia and Adrian. Richard held out his arms.

'Well, ladies, shall we go on?'

His laughing glance made Phyllida grind her teeth but she had no choice, she must accept gracefully. The alternative would be to face questions from Ellen, questions which she had no intention of answering with Richard Arrandale standing by. Such was her distraction that when they passed Sir Charles Urmston in Argyle Street, her response to his pleasant greeting was no more than a distant nod.

Phyllida said little as they made their way to Milsom Street, allowing Ellen to chatter on. When they reached the milliners Richard accompanied them inside to inspect the bonnet that had caught Ellen's eye. It was a ruched bronze-satin creation decorated with an overabundance of flowers and tassels. Phyllida declared she thought it far from tasteful, but it was the doubtful look on Richard's face that made Ellen change her mind and decide the bonnet was not for her after all. Phyllida was relieved, but perturbed by the thought that she should be grateful to Richard Arrandale.

They went on to the haberdashers, where Ellen browsed the rainbow of coloured ribbons that the assistant spread out for her inspection. There was barely room for two people to stand together at the counter and Phyllida hesitated before stepping back to let Richard move in and advise Ellen on her choice. Let that be his reward for dissuading her from buying the unsuitable bonnet.

Phyllida stood out of the way by a side door until Ellen had made her purchase, then she accompanied them out of the shop.

'Well…' She smiled. 'Which ribbon did you decide upon?'

'This one.' Ellen opened the package to show Phyllida. 'I could not decide between this and the primrose but in the end I chose the cornflower blue. Is it not a lovely colour?' She added in an innocent voice, 'Mr Arrandale said this matches my eyes.'

Ellen's laughing glance was somewhat reassuring. Phyllida knew her stepdaughter was not taken in by such compliments. Not yet.

'And he is right,' she agreed, keeping her tone cool. 'Shall we go on?'

They had not gone many yards down Milsom Street when Ellen gave a loud sigh.

'Is it not always the same? Now that I have left the shop I am sure I should have bought the primrose ribbon as well as the blue.'

'Well, it is too late to return now,' said Phyllida. 'I think it is going to rain. 'Let us get on now, we can always come back tomorrow.'

Richard stopped.

'I have an errand of my own to run,' he said. 'If

you would like to continue with your shopping, I shall catch you up.'

He strode away before they had time to argue. Ellen giggled.

'I do believe he is going back to buy the primrose ribbon for me.'

'Oh, I hope not,' said Phyllida. 'I really do not wish to be beholden to Mr Arrandale.'

'For a few pennies' worth of ribbon?' declared Ellen. 'What harm can there be in that?'

'He is not related to us, Ellen.'

'But he is related to Lady Hune, who is a great friend of yours,' argued Ellen.

They walked on, gazing into shop windows, marvelling at the variety of goods available in Bath and before too long Richard caught up with them.

'Here we are.' He handed Ellen a small packet. 'Your primrose ribbons, Miss Tatham. And for you, ma'am,' He handed a second even smaller package to Phyllida.

Peeping inside she saw a neatly rolled length of dark-green ribbon.

'I thought of the gown you were wearing the first time I saw you,' he murmured. 'The colour became you so well.' She raised her brows and he quickly corrected himself. 'The first time I saw you in Bath, I mean.'

'Oh?' Ellen was immediately attentive. 'I did not know you were already acquainted.'

'Oh, yes,' Richard nodded. 'I knew your step-mama at her come-out. We danced together at Almack's.'

His blue eyes bored into Phyllida, challenging her to contradict him, but in truth she could not speak, for his look heated her blood and sent her imagination skittering towards secret trysts and stolen kisses. Outrageous thoughts that had no place in a chaperon's mind.

'Oh, that is famous!' cried Ellen, 'Phyllida, why did you not *tell* me? If that is so I am sure there can be no objection at all to accepting Mr Arrandale's gifts. I am very grateful for my ribbons, thank you, sir. Philly? Are you not going to thank Mr Arrandale?'

'Well, Lady Phyllida?'

His eyes continued to hold her gaze, saying so much more than words. In their blue depths gleamed a mixture of amusement and understanding, an invitation for her to share the joke, to accept his friendship. Perhaps even more than that. All of it lies, of course. She had to believe that, or she was lost.

Richard waited for her answer. It would not have surprised him if she had handed the ribbon back but in the end she thanked him, albeit grudgingly, and they continued on their way. He escorted the ladies to Charles Street, left them at the door and turned to make his way back to Queen Square, well satisfied with his progress.

As soon as they were indoors, Phyllida dashed off to her bedchamber, saying there were letters she must write. She knew Ellen would want know about her acquaintance with Richard Arrandale and she needed to prepare her answers. She kept to her room and was thus able to avoid saying anything at all until after dinner.

When they were alone in the drawing room, Ellen placed a footstool before Phyllida's chair and sat down upon it.

'Now,' she said, taking Phyllida's hands, 'why did you not tell me you and Mr Arrandale were old friends?'

'We are not,' Phyllida replied. 'We are acquaintances, merely.'

'But he says you danced together. Did you know him before you met Papa?'

'I met them at the same time. It was my come-out. One dances with a lot of gentlemen in one's first Season, as you will discover when we go to town next year.'

Ellen was not to be distracted. 'And was Mr Arrandale as handsome as he is now?'

Phyllida had been managing rather well to stay calm and matter of fact, but this question caught her off guard. Her cheeks burned. She had not blushed for years, but these days she could not stop!

'I—I suppose he must have been. I really cannot remember.'

But she could. She recalled every painful, tongue-tied moment she had spent with him. He had been charmingly polite, while she had been unable to do more than utter one or two stilted sentences.

'I knew it!' Ellen clapped her hands. 'You fell in love with him!'

'I did not!'

'Then why are you blushing?'

Phyllida managed to laugh. 'I was remembering what a gauche, awkward creature I was in those days.' That much at least was true. 'Now, Ellen, it is most improper for you to quiz me on this. As I told you, a girl in her first Season meets a lot of gentlemen but once she is married she forgets them all. I was very happy with your father, and I hope he was happy with me.'

'But it was not a love match, was it?' Ellen persisted. 'I was only twelve years old at the time but I remember people saying so.'

'Not everyone marries for love, Ellen, and not every family is as happy as we were at Tatham Park.'

Phyllida thought back to her own childhood.

She was a younger daughter and not particularly pretty. She had also been painfully shy and constantly afraid of incurring her parents' displeasure. It had been a relief when Sir Evelyn had offered for her and by the time her parents died two years later she was happily settled with Sir Evelyn. At his coaxing she had left off the pale pinks and blues her mother had chosen for her and given up the nightly ritual of tying up her hair in rags to produce a mass of unbecoming ringlets. Now she wore her hair swept up smoothly with only a few soft curls falling on to her neck. Sir Evelyn had given her a great deal, including confidence.

She said now, 'Be assured that I was much more comfortable with your father than I had ever been at home.'

'That is because they bullied you,' replied Ellen. 'Did they force you to marry Papa?'

'Not at all, but I was expected to marry well.'

'Well, that is quite, quite *Gothic*,' declared Ellen. 'I shall not allow anyone to force me into marriage.'

She looked so absurdly young that Phyllida smiled. She squeezed her hands.

'I hope when the time comes you will fall in love, Ellen, but I also hope you will not be in too much of a hurry to do so.'

'Oh, no. I am enjoying myself far too much to think of such things yet.'

Phyllida was relieved to hear this, but she did not say so and turned Ellen's thoughts by asking her what she intended to wear to the Italian concert the following evening.

To Phyllida's secret pride, Ellen was proving to be universally popular. The house in Charles Street was besieged by visitors and there were entertainments every day. It was becoming clear that several gentlemen were vying for Ellen's attention, including Richard Arrandale, and Phyllida was relieved, if a little surprised, that the other young ladies of Bath were not more jealous of her success. However, she was perturbed to see how much attention the gentlemen lavished upon Ellen and could only be glad that her stepdaughter appeared to take it all in her stride.

Phyllida insisted that Ellen should be chaperoned at all times. When the party comprised young people under the aegis of careful mamas like Mrs Desborough or Lady Wakefield Phyllida was happy to allow Ellen to go unattended, but at the public breakfasts and dances Phyllida was always there to ensure no gentleman stepped out of line. As an heiress, Phyllida had always known Ellen would attract attention, but there were a number of married men amongst her admirers, and that was a puzzle.

Her puzzlement turned to concern when they attended the recital at the Assembly Rooms the evening following their walk in Sydney Gardens and Phyllida returned from a break for refreshments to find her stepdaughter in an antechamber with Mr Cromby. The gentleman was holding Ellen's hand and paying her the most fulsome compliments. Phyllida lost no time in carrying Ellen away, but when she remonstrated with Ellen later she merely laughed.

'We were only a step away from the main room, Philly. You really did not need to worry. We had gentlemen far older than Mr Cromby flirting with us at Mrs Ackroyd's Academy.'

'That is not the point,' objected Phyllida, despairing. 'Bath is a hotbed of gossip and you will do your reputation no good at all if people think you fast.'

In no wise chastened, Ellen threw her arms about Phyllida and hugged her.

'Very well, I will try to behave, for your sake, darling Stepmama. But I do enjoy being the centre of so much attention!'

There was no doubt that Ellen was indeed in demand. The parties and entertainments, together with Ellen's dancing, singing and Italian lessons, gave Phyllida little time for leisure. Ellen thrived upon the activity and Phyllida made sure she was always accompanied whenever she stepped out of the door. However, she soon discovered that even the presence of Ellen's maid did not keep Richard Arrandale away. She was in the morning room waiting for Ellen to return from her dancing lesson when she saw him pass the window with Ellen on his arm. He left Ellen at the door but Phyllida watched in growing alarm as he raised Ellen's fingers to his lips before striding away.

Phyllida was dismayed at her reaction to this gesture but she was honest enough to admit that the emotion uppermost in her was envy. She stifled it immediately, composing herself as Ellen burst into the morning room with her sunny smile quite undimmed.

'Did I see Mr Arrandale at the door with you?' Phyllida kept her voice light, determined not to show undue anxiety.

'Yes. We met in Wood Street and he insisted upon escorting me home. Was that not kind of him?'

'Yes, very.'

She said no more at the time, but as the conversation moved on Phyllida knew she must speak to Matlock about the matter.

* * *

However, when she did so Matty's response was typically blunt.

'What would you have me do, my lady? Miss Ellen greeted him like a friend and I could hardly forbid him to walk with us. And even if it had been in my power I would not have done so, for nothing is more certain to make a spirited girl want something than to tell her she can't have it.'

Phyllida nodded. 'I am well aware of that, Matlock. And Miss Ellen is definitely spirited.'

'But nothing untoward happened,' added the maid. 'I can assure you of that, ma'am. In fact, I was pleasantly surprised in Mr Arrandale, after all I had heard about the man.'

'Oh, Matty, pray do not tell me you are falling under his spell, too.'

The older woman gave a grim little smile.

'No, no, I'm too long in the tooth to be taken in by a handsome face, my lady, but credit where 'tis due, the gentleman never said anything out o' place while he was escorting Miss Ellen. And he made no attempt to lower his voice to avoid my hearing it, either.'

'Well, perhaps there is some good in the man, after all,' murmured Phyllida, but she added, her suspicions not completely allayed, 'Or perhaps he is playing a deep game.'

Chapter Five

Phyllida had still not made up her mind about Richard Arrandale by the time they rode to Farleigh the following Monday. Her groom Parfett brought the horses around from the livery stables, warning that they were very lively since they had not been ridden for some time. Phyllida was soon in control of Sultan, her own rangy chestnut gelding, but she watched anxiously as Ellen's spirited grey mare pranced and sidestepped playfully.

'No need to worry about Miss Ellen,' said Parfett, observing Phyllida's frown. 'You know there wasn't a horse in her father's stable she couldn't master. She's at home to a peg.'

As if to prove him correct, the mare quickly grew quiet under Ellen's confident handling and they set off to meet up with the rest of the party at Laura Place, where they found the Wakefields already mounted and waiting for them.

'Our little riding party has grown to nine,

Lady Phyllida,' Lady Wakefield greeted her with a cheerful smile. She waved her hand towards the pretty brunette talking with Julia and Adrian. 'Mrs Desborough has allowed Penelope to join us, and Mr Henry Fullingham came up to me just yesterday and begged to be allowed to join us. Here he comes now, with Mr Arrandale.'

Phyllida looked back to see the two gentlemen approaching. Surely it was not merely her fancy that of the two men, Richard had the advantage? It was not only his superior height, nor the way his blue riding coat moulded to his form. He looked relaxed and at home in the saddle, completely in control of the powerful black hunter he was riding. She thought it could not be a livery-stable horse, and this was soon confirmed when Mr Arrandale rode up to Lady Wakefield as the party prepared to set off.

'I do not know the country,' he said. 'Will we be able to give the horses their heads? I was going to hire a hack, but in the end I sent for my hunter. He has been eating his head off at Brookthorn Manor and could do with the exercise.'

'There are a couple of places one can gallop, although Wakefield and I will not do so,' replied the lady. 'And I should warn you that Miss Desborough and Julia are rather nervous riders, so I pray you will not encourage them to join you.'

Phyllida knew Ellen was anything but nervous

and would undoubtedly wish to gallop across the country with the gentlemen. She made up her mind that if Lord and Lady Wakefield would not accompany them, then it would be up to her to do so. She patted Sultan's glossy neck, reflecting that neither she nor her mount would consider it a penance to career across the countryside.

They rode out of Bath at a sedate pace. Mr Fullingham and Mr Arrandale both looked as if they would like to ride with Ellen but she remained happily between Phyllida and Penelope Desborough. Phyllida considered the picture they must make. Penelope's plum-coloured habit was sober enough, but Ellen's sky-blue velvet with its matching hat was quite eye-catching, and there was no doubt that the colour accentuated her flawless complexion and shining curls. Phyllida thought her own dove-grey habit must look very dull by comparison and was obliged to stifle a pang of regret. She felt a little envious, then scolded herself for such nonsense. As a girl she would never have been confident enough to choose bright colours, even if Mama had allowed it. She glanced again at her kerseymere skirts. She was out of mourning now, there was no reason why she shouldn't order a new riding habit. Something a little more…showy.

What on earth am I thinking? I am Ellen's chaperon. I do not wish to draw attention to myself.

But at that moment her gaze fell upon Richard Arrandale and she knew that she was not being quite honest. Phyllida glanced again at her step-daughter. Ellen was looking particularly lovely today, her eyes sparkling, her countenance so animated that Phyllida thought no man would be able to resist the attraction. She would have to keep her under close scrutiny. She passed the gentlemen in the party under quick review. Lord Wakefield and his son posed no threat, she decided, but Messrs Fullingham and Arrandale were a different matter. They were both fashionable men with considerable address and Phyllida had no intention of allowing either of them to spend time alone with Ellen.

This was not a problem until they reached the first stretch of open ground where Lord Wakefield indicated it would be safe to gallop.

'Our route lies along the road here,' explained Lady Wakefield, 'so those of us who do not wish to race may walk on at a respectable pace. The rest of you may gallop over to that copse yonder and back again.'

'But there will be no racing,' Lord Wakefield reminded them.

'Actually I think I will remain on the road,' said his son, drawing closer to Penelope Desborough.

Lord Wakefield turned his attention to the

other two gentlemen. 'We have a long way to go,' he barked. 'I do not want to be turning back because one of you young dogs has broken his neck.'

He frowned so direfully at Mr Fullingham that the young man flushed.

'No, no, sir. Wouldn't dream of it.' His glance flickered towards Ellen who was trotting up. 'Especially when we will have ladies with us.'

'Oh, do not hold back for me, I want no special treatment,' replied Ellen, laughing.

'Your stepmama may not agree with you,' said Lord Wakefield.

Ellen looked around, her brows rising when she saw Phyllida approaching. 'Oh, are you coming with us Philly?'

The surprise in her tone irked Phyllida and roused a tiny spurt of rebellion.

'Coming with you?' She kicked her horse on. 'Catch me if you can!'

Sultan was fresh and leapt forward without a second bidding. Phyllida heard the cry of delight from Ellen and a startled call from Lady Wakefield for her to take care but she ignored them both. She felt suddenly, gloriously free as the gelding flew across the turf. She glanced behind. Three riders were following, Ellen's grey mare galloping beside Mr Fullingham's bay but in front of them and closing fast upon her was Richard Arrandale on the black hunter. Phyllida turned back, crouching lower over Sultan's neck, urging the horse on. She could hear the hunter thundering up behind her. The copse was approaching all too quickly, but she did not want to rein in Sultan. Her only relief during her year of mourning and self-imposed exile at Tatham Park had been her early morning gallops. She had missed them when she had come to Bath and now she wanted the feeling of excitement to go on for ever.

'Don't pull up,' Richard shouted. 'We'll go on to the barn yonder!'

It was madness. She was setting a poor example to Ellen, but with the wind in her face and the exhilaration of the ride firing her blood, Phyllida could not resist prolonging the race. She touched her whip to Sultan's flank and they shot past the copse and on towards the barn in the distance. Above the thud of Sultan's hoofs she was aware of the hunter closing up. The black nose was at her shoulder. She pushed Sultan on, urging him to make one last effort and they thundered past the barn neck and neck.

The horses slowed and Phyllida straightened in the saddle, unable to hold back a laugh of sheer delight.

'Impressive, Lady Phyllida.' Richard had brought his hunter alongside and was grinning at her. 'And unexpected.'

She met his eyes, still exhilarated by the race.

The glowing, soaring elation intensified when she saw the admiration in his glance. She could not stop smiling at him. They were very close, his muscled thigh encased in tight buckskin was so near that she might reach out to touch it. Phyllida was startled to realise how much she wanted to do so. How much she wanted *him*.

The urge to smile disappeared. In a panic she dragged her gaze away and stared determinedly between Sultan's ears.

She said remorsefully, 'It was very bad of me. Lord Wakefield expressly forbade us to race. And then to extend it here, out of sight of the road.' The pleasure of the moment had subsided and she bit her lip, suddenly mortified at her lack of decorum.

'Console yourself with the fact that the others did not follow us,' said Richard. 'They are obediently waiting at the copse even now. Shall we go back?'

'I suppose we must.'

His look was searching as they turned about and Phyllida realised she had sounded quite regretful. Heavens, she hoped he did not misunderstand her and think she wanted to keep him by her side. She rushed into an explanation.

'It is a long time since Sultan has raced against another horse. When Sir Evelyn died the family thought it would be best to sell all the horses except Sultan and Ellen's mare.'

'Surely that was your decision?'

'Yes. Yes, of course.'

And it *had* been her decision, but she could acknowledge now the pressure that had been brought to bear, while she was still coming to terms with her loss. It was not just from Sir Evelyn's family, but her own, too. She had been brought up to believe that a man must be head of the family and his word was law, that she should always bow to his will, but marriage had changed her. She had enjoyed being mistress of her own house and had grown more confident under Sir Evelyn's benevolent protection. He had encouraged her to think for herself.

Her parents had died by the time Phyllida became a widow, but her family had descended upon her, discussing with Sir Evelyn's relatives what would be best for her and it had taken all her newfound strength to stand out against them. Thank goodness she had not allowed them to persuade her to give up Sultan, or to sell Tatham Park.

Richard was silent, watching the play of emotion on Lady Phyllida's countenance. The excited glow died from her eyes and her cheeks lost their hectic flush. He thought there was a shadow of sadness about her. She was thinking back to her dead husband, perhaps. Did she miss him? Had she loved him?

Richard shifted in the saddle, uncomfortable with the thought. A sudden and unfamiliar feeling swept through him. He wanted to protect her, to keep her safe. To make her happy.

The others were waiting for them at the copse, keeping their horses in the shade of the trees. As Phyllida and Richard approached Ellen called out, 'Philly, are you all right? When I saw you racing on I wanted to follow but Mr Fullingham thought we should wait here, since this is where we agreed to stop.'

'We were afraid Sultan had bolted with you,' added Mr Fullingham.

'No such thing,' said Richard. 'We were enjoying the race and decided to go on.' He glanced at Phyllida. 'It was my fault, and I beg your pardon.'

'I knew you were in no danger, Philly,' said Ellen comfortably. 'You were always a clipping rider, I had forgotten just how good you are!'

Phyllida chuckled and shook her head. 'It was most irresponsible of me, but I cannot deny that I enjoyed it.'

Ellen looked back towards the road. 'I think we should be getting back to the others. I am not sure how much they will have seen…'

'Not the race to the barn,' said Richard. 'That would have been screened by the copse.'

Ellen giggled. 'Then we shall not tell them how reprehensibly you both behaved.'

'Thank you,' said Phyllida meekly.

'And it has done you good, Philly,' Ellen continued. 'I have never seen you looking better.'

Richard grinned. He had to agree, Lady Phyllida was looking radiant. She had surprised him and he thought that perhaps she was not such a mouse after all. He fell in with the others, but as he did so he caught Henry Fullingham's eye and the fellow winked at him. Richard's jaw tightened and he cursed inwardly. By allowing himself to gallop off with the widow he had left the field free for Fullingham to advance his cause with Ellen Tatham. And if that smug expression was anything to go by, he had taken full advantage of it.

Richard hoped for an opportunity to draw Ellen away as they continued towards Farleigh but she fell in beside her stepmother. Phyllida's unexpected escapade had clearly impressed her and the two ladies rode together, laughing and chattering. Watching them, and listening to them reminisce about past rides and excursions, Richard was again struck by Phyllida's youthfulness. She could only have been about Ellen's age when Sir Evelyn had married her. She and Ellen were obviously good friends and he wondered if that had been a comfort to the young bride in the early days of her marriage.

The question was still in his head when he finally managed to ride beside Ellen, and instead of taking the opportunity to engage her in a gentle flirtation he remarked that she appeared to be on very good terms with her stepmother.

'Yes. Philly has always been much more like an older sister than a mama to me.'

She turned her head and regarded him for a moment with unwonted seriousness. 'I would do nothing to hurt her, Mr Arrandale.'

'I am sure you would not.' He added, surprising himself, 'I hope that will always be the case, because it might well prevent you from getting into any serious scrapes.'

She thought about this for a moment.

'Sometimes I think I am much more worldly-wise than Philly. In fact, I have decided to promote her happiness.'

His lips twitched. 'And how do you propose to do that, Miss Tatham?'

The solemn look fled and she shook her head, eyes gleaming with mischief.

'I shall not tell you. It is always best to play one's cards close to one's chest, is it not?'

He frowned. 'Now where did you learn that expression?'

'From my teacher, Mrs Ackroyd. She explained to us about games of chance. Cards, and dice and the like.'

'Ah, I did not think you would have heard Lady Phyllida say such a thing.'

'Goodness, no. Sometimes I think Philly needs me to look after her, not the other way round.'

Before he could respond, a call from Lord Wakefield informed them that they had reached Farleigh and the party reorganised itself to ride up the drive to the house. They were met at the door by the housekeeper, who confirmed that the family were not at home but that refreshments were waiting for them, if they would care to step inside for a little while before they inspected what was left of the castle and the chapel.

Phyllida moved closer to Ellen. She had observed her talking to Richard during the ride, seen the looks, brimful with laughter, that Ellen had thrown at him and she had been conscious of a strong feeling of desolation. It had formed itself into a hard, unhappy knot deep inside. Phyllida wanted to snatch Ellen away but that would do no good at all. She was Ellen's chaperon, not her gaoler, and would never prevent her merely talking to a gentleman. So she entered the house beside Lady Wakefield and left the younger ones to chatter together while they enjoyed the cold collation that had been set out for their delectation.

Afterwards, when they went off to look at the ruins of the castle, she made no attempt to keep Ellen at her side, but watched her scamper off with the other girls. Adrian, Mr Fullingham and Richard Arrandale accompanied the group to help them over the uneven ground while Phyllida followed a short distance behind with Lord Wakefield and his lady.

'Oh, dear,' murmured Lady Wakefield when the breeze brought snatches of the young people's conversation floating back to them, 'Adrian is recounting the castle's gruesome history. Should we tell him to stop? I would not wish him to give the girls nightmares.'

'Do not silence him on Ellen's account,' replied Phyllida, thinking of the copy of *The Monk* currently secreted in her stepdaughter's bedchamber, 'She will enjoy the horrid stories immensely.'

'As will Julia and Penelope,' added Lord Wakefield, with a complacent chuckle. 'Do not worry, ladies, the children will not come to any harm here.'

Phyllida wondered if that were true, but she soon saw that the young ladies were much more interested in clambering over the ruins and listening to Adrian Wakefield's blood-curdling tales than in dalliance with any of the gentlemen.

There was little to see of the castle except the gatehouse and what remained of the thick walls. The rest was merely piles of rubble, much of it overgrown, but this did not prevent the younger members of the party from scrambling around like excited children.

'Which is what they are,' remarked Lady Wakefield, watching them with smiling indulgence. 'The girls are barely out of the schoolroom and Adrian is only a couple of years their senior. I wish I had their energy! The ride and then the refreshments have left me feeling quite languid, so Wakefield and I are going to find a convenient stone block to sit upon, Lady Phyllida, if you would like to stay with us?'

Phyllida declined gracefully. She was not at all fatigued by the ride and glad to have some time to herself. She wandered off, enjoying the solitude. She loved Ellen dearly, but having responsibility for such a pretty girl, and an heiress at that, was proving more arduous than she had thought. Having spent the past year living on her own at Tatham Park she had thought having Ellen to live with her would provide her with the companionship she had lacked since Sir Evelyn's death, and it did, but Phyllida knew now that it was not enough. Ellen was not a kindred spirit, they could not converse upon equal terms, because Phyllida could never forget that Ellen was her responsibility.

She did not regret taking Ellen to live with her and she would devote herself now to looking after her. But later, when Ellen was married and she could look to her own happiness, what then? Perhaps she should marry again. Sir Evelyn had proved himself a kind and considerate husband but Phyllida knew that only the deepest love would make her give up her independence now, and ladies who had reached the advanced age of four-and-twenty did not readily fall in love, did they? The question hovered and impatiently she closed her mind to it. The future must look after itself. She was comfortably situated and had sufficient funds to do whatever she wished.

Such as wandering around ruined castles all alone?

Yes, she told herself firmly, and set off to prove it was possible.

The area adjoining the gatehouse was now a farmyard so Phyllida made her way in the opposite direction, where trees and bushes obscured what was left of the thick curtain wall. Stones from the ancient building were scattered around, making the ground uneven and she gathered up her voluminous skirts to avoid snagging them on the rampant vegetation.

'Exploring, Lady Phyllida?'

Richard Arrandale was coming towards her. She quickly dropped her skirts, but not before she was sure he had glimpsed her stockings and half-boots.

And what of it? No doubt he has seen scores of ladies' ankles in his career.

She told him, 'I wanted, if I could, to discover something of the size of the castle.'

'It is quite extensive. Here, take my hand and let me help you over these stones. We may find the path a little easier further on.'

'Perhaps I should be getting back. Ellen—'

'Miss Tatham is safely under the eye of the Wakefields,' he replied. 'And Fullingham has taken himself off to smoke a cigar.' He said solemnly, 'You are at liberty to enjoy yourself, Lady Phyllida.'

Tentatively she put out her hand. As his fingers closed around her glove she felt his thumb moving over the soft leather. The slow sensual strokes made her want to purr and she had to struggle to ignore it. He led her on through the ruins, pointing out portions of carved stone amongst the rubble and the outline of walls that were now no more than ridges in the ground.

'You are very well informed, Mr Arrandale.'

She cast a suspicious look up at him. 'When Lady Wakefield told you of this excursion you gave the impression you had not been here before.'

'Did I?'

She stopped. His expression was innocent enough but there was laughter in his eyes. She said severely, 'You know very well you did.'

He laughed.

'Very well, I admit it. My great-aunt brought me here several times when I was younger. I explored the ruins then.'

'Oh? Did all your family visit here?'

'Good God, no. My father would have thought this place beneath him. He and my mother were too busy enjoying themselves in town to bother with their children.'

She tried to ignore the bitterness in his response.

'Did your brother come here too?'

'No. By the time I visited here Wolf was at Oxford, causing mayhem.'

'Ah.' She smiled. 'The Scandalous Arrandales.'

'Quite. However, unlike me, he wasn't sent down. He saved his disgrace for something far more serious.'

He looked so grim that she could not prevent herself from squeezing his hand.

'I am very sorry.'

'You need not be.'

He spoke roughly and she knew he wanted to pull away from her. It was an almost imperceptible movement but she was aware of it and immediately she released him. He took a couple of paces towards one of the low stretches of wall rising up through the grass and rested one booted foot upon the stones.

He said with feigned carelessness, 'It gives one a certain...standing, don't you know, to have a murderer for a brother. I attracted all the choicest spirits at Oxford, most of 'em older, all of them ripe for mischief. I did not last a year before they kicked me out.'

'Why, what did you do?' The question was voiced before she could prevent it.

'Gambling, drinking. Women. Then I moved on to London, where I found even more of the same pleasures to be enjoyed.' His mouth twisted. 'After all, I had to maintain the family reputation. Although *I* stopped short of murder.'

Her heart went out to him.

'I do not believe the Arrandales are as black as they are painted. As for your brother—it was a long time ago but I know the whispers, the rumours, continue.' She tried to smile. 'They are probably much worse than what actually happened.'

'I doubt it.'

'Would you like to tell me?'

She spoke the words softly and wondered if he had heard them for he ignored her, idly swiping at a thistle with his riding crop. Phyllida waited and eventually her patient silence was rewarded.

'I am no better informed than you about how my sister-in-law died. I was spending that winter with my great-aunt at Shrewton and my parents decided it would be best if I remained in ignorance of what had happened. Of course that state of affairs could not last, Sophia's acquaintances soon informed her of the situation and she took me back to Arrandale but by then it was too late. Florence, my sister-in-law, had been dead three months and my brother was gone.'

He turned and began to stroll on. She fell in beside him.

'How did she die?'

'Fell down the stairs. Florence was pregnant at the time and the fall brought on the birth. The child survived but Florence died that night. Everyone thought Wolf had killed her. Oh, the death was recorded as an accident, my father saw to that. After all he'd had plenty of practice covering up his own transgressions.' His lip curled. 'I come from a family of wrongdoers, Lady Phyllida. My family history is littered with murder, abduction and thievery, the stories of Farleigh Castle pale in comparison. Wolf was merely following the family tradition.'

She shook her head, but did not contradict him, merely asked what had happened to his brother.

'My father sent Wolf abroad immediately after the tragedy. Then Florence's parents demanded the return of a diamond necklace. It was a family treasure, apparently, to be passed to the heir, in this case Florence's twin, but she had borrowed it for her wedding and had kept it to wear on grand occasions. Only it wasn't there. It would seem that Wolf took it to pay his way abroad.'

'And do you believe that?'

His scornful glance scorched her.

'Does it matter what I believe? My father refused to talk of it. I was sent back to Shrewton Lodge with a tutor to finish my schooling, then I was packed off to Oxford and by the following spring my parents were dead. Officially it was scarlet fever, there had been a particularly bad outbreak at Arrandale, but I think it was more likely the shame of it all that overcame them, at least for my mother.'

'Or the heartbreak,' she murmured sadly, thinking of how the tragedy must have ripped apart the family. 'What happened to the baby?'

'It was a girl. When my parents died she was sent to live with a distant cousin, the Earl of Davenport.' A wry smile broke through for a moment. 'Another Arrandale, but James is as sober as the rest of us are dissolute and he was thought the best guardian for the girl. He has a daughter of the same age, so it was deemed the best thing to do with the child.'

'And Wolfgang? Where is your brother now?'

He spread his hands. 'We never heard from him again. I made enquiries, hired men to search for him, sent letters.' A muscle worked in his jaw. 'It may be that he did not want to be found. Or he may well have been drowned on the crossing to France, there were some exceptionally vicious storms that winter.'

'How sad, that he never had a chance to explain himself.'

Richard stopped.

'I desperately want him to be innocent,' he burst out. 'Wolf is seven years my senior and I always looked up to him. Oh, I know he was hot tempered and rash, but he was never unkind, not intentionally. And I really cannot believe—'

He broke off. Phyllida saw the muscle working in his cheek. He was wrestling with profound grief and she wanted only to comfort him.

'You really should believe he is innocent, Mr Arrandale, until it is proven otherwise.'

He did not answer. He did not appear to have heard her but remained staring at nothing, his thoughts clearly elsewhere. Unhappiness wrapped about him like a cloak and there was nothing she could do to relieve it. A small cloud momentarily blocked out the sun and Phyllida shivered. The faint movement recalled his wandering attention. He was once again his usual, urbane self.

'You have not yet seen the chapel, Lady Phyllida. Perhaps we should go back there now, if you have seen enough?'

He extended his arm.

'Yes, please.' She slipped her hand on to his sleeve. 'These broken walls have lost their charm for me.'

As they made their way back across the ruins she noted that Lord and Lady Wakefield were still sitting on their stone seat. Ellen, Penelope and the two younger Wakefields were exploring what was left of the gatehouse. She eased her conscience with the thought that she was keeping Richard Arrandale away from Ellen. Wasn't she?

The little chapel was built within the curtain wall of the castle and had been restored sufficiently for visitors to go inside. Richard stood back for Phyllida to pass before him into the narrow building. Odd that he had told her about Wolf. He had never said as much to anyone before. After all, what was the point? Everyone believed Wolf was guilty, he was just another in the long line of scandalous Arrandales. So why had he spoken so freely to Phyllida? Was it because she had seemed genuinely interested, prepared to think something other than the worst of an Arrandale?

Richard followed her into the centre of the chapel. Her soft boots made no sound on the stone flags, her skirts floated out as she moved, a silent figure in pale grey. She looked so ethereal that he could not help himself. He reached out and touched her shoulder. She turned and he found himself subjected to her enquiring gaze.

'I beg your pardon,' he said. 'I needed to reassure myself that you were real.'

'Of course I am real.' Her mouth curved into a smile. 'Did you think me a ghost?'

'No, an angel.'

An angel sent to redeem him.

She was surprised into a laugh. The warm, delicious sound echoed around them, breaking the sepulchral calm of the stone building. Quickly she put a hand over her mouth but her eyes still gleamed with merriment, green as emeralds. His blood quickened. She no longer looked ethereal, she was a living, breathing woman and he wanted to pull her into his arms and kiss her.

He was aware of the change immediately and he knew she had read his thoughts. Her eyes were no longer alight with laughter but something else, an instinctive response to him. He felt the connection, the sizzle of excitement that held them immobile. They were less than an arm's length apart, beneath her mannish jacket and white shirt her breast rose and fell as she took a deep, ragged breath. When she lowered her hand he reached for it, felt the quiver of excitement as their fingers touched, not in the least dulled by the soft kid of their gloves. They were caught in a bubble that tightened around them, moving them slowly but inexorably together.

The air shimmered with anticipation. He saw the tip of her tongue flicker nervously over her lips, as if she knew that they would kiss, that it was inevitable and there was nothing she could do to prevent it. Looking into her eyes, he saw a shy smile there and he knew with startling clarity that she did not *wish* to prevent it. He was holding her hand, drawing her closer. They were breast to breast, he had only to lower his head now for the sweetness of a first kiss from those full, inviting lips.

Laughter, the chatter of familiar voices intruded upon the silence, breaking the spell. Phyllida jumped back, shaken. She felt very much as she did when she dreamed of falling and awoke with a start. What was she doing, standing so close to this man, wanting him to kiss her? She forced herself to turn away, to face the door where the Wakefields now appeared, the others crowding in behind them. Thankfully they all stopped in the doorway, blinking as their eyes grew accustomed to the dim light and that gave her the opportunity to recover herself and school her face into a semblance of calm.

'Why, Lady Phyllida, you are here before us. We thought you were still wandering through the ruins.'

She forced herself to acknowledge Lady Wakefield's cheerful greeting, to smile and make a suitable reply. The moment was gone, the small chapel was now full of people and noise. Phyllida linked her arm with Ellen's and accompanied her around the small church, admiring the ancient tomb and the arched window with its elegant tracery. She did not look back at Richard. She could hear his voice, cool and steady with just a hint of amusement, but in her mind's eye she recalled his face when they had stood alone in the chapel. The blaze of passion that had set her heart racing and then something quite different when they were interrupted. The look of shock, of horror, at what had almost occurred.

They did not tarry in the chapel and soon the party made its way back to the stables to collect the horses. Henry Fullingham was waiting for them, sitting on a mounting block and chatting with Parfett and Lady Wakefield's groom. Phyllida blinked. She had not even noticed he was not with the others. To be honest she had noticed very little since that moment alone with Richard in the chapel. She heard Lady Wakefield murmur to her husband as they followed Phyllida into the stable yard.

'If you were to ask me, Mr Fullingham is not at all interested in the romantic ruins.'

'I quite agree, my dear,' chuckled Lord Wakefield. 'He lounged off in a sulk when it was clear the girls preferred Adrian's ghoulish tales to his flirting. And look now, if he was hoping to help any young lady on to her horse he is foiled again, for the grooms are there before him!'

Lady Wakefield turned to Phyllida, saying as they watched the younger ones mounting up, 'Well, ma'am, are you glad you came?'

'I have enjoyed it very much, ma'am. I am grateful to you for arranging it.'

'Thanks, too, should go to Lady Hune for her introduction,' put in Lord Wakefield. 'Without it I doubt our reception would have been quite so hospitable. The refreshments were truly exceptional. Pray, Mr Arrandale, tell Lady Hune we are obliged to her, when you get back to Royal Crescent.'

Phyllida had been lost in her own thoughts and had not realised Richard was so close. He had filled her thoughts and now the unexpected sight of him at her shoulder caught her unawares. The erratic beat of her heart disturbed her breathing. She was obliged to concentrate very hard to prevent herself from simpering and blushing like a schoolgirl when he asked if he might help her into the saddle.

She accepted in as dignified a manner as she could manage, trying not to think how strong he must be to throw her up so effortlessly. She forced herself to appear calm and unruffled while he checked the girth and adjusted her stirrup but her nerves were still on edge. She could not prevent her thoughts from racing ahead. What if he helped her down when they reached Charles Street? She would slide into his arms. They would envelop her, of course, and hold her close while he smiled down at her. His eyes would be gleaming with tender amusement and that would draw from her an answering smile before he bent his head and…and…

'We must behave ourselves on the return journey, Lady Phyllida.'

Richard's quiet words made her jump guiltily. He was standing beside Sultan, one hand resting on the gelding's neck and only inches from her knee. She looked down at him, dazed, and saw just such laughter in his eyes as she had imagined. It stirred something deep inside her, something that disturbed and excited her in equal measure.

From across the yard Ellen called out with

mock severity, 'Indeed you must, Stepmama. Such a bad example you would be setting us!'

Phyllida was at a loss to answer her. She knew Ellen was referring to the madcap race across the turf, but she was aware that in the chapel she had come perilously close to being discovered locked in an embrace with Richard Arrandale. The look of smiling understanding in that gentleman's eyes compounded her confusion. There was such warmth, such friendship in his glance that she could not resist smiling back at him, but as they set off on the long ride back she regained command of her senses and forced herself to face the depressing reality of the situation. Richard Arrandale had no interest in her, he was merely trying to put her at her ease in order to advance his pursuit of Ellen.

Chapter Six

The afternoon was well advanced by the time they rode into Bath and the party broke up in Laura Place.

'What a delightful day,' exclaimed Ellen. 'Thank you so much for inviting me, Lady Wakefield.'

'It was a pleasure to have you with us, my dear.' Lady Wakefield's smile encompassed everyone. 'I think we all enjoyed it.'

'Well, Lady Phyllida?' Richard brought his horse alongside Sultan. '*Did* you enjoy yourself?'

She had had time to regain her composure and now answered cautiously, 'The castle was well worth seeing.'

'But originally you did not intend joining the party. Why did you change your mind?'

'Does there have to be a reason?' she parried lightly.

'Well, I am very glad you *did* come,' he said. 'I have enjoyed renewing our acquaintance, my lady.'

Her brows went up.

'Trying to turn me up sweet, Mr Arrandale?'

He grinned. 'Could I do so?'

'Never.' She was in control of herself now, and felt confident enough to add, 'I am no longer a shy *ingénue*, sir, to be impressed by your blandishments.'

She inclined her head, dismissing him, and walked Sultan across to where Ellen was taking her leave of Julia and her family. A brief word with Lady Wakefield and she drew her stepdaughter away, saying it was time they went home.

'Oh,' said Ellen. 'Perhaps Mr Arrandale and Mr Fullingham would like to—'

'No, I think not. We have imposed upon them quite long enough today. Good day, gentlemen.' Phyllida's voice was firm, she would brook no argument.

Richard touched his hat as they rode past him and once he had taken his leave of the Wakefields he was left with only Henry Fullingham for company. They turned their horses and made their way together towards Pulteney Bridge. Fullingham chuckled.

'Well, I am indebted to you today, Arrandale. In trying to ingratiate yourself with the mother you left the field clear for me to cut you out with the heiress.'

'Perhaps that was my intention,' drawled Richard. 'I knew she would soon grow weary of your inane chatter.'

'Not a bit of it. Miss Tatham was as friendly as can be.'

'Not when we were at the castle,' Richard pointed out.

Fullingham scowled at him.

'Not *then*, perhaps, but on the ride there and back she was clearly delighted with my company. Urmston's right, she is a ripe plum, ready for plucking.'

'Do not be too sure. There is a sharp intelligence behind Miss Tatham's pretty face. She'll not easily fall for your charms, Fullingham.'

'Pho, Arrandale, that is sour grapes.' He laughed. 'Admit it, man, you have caught cold on this one. The widow has your measure. She'll be spending her time keeping you away from her precious daughter and won't spare a thought for the rest of us!'

They had reached the junction and Fullingham went on his way, still laughing. Richard rode slowly to the stables behind Royal Crescent. He couldn't help thinking that the fellow was right, Phyllida might well be blind to the danger posed by the other men. She might even welcome their attentions towards Ellen, even those of Sir Charles Urmston. There was no doubt the fellow could be very charming, but underneath he was a villain. Richard's mouth tightened. He meant to win this wager. When it came to women he had never yet lost out to a rival, and he had no intention of starting now.

And what of Phyllida?

Richard's hand tightened on the reins. That incident in the chapel should never have happened. He had felt curiously lightheaded, probably from the wine they had been served at the house. It could certainly not have been anything else; he was not one to lose his head over any woman, especially one who was only tolerably pretty.

Although she did have particularly fine eyes.

And her smile. When she smiled she illuminated a whole room—

No! His only interest in Lady Phyllida was as Ellen Tatham's guardian and as a friend of his great-aunt. If she were to confide her worries to the dowager that would make life difficult. Not impossible, but he should not like to fall out with Sophia. A bitter, humourless smile twisted his mouth. Phyllida had told him she did not believe the Arrandales were really so scandalous. This little adventure would show her how wrong she was.

For the next few days he concentrated upon fixing his interest with Miss Tatham. He paid morning calls in Charles Street, and when Ellen hinted they were going shopping he tarried in

Milsom Street until they arrived, or he sought them out at the Pump Room and curtailed his own visit to walk them home. Lady Phyllida was cool, even a little reserved, but not overtly hostile and when Ellen informed him innocently that she and Lady Phyllida would be taking a stroll in Sydney Gardens with Julia Wakefield the following morning he made sure he was there, just in case he needed to head off any of his rivals.

'Mr Arrandale, what a surprise to find you here,' declared Ellen when she saw him approaching, not long after they had entered the gardens.

'Yes, isn't it,' muttered Phyllida.

'We are going to the labyrinth,' explained Julia Wakefield.

'Then I will walk with you, if I may.'

'But we are going in the opposite direction to you, Mr Arrandale,' Lady Phyllida pointed out. 'Are you sure you have time?'

He ignored the challenge in her eyes and replied with a smile as false as her own, 'All the time in the world, ma'am.'

He turned to walk with Ellen but Phyllida stepped between them.

'Then that is very civil of you, Mr Arrandale.'

She proceeded to converse with him as they strolled along the wide path. Occasionally they were obliged to move aside to allow a carriage to pass, but every time they recommenced their walk she was there, at his side, and engaging him in conversation.

He wondered briefly if she was trying to fix his interest, following their time together at Farleigh Castle but he soon dismissed the thought. Then she had been open and relaxed with him. Now her cool friendliness did not ring true. She was on her guard and he thought it much more likely that she was suspicious of his motives. Clearly she did not intend to allow him a chance to converse with either of the young ladies and he knew better than to attempt it. When they arrived at the labyrinth he thought it politic not to offer to accompany them inside, and prepared to take his leave.

'Oh, but you must stay and keep Phyllida company,' Ellen protested. 'She does not like the maze and means to wait for us outside.'

'No, Ellen, that will not be necessary. I am sure Mr Arrandale has better things to do with his time.'

Lady Phyllida's answer was delivered firmly. Clearly it was designed to dismiss him. He knew he should retire with good grace but his particular devil prompted him to stay.

'I should be delighted to wait for you, Miss Tatham.' He patted his pocket. 'And I have a plan of the labyrinth, so if you get lost you only need to call out and I shall come to your aid.'

Phyllida's eyes sparkled with indignation, but Ellen was duly admiring.

'How gallant, and enterprising,' she remarked. 'Come along, Julia. Phyllida, pray you, wait on that bench for us—we will not be too long.'

The girls ran off, leaving Phyllida with Richard Arrandale. It was the first time they had been alone together since the chapel at Farleigh, when she had come close to making a complete fool of herself. It had not been mentioned, of course, and since then she had been careful to keep a distance between them. Until today, when she had put herself in his way and kept him talking. She had not been comfortable about it, but she was determined that he should not be allowed to give his arm to Ellen or Julia Wakefield.

She had to admit that he had taken it in good part and had behaved like the perfect gentleman, conversing with her as if there was nothing he would rather do. He had a knack of setting her at her ease, of making her feel important. Cherished. That was what made it so difficult to dislike him.

Yet it did not mean she should encourage him. She moved towards a bench.

'I must not take up any more of your time, Mr Arrandale, so I will bid you good day.'

'I assure you, Lady Phyllida, I am at your disposal.'

She sat down, saying with finality, 'Really, Mr Arrandale, it is not at all necessary for you to wait with me.'

'But I have a plan of the labyrinth.'

It gave her no little satisfaction to respond, tapping her reticule. 'So, too, have I.'

'Ah.'

It was then she made the mistake of peeping up at him. She saw his rueful look and burst out laughing.

'Admit it, sir, you have been brought to the *point non plus*. There is no reason to stay now.'

'Would you have me be so unchivalrous as to agree with you?' he said, sitting down on the bench beside her. 'It has never been my practice to abandon a lady when she is on her own.'

'But I shall not be on my own once the girls return.'

'Then I shall keep you company until then.'

His cool response flustered her.

'But I do not wish for your company.'

He shifted to the far end of the bench and twisted in his seat to look at her, resting one hand negligently along the backrest. Phyllida remained rigidly upright, staring straight ahead. He really was the most infuriating man. Well, she hoped he appreciated her profile.

'We could converse,' he said at last.

'We have already done so, on the way here.'

'But there must be something we have not yet talked about.'

'No.'

She could feel the warmth of his gaze upon her. It sent little shards of excitement to pierce the armour of cool civility with which she had surrounded herself. If only he would go away! She recalled reading somewhere that the best form of defence was attack and she turned to face him.

'Yes, there is something. Why do you remain in Bath, Mr Arrandale?'

'I enjoy spending time with my great-aunt.'

'Is that truly the reason?' She subjected him to a searching look.

'Yes, truly. She was laid very low when Cassandra eloped, and I know how cruel the gossipmongers can be. None better.' He raised his brows. 'You look sceptical, Lady Phyllida. Do you not believe me?'

She pursed her lips.

'I can believe you came to Lady Hune's assistance when she wrote to you, but she is much better now and the image of you playing companion to an elderly lady does not quite fit with your reputation.'

'Perhaps you should not put too much store by all you hear of me, ma'am. I am extremely fond of Lady Hune. When I was younger she was the only one of my family who had any faith in me and while she needs me I shall remain in Bath.'

'But it is hardly London, is it? Do you not find it dull here? After all, Lady Hune demands very little of your time.'

'True, but there are gambling hells, if one knows where to look, and—'

'And heiresses to chase.'

'That is not what I was going to say.'

'No, I thought I would save you the trouble.'

'There is sufficient society in Bath to entertain me for a few weeks, Lady Phyllida. I am not so very exacting.'

Oh, heavens, he was smiling at her, just as he had done in the chapel at Farleigh. She could feel the tug of attraction building again. It must not, could not happen. With relief she heard Ellen and Julia's girlish laughter near at hand. It gave her the strength to look away and she observed the girls running towards her.

'We lost all track of the time, Lady Phyllida,' said Julia guiltily. 'I do hope we were not gone too long.'

Phyllida rose to her feet and replied with determined cheerfulness, 'Not at all. I am glad I did not have to resort to my map to find you and bring you out. However, we had best be getting back now.' She turned to Richard. 'We can trespass on your time no longer, sir. I am going to escort Miss Julia home now.'

'Too soon, Lady Phyllida. My way lies with you. It would look very odd if I were to follow you all the way to Laura Place, would it not?'

'It would indeed.' Ellen giggled.

She showed no desire to release Julia's arm in favour of Richard Arrandale's, which relieved Phyllida's mind of its greatest worry, but the gentleman was in no way discomposed and merely fell into step beside Phyllida, which threw up quite a different anxiety.

She felt such conflicting emotions about this man. She knew he was a rake and even though she suspected—nay, she was sure—he was pursuing Ellen, she could not dislike him. Just having him at her side set her pulse jumping. She thought it would be easier if she cut the acquaintance altogether, but that might well precipitate the thing she was most anxious to avoid. Phyllida knew Ellen liked Richard Arrandale, but at present it was no more than that. If Phyllida was to forbid Ellen to have anything more to do with him she was very much afraid it would invest Richard with an air of danger and illicit excitement that a spirited young girl would find irresistible.

Her companion showed no desire to talk, so Phyllida was able to consider her dilemma in peace, until she realised they had traversed almost the length of Great Pulteney Street in silence. Even worse, Ellen and Julia were nowhere in sight.

'They hurried on ahead and are by now at Lady Wakefield's house,' Richard told her, as if aware of her alarm.

He kept up with her easily as she quickened her step and they reached the Wakefields' door just as the two girls emerged and Julia very prettily requested that Ellen might join them for dinner.

'I have asked Mama,' she added, 'and she says she will send Ellen home in the carriage, if you will allow it, Lady Phyllida.'

Ellen clasped her hands and subjected Phyllida to a beseeching look.

'Please tell me I may stay, *darling* Stepmama. And I am sure Mr Arrandale will accompany you, so you need have no worry about walking back to Charles Street unattended.'

'I should be delighted to escort Lady Phyllida,' he responded promptly.

Ellen beamed at him.

'Then it is all settled to everyone's satisfaction!' Ellen reached up and gave Phyllida a hasty kiss on the cheek, then ran indoors with Julia.

Speechless, Phyllida watched them go. This was not at all to her satisfaction. Richard held out his arm to her and silently she placed her fingers on his sleeve. They began to walk.

'Are you going to tell me that you are quite capable of walking back to Charles Street unattended?'

'I should not say anything so uncivil,' she replied loftily.

'That's put me in my place.'

She caught herself up on a laugh.

'You are quite shameless, you know.'

'I fear you are right. And I am going to prove it by asking you why you married Tatham.'

It was an impertinent question and Richard wondered if he had gone too far. She had every right to protest. She might even snatch her arm away and refuse to walk further with him. Instead she answered him quietly.

'Because he offered for me. I didn't *take*, you see, amongst the *ton*, but I had very little to recommend me. If you really do remember then you will know how gauche and awkward I was then.'

'So Sir Evelyn proposed.'

'Yes. He was rich, but he was also kind, much kinder to me than my parents were. To them I was nothing more than a commodity, to be used to the family's best advantage.'

Richard's jaw clenched tight. Knowing his world he was well aware of what might have happened to her, sold to the highest bidder.

'And was it a good marriage?'

'I think so. I believe I made Sir Evelyn happy, even though I failed to give him the heir he wanted.'

'I am not interested in Tatham,' he said roughly. 'What about *you*, were you happy?'

She smiled. 'Why, yes, why should I not be?'

'Did you love him?'

The little hand resting on his sleeve trembled.

'I did not dislike him, and that is very important.'

Her cool, reasonable response angered him. Smothering a curse he stopped and pulled her round to face him.

'How old are you, Lady Phyllida?'

She blinked. 'I am four-and-twenty, not that it is any concern of yours!'

'No, but it concerns me that you should be dwindling into widowhood before you have even lived.'

'Mr Arrandale, I assure you I am not at all unhappy with my lot.'

He shook his head at her.

'I saw your face when we raced the horses the other day. How often have you felt like that? When was the last time you really enjoyed yourself, dancing 'til dawn, walking in the moonlight, being kissed senseless—?'

Her eyes widened at that and she drew away from him.

'You should not be talking to me in this way.' She looked around. 'We—we are at Charles Street. Thank you for your escort. Forgive me if I do not ask you to come in.'

With that she left him, almost running the last few yards to her door, where she was soon lost to sight.

Damn, damn, damn! What was he thinking of? Richard turned on his heel and strode away. He was supposed to be making a friend of her, preparing the ground so that she would support him when he made Ellen an offer. Instead he was saying all the wrong things.

What in hell's name had got into him?

September advanced and the invitations continued to flood into Charles Street, including an urgent message one morning from Mrs Desborough, inviting them to take advantage of the continuing good weather to drive out of town and enjoy a picnic that very day. The Wakefields were going, which made Ellen keen to go and even Phyllida found the idea too tempting to resist.

'I always think these things are so much better *impromptu*,' declared Lady Wakefield as they made themselves comfortable on the rugs and cushions spread out upon the grass. 'I am so pleased Mrs Desborough suggested it, and such a pleasant spot, too.'

Phyllida could not deny the spot was indeed delightful, a sloping meadow near the little village of Claverton, but she was not quite so happy with some of the company. Mrs Desborough had laughingly explained that Mr Fullingham had come upon her as they were about to set off.

She continued. 'I had not the heart to say him nay, not when young Mr Wakefield had already asked Mr Arrandale to join us. After all, there is space enough here for everyone, is there not?'

'And you have refreshments enough for an army,' chuckled her fond spouse, eyeing the array of hampers set out before them. 'But it is not only good food she has arranged for us, is that not so, my dear?'

'Well, I did think that afterwards the young people might like to gather blackberries. The hedgerow is positively thick with them.' She chuckled and beckoned to one of the servants who came forward. 'You see I have brought three small baskets for you to fill, and to save you young ladies ruining your gowns there are aprons for you to put on.'

Lady Wakefield laughed. 'Then there can be no objection. You have thought of everything, ma'am!'

They dined well on cold meats and cakes washed down with wine or small beer, but soon the effects of good food and the heat of the day took their toll. The party became less noisy and conversation began to die away to a soft murmur that Phyllida found quite soporific. Her eyelids were beginning to droop when she heard Penelope Desborough's eager voice.

'May we go and collect blackberries now, Mama?'

Mrs Desborough and Lady Wakefield were nodding sleepily, their spouses already snoring gently in the warm sunshine. As the young ladies donned their aprons Phyllida glanced across at the hedgerow. It meandered away for quite some distance and she was suddenly struck with misgiving. Of course, the gentlemen might not go to help, but Mr Fullingham was already on his feet, followed quickly by Adrian Wakefield and Richard Arrandale.

She jumped up, which caused Mrs Desborough to exclaim, 'What's this, Lady Phyllida, do you wish to collect berries too? I made sure you would want to rest a little.'

'No, no, I am not at all tired,' Phyllida assured her.

Mrs Desborough sat upright, looking perturbed.

'But there are only three baskets, and I have no more aprons, ma'am, your gown—'

'Oh, that is of no consequence,' she replied airily.

Ellen laughed. 'I doubt if Matlock will agree with you, Philly! But never mind that. Here, you may have my basket, and I shall share with Penelope.'

The arrangements settled, they moved off towards the hedgerow.

Richard fell into step beside her.

'Three gentlemen, four ladies,' he murmured.

'Even numbers are not required for berry picking, Mr Arrandale.'

'Nor is a chaperon, Lady Phyllida.'

She put up her chin. 'That, sir, depends upon the company.'

Ellen had stopped by the hedge and her voice floated across on the still air.

'Adrian, will you help me and Penelope to fill our basket?'

Mr Fullingham stepped up. 'Allow me, Miss Tatham—'

'Ah, sir, I was hoping you would help Julia, because you see that she cannot quite reach those berries at the very top, there, and they look so delicious...'

He was subjected to a dazzling smile and Phyllida smothered a laugh as the gentleman went off to do as he was bid. She glanced towards

Richard and saw that he was grinning at her. Caught off guard, she blushed and looked away, but her confusion increased when she heard Ellen's next words.

'That leaves Mr Arrandale to help Phyllida.'

That could *not* please him any more than it pleased Phyllida. He would surely protest. She waited, but after a brief hesitation he swept a low bow.

'Your wish is my command, Miss Tatham.'

Phyllida glared at him and without another word she hurried away to begin filling her basket.

Mrs Desborough was right, the tall hedgerows were thick with ripe blackberries and Phyllida worked steadily. Her gloves were soon stained with berry juice and she had to take care to prevent herself from becoming caught up on the brambles. Richard Arrandale was only feet away from her. His body and the lush, straggling hedgerow hid the others from her sight although their voices floated to her from time to time. They were distant, unimportant. All that mattered, all that she could think of, was the man beside her. He had removed his gloves to pick the fruit and she found herself watching his long lean fingers as they gently plucked each soft, plump berry.

They worked in silence. Phyllida had placed the basket on the ground between them and was surprised at how companionable it felt. She was aware of the birdsong, of the hum of insects and the warmth of the sun on her back, but more than anything she was aware of Richard at her side. Occasionally he moved closer and pulled down the higher stems for her to collect the soft fruit, or held aside the thick branches so she could reach deep into the heart of the bush.

Clearly, it was her duty to keep Richard Arrandale away from Ellen, but there was no denying that she was enjoying herself, more than she had done in a long time. The thought surprised her and she realised how staid her life had become, not only the twelve months she had spent in mourning at Tatham Park but the years before that. Years spent running a household and looking after an ageing husband.

I became a matron at eighteen, she thought, as she reached between two long branches to pluck a few particularly juicy berries. *I was caught up in the duties of being a wife and mother as soon as I left the schoolroom, with no time for frivolous pastimes.*

'Oh!'

A thorn had penetrated the soft kid of her glove and pierced her finger.

'Keep still.'

Richard was at her side immediately and she found it impossible to remain silent.

'I fear I have no choice but to obey,' she told him. 'The thorns have caught at my sleeve.'

He stepped closer and she was painfully aware of the hard wall of his chest against her back. Her mouth dried, he filled her senses. She breathed in the masculine smell of him, the mix of soap and leather and an indefinable hint of musky spices. Surely she was imagining the thud of his heart against her shoulders, but she could feel his breath on her cheek and she trembled.

'Steady now.'

One hand rested on her shoulder while the other reached past her to lift away the offending thorny tentacle.

'There, you are free.'

Free? How could she be free when her whole body was in thrall to him? When he was so close she could feel the heat of him on her back? Phyllida shook off the thought and carefully withdrew her arm from the briars. When Richard removed his hand from her shoulder she felt it immediately, a yearning chill and an emptiness that was almost a physical pain. She stepped back and turned, only to find that he was close behind her, less than a hand's width away, his broad chest and powerful shoulders filling her view, like a cliff face. She was distracted by detail, the fine stitching of his exquisitely tailored blue coat, the double row of buttons on his pale waistcoat, the snowy folds of linen at his neck. The hammering of her heartbeat thrummed in her ears. Surely he must hear it, see how shaken she was? She tried to speak lightly to divert his attention and her own.

'Thank you, sir. I fear I could not have extricated myself without ruining this gown.'

She stretched her cheeks into a smile and looked up, confident she could ask him calmly to let her pass, but her gaze locked on to his mouth and the words died in her throat as she studied the firm sculpted lips. She was distracted by imagining how they would feel on her skin. She swallowed, forced her gaze upwards but that proved even more dangerous, for his blue eyes held her transfixed. She was lost, unable to move. She could no longer hear the skylark's distant trill, nor the laughing voices of those picking berries further along the hedgerow. The world had shrunk to just the two of them. Anticipation tremored through her when he ran his hands lightly up her arms and the skin beneath the thin sleeves burned with his touch. His fingers came to rest upon her shoulders, gently pulling her towards him as he lowered his head to kiss her. She made no effort to resist. Instead her chin tilted up and her lips parted instinctively as his mouth came closer.

It was the lightest contact, a slight, tantalising brush of the lips, but Phyllida felt as if a lightning bolt had struck her, shocking her, driving through her body and anchoring her to the spot. She kept her hands at her sides, clenched into fists to prevent them clinging to him like a desperate, drowning creature. She found herself straining upwards, trying to prolong the contact but it was over almost as soon as it had begun and as he raised his head Phyllida felt strangely bereft. The kiss had been the work of a moment, but it had shaken her to the core and she struggled to find a suitable response.

'You, you should not have done that.'

There was a faint crease at one side of his mouth, the merest hint of a smile.

'No one saw us.'

That was not what she meant at all, but it brought her back to reality. The thorny brambles were at her back so she sidestepped, breaking those invisible threads that had held her to him, even though it was like tearing her own flesh to move away from him. Distance gave her the strength to think properly again.

'I did not mean that and you know it. Your behaviour was ungentlemanly, sir.'

'You could have said no. You could have resisted.'

She scooped up the little basket and began to walk away.

'I should not have had to do so.'

He laughed softly as he fell in beside her.

'I believe I deserved some reward for rescuing a damsel in distress.'

She stopped, saying angrily, 'What you deserve, sir—'

'Yes?'

He was smiling down at her, sending her thoughts once more into disorder. Alarms clamoured in her head, it was as much as she could do not to throw herself at him and the glint in his blue eyes told her he knew it. With a hiss of exasperation she walked on.

'You deserve to be shamed publicly for your behaviour.'

'Ah, but the Arrandales have no shame, did you not know that?'

He spoke lightly, but there was something in his tone, a faint hint of bitterness that undermined her indignation. It could have been a ploy, a trick to gain her sympathy, but somehow she did not think so. With a sudden flash of insight she thought he was like a child, behaving badly because it was expected of him.

'Oh, how despicable you are!' she exclaimed. 'I should be scolding you for your outrageous behaviour and instead—' She broke off.

'Yes?' he prompted her gently.

I want to take you in my arms and kiss away your pain.

Phyllida was appalled. She had come very

close to saying the words aloud. With a tiny shake of her head she almost ran the last few yards to where Mrs Desborough and Lady Wakefield were sitting under a large parasol.

The two ladies greeted Phyllida cheerfully and although they noted her flushed countenance, they put it down to too much sun and suggested she should come and sit with them in the shade. Mr Desborough, who was now awake and enjoying a glass of claret, invited Richard to join him.

As the ladies admired her basket of blackberries, sympathised with her ruined gloves and uttered up thanks that she had not spoiled her gown, Phyllida recovered her equilibrium. She decided not to say anything about Richard's disgraceful behaviour, especially since it did not reflect well upon her own judgement in allowing him to take such a liberty.

No, she thought, as the others returned and they prepared to make their way back to Bath, she had learned a valuable lesson and she would be sure Richard Arrandale had no opportunity to repeat it, or to try such tricks upon her stepdaughter.

Chapter Seven

The season had not yet started in Bath but the Assembly Rooms were crowded for the latest ball. Lady Wakefield had offered to include Ellen in her party, but Phyllida had decided she should go, too. She was concerned at the number of gentlemen who were vying for Ellen's attention, so much so that she had mentioned it to Lady Hune, when they had met a few days earlier. Ellen was attending her dancing class and Phyllida had taken the opportunity to call upon Lady Hune and enquire after her health, but the dowager's kindness encouraged Phyllida to confide in her.

'I had not thought there would be so many gentlemen in Bath on the lookout for a wife,' she admitted. 'Ellen's inheritance is held in trust until she attains her majority in four years' time but even that knowledge does not seem to deter them.'

'And does Ellen favour any of these gentlemen?'

'No, she doesn't, and that is the most comforting thing, ma'am. She is a minx, and willing to flirt with them, although I make sure she does not go too far, and I allow none of them to be alone with her.' Phyllida stopped, frowning, trying to make sense of her worries. 'I wonder if perhaps I made a mistake in bringing her to Bath. Only, she could no longer remain at the school, and to incarcerate her at Tatham Park would have been too cruel. You see, the families of her close friends have moved away and the society there is somewhat limited now.'

'As you have discovered in the past year.'

She gave a reluctant smile. 'Precisely, ma'am. Oh, I know I was in mourning, but it would have been a comfort to have at least a few families I could call upon, instead of having to entertain my husband's relatives.'

'Is that Walter Tatham?' asked Sophia. 'He was always a pompous slow-top. I never met his wife but I suppose she is the same—you need not say so, my dear, I can tell by your face that it is the case.'

'I do not mean to be unkind, but when one has been the mistress of one's own household for years…'

'They tried to browbeat you, I suppose.' The dowager gave a little huff of exasperation.

'The thing is, they were against my bringing

Ellen to live with me, and I…' Phyllida bit her lip
'…I wonder now if they were right.'

'Nonsense, it is doing you the world of good to
be out in society again. You have regained your
glow.'

'You are very kind, ma'am, but it is not about
me.'

'From what I know of your stepdaughter she
is well able to look after herself,' retorted Sophia. 'She is a very pretty-behaved young lady,
confident, yes, and spirited, I always like that in
a girl, but she also appears to be quite sensible.
She will do very well, as long as none of these
fellows steals her heart.' She fell silent and from
the shadow of pain that crossed her face Phyllida
thought that perhaps she was thinking of Lady
Cassandra, her granddaughter. Phyllida waited,
not wishing to disturb the old lady's thoughts and
after a few moments the dowager gave herself a
little shake and resumed, saying briskly, 'Let her
enjoy herself, within the bounds of propriety, and
she will do very well.'

Sophia had hesitated for a moment, then
changed the subject. Looking back, Phyllida wondered if she had been about to ask if Richard Arrandale was one of those paying court to Ellen,
but the old lady was sharp enough to know the
answer to that. If Lady Hune would warn him
off, then all to the good, thought Phyllida now,

as she watched Ellen going down the dance with Henry Fullingham.

Phyllida felt a little guilty because her concern over Ellen was not the only reason she had decided to attend the ball. She had given in to the temptation to put on one of her old ball gowns. When she had seen that Phyllida was prepared to dance, Lady Wakefield had immediately found her a partner, and since she had assured her that she was perfectly able to keep an eye on Ellen as well as Julia, Phyllida gave herself up to the enjoyment of the music. She was not quite lost to all sense of her responsibilities, but Ellen appeared to have a partner for every new set, so Phyllida salved her conscience with the thought that the child could come to very little harm while she was dancing.

Richard saw Phyllida as soon as he entered the ballroom. She was on the dance floor, the folds of her peach-coloured gown flowing gracefully around her elegant figure as she moved. She was laughing at something her partner was saying, her face was positively glowing with happiness and his breath caught in his throat. She might not be an accredited beauty but there was an elusive charm about the lady that made her stand out from the crowd.

He dragged his eyes away. This was not why

he was here, his goal was to secure a fortune by winning the hand of Ellen Tatham. The previous evening at Burton's gaming hell he had heard the other fellows complaining that it was impossible to get the heiress alone. She was friendly to a fault, blushed adorably at their compliments, but made no effort to dismiss her maid when they were out together, nor would she allow herself to be separated from her friends. And if she was escorted by her stepmother the two were well-nigh inseparable.

Richard had said nothing but he was faring no better. In fact, whenever he met Ellen and Lady Phyllida the chit seemed to delight in palming him off on her stepmama. No, the only chance of a private word with Miss Ellen Tatham was on the dance floor and he quickly scanned the room for her. She was partnered by young Naismith, who was gazing at her with blatant adoration as they trod the final measure of a lively country dance. The music was ending and Richard saw his chance. He moved forward as Naismith escorted his partner from the floor. Ellen was already smiling but her smile widened when she saw him. Naismith was dismissed even before Richard had begged the honour of leading her out for the next set.

'Mr Arrandale, how delightful!' She tucked her hand in his arm and began to walk away with him. 'I would be very happy to stand up with you, sir, but first you must dance with my stepmama.'

'What?'

His step faltered but the little hand on his sleeve pulled him on. He could see Phyllida standing only feet away. She had just walked off the floor on the arm of an elderly brigadier.

'It is a rule I have made for tonight,' Ellen told him. 'Stepmama, here is your next dance partner!'

The brigadier bowed and walked away. Lady Phyllida looked around, her smile slipping a little when she saw Richard arm in arm with her stepdaughter. Then, as the meaning of Ellen's words sank in she blushed scarlet.

'My dear child, do not be absurd!'

'I told you I would not stand up with any gentleman tonight unless he had first danced with you.'

'Does that include the brigadier?' murmured Richard.

'No, but he pounced on Phyllida without my having to ask him.'

'Ellen, you cannot order people around in this way!' hissed Phyllida, frowning at her.

Richard put up his hand.

'Believe me, ma'am, I should be delighted to stand up with you.'

'Thank you, sir, it is not at all necessary.'

'Yes, it is, Philly, or I shall not be able to dance

with Mr Arrandale, and you said yourself he is quite the best dancer in Bath.'

'I said no such thing! Really, Ellen—'

Lady Phyllida was looking very flustered and Richard felt obliged to protest.

'Miss Tatham, I cannot dance with Lady Phyllida if she is averse to it.'

Ellen's face grew suddenly serious. She reached out and took Phyllida's hands.

'I only want you to enjoy yourself, Philly. Do you truly not wish to dance any more tonight?'

Phyllida hesitated. She could lie, and spend the rest of the evening sitting on the benches, watching everyone else enjoying themselves.

'I would, of course, like to dance…'

'There, I knew it.' Ellen was triumphant. She stood back. 'Off you go now. And, Mr Arrandale, I shall save the next dance for you!'

This was said so much in the manner of granting a child a treat that Phyllida, catching Richard's eye at that moment, burst out laughing. It relieved the tension and he grinned back at her.

'We have been outmanoeuvred, Lady Phyllida.' He took her hand and led her away. 'Your stepdaughter is very persuasive.'

'She is outrageous,' replied Phyllida. 'I do not know what she is thinking of.'

'Your happiness,' said Richard, remembering

the conversation he had had with Ellen during the ride to Farleigh.

She shook her head at that and took her place opposite him. The hot blush had cooled to a faint staining of her cheeks. It was very becoming, and in keeping with the smile that curved her lips and glowed in her eyes.

The music started, they saluted one another, stepped up, back, joined hands, moved away. They were in perfect time, thought Richard, their steps matching as if they had always danced together. A memory surfaced, clear as crystal. He suddenly remembered Phyllida at her come-out seven years ago: pale and shy in a room full of strangers. He had been pursuing his latest quarry, a dashing matron who had been throwing out lures to him for weeks, but every time he entered the hallowed walls of Almack's the patronesses seized upon him and he was obliged to dance with any number of débutantes before he was allowed to escape. Some became simpering idiots as soon as a man spoke to them, others were so forward he indulged them in a fast and furious flirtation before disappearing into the crowd.

One night there had been a débutante who neither simpered nor flirted. She was tall and thin, pale as her gown, pushed forward by her mother and clearly being offered up to anyone looking for a bride. No wonder they called the place the

Marriage Mart! Richard had taken pity on the girl, treated her kindly and taken her back to her dragon of a mother when the dance was over. Then he had returned to his dashing matron and forgotten all about the poor little dab of a girl.

Except, he recalled now, how it had felt to dance with her. True, during the first few bars of the music she had made a mistake and cannoned into him, but he had recognised that she was crippled with nerves and he had exerted himself even more to put her at her ease. After that she had danced beautifully, so beautifully he had thought at the time it was like holding hands with an angel.

That same angel was dancing with him now, holding his hand, circling, crossing, skipping around him. How could he have forgotten? All too soon the dance ended. Richard was unprepared for it, he was still confused by his memories. Mechanically he made his bow to his partner. Phyllida was not smiling, she did not meet his eyes and was reluctant to take his hand. In fact, he thought with dismay, she could not wait to get away from him.

Ellen was waiting as they left the dance floor, compliments on their dancing tripping from her tongue.

'Yes, well, now I have done my duty and it is your turn,' Phyllida responded, a shade too brightly, Richard thought, before excusing herself and hurrying away.

He led Ellen out to join the next set but he found it difficult to concentrate. His head was still full of Phyllida, how well they danced together, how he had enjoyed having her tall, graceful figure beside him. The way the candlelight glinted on the golden strands in her hair, the elusive, seductive scent of her. For pity's sake he must stop this sentimental yearning and concentrate upon his partner. After all, Ellen Tatham was the prize he had set himself to win. Never had a dance seemed longer, or less enjoyable, but at last it was over. Richard surrendered Ellen to her new partner and took himself off to the card room, but the games held no allure and after a wasted hour he returned to the ballroom, his eyes immediately seeking and finding Phyllida, who was dancing with Sir Charles Urmston.

Richard frowned. Was that at Ellen's instigation? If she was playing off her tricks on Urmston she might find herself undone. He stationed himself against one wall and watched until the dancers reorganised themselves for the next set and he was relieved to see Ellen stand up with Adrian Wakefield. Phyllida, he noticed, had detached herself from Urmston and was standing on the far side of the room. She looked composed now. Had she enjoyed dancing with Urmston? More so than standing up with himself? The idea annoyed him.

As if aware of his scrutiny she looked across at him and their eyes met, but she looked away again immediately. That annoyed him, too, as did the temptation to cross the room and join her. What was he thinking? A little dalliance was one thing, sufficient to win the lady over, but anything more would not help him to win Miss Tatham's hand and that was his objective. Wasn't it?

He wanted to leave, to clear his head, but Tesford and Cromby were clearly waiting to pounce on Ellen when the dancing ended and he knew he should stay. It was not in his interests to let any of them gain an advantage with the heiress. He glanced at his watch. There would be a break for refreshments next and Richard knew what to do. A quiet word with George Cromby came first, telling him that his wife's bosom friend was looking for him. That sent the fellow scuttling away to the card room. The music faded and young Wakefield was leading Ellen back to Phyllida. Urmston and Tesford were already closing in, determined to escort the ladies into supper. Richard made his move. A judicious nudge sent a waiter's tray flying and claret cascaded over Tesford's white-quilted waistcoat, forcing him to retire. He then intercepted Sir Charles on the pretext of asking him about the mare he was selling. By the time

Urmston had shaken him off it was too late for him to do any harm: young Wakefield had carried off Ellen and her stepmother to join his family. Richard sank down on the fast-emptying benches in the ballroom. He needed to think.

Phyllida listened to Ellen chattering away to the Wakefields but the words did not make sense. Nothing had made sense since she had danced with Richard Arrandale. The moves, the touch of hands, the closeness of their bodies when the dance brought them together—it had stirred emotions within her that she had never felt before. The crowd had disappeared; for a while it had been just her and Richard, alone together. Of course it did not last and she was foolish to wish it could. It was just a dance and however much he might smile into her eyes, however much she might read into his look, he was merely being courteous, as he had been all those years ago.

Even worse, she knew his courtesy had an ulterior motive, to gain her approval for his courtship of Ellen. That was out of the question. Ellen would make her come-out next year and Phyllida would ensure she enjoyed at least one Season in town before she decided on a life partner. Ellen herself had declared that it was not her intention to marry too soon, but Phyllida knew that hearts were fickle. A look, a touch was enough to send all sensible plans flying out of the window. Phyllida watched her stepdaughter as she chatted happily to Julia and Adrian Wakefield. She showed no signs of having lost her heart and Phyllida sent up a silent prayer that she would not do so for a long time yet.

Phyllida's head was aching. She longed to go home but the dancing had recommenced and her stepdaughter was once more in great demand. She watched with dismay as Richard Arrandale cut out Henry Fullingham and carried Ellen off for a second time. That was enough. She dared not allow Ellen to stand up with him again. It was not pique or jealousy, she told herself. Tongues would wag if any one admirer became too particular.

'Lady Phyllida, you are looking very pale, are you unwell?' Lady Wakefield's voice interrupted her thoughts.

'No, ma'am. I am a little tired perhaps.'

'Why do you not go home? I can easily convey Ellen to Charles Street later.'

'No, I am her guardian, I must be here to look out for her.'

She shook her head, but that made it ache even more horribly.

Lady Wakefield touched her arm. 'My dear, you look positively white. Do, at least go into the tea room and sit down quietly for a little while.'

When Phyllida hesitated she said bluntly, 'You are concerned for Ellen, having seen her stand up again with Mr Arrandale.'

'I know it is only a second dance,' said Phyllida. 'Perhaps I refine upon it too much, but...'

Lady Wakefield patted her hand.

'I shall make sure he does not dance with her again, nor any of the other gentlemen who have had their two dances. There are several young friends of Adrian's who have not yet danced with Ellen and I will make sure they get their turn. Off you go and look after yourself.'

'Ah, you understand,' murmured Phyllida, with a grateful smile. 'I will do as you suggest, ma'am, and find somewhere quiet to sit for a while.'

She slipped away through the door to the Octagon, but this was quite as noisy as the ballroom and she moved on to the tea room, where there were fewer people but their jackdaw-like chatter echoed around the lofty space. Quickly she passed on to the antechamber. It was empty for the moment and she sat down on one of the benches there. After a while the pain in her head subsided, but the hard knot of unhappiness in her chest did not. She closed her eyes as regret, deep and bitter, welled up. For a brief moment she wished that at seventeen she had been as beautiful and confident as Ellen. Then perhaps some young and attractive gentleman might have made her an offer, instead of a man old enough to be her father. Perhaps even Richard might have been tempted.

But there her sensible nature fought back. Richard Arrandale was a rake. If she had been pretty enough to attract his attention then the hard truth was that he would have seduced her. Phyllida sighed. The past was gone, it could not be brought back. Sir Evelyn had been a good husband, and even though they had not been in love they had been happy. He had treated her very well and given her the confidence and the means to stand up to her relatives and choose to live alone. She would always be grateful to him for that. And she would always be grateful for Ellen. She had become very fond of her stepdaughter and would do her best to make sure she was happy.

A familiar, amused drawl interrupted her reverie.

'I wondered where you had gone. Do you consider it safe to let Miss Tatham out of your sight?'

Her eyes flew open. Richard Arrandale was standing before her, looking so devilishly handsome in his close-fitting dark coat that her heart missed a beat and a wave of desire washed over her, so strong she thought she might faint. Afraid he might read her thoughts if she looked into his eyes, Phyllida fixed her gaze upon the single diamond winking from the folds of his snowy neckcloth as she responded.

'She will come to no harm while she is dancing.' Her voice at least was under control. 'Are you leaving?'

'Yes. That should relieve you of one worry, at least.'

'I have no idea what you mean.'

'Do you not?' To her alarm he sat down beside her on the bench. 'I have the distinct feeling you do not trust me. Is that why you are always putting yourself in my way, claiming my attention when we meet?'

'How…how absurd.'

He continued as if he had not heard her faint protest.

'And is that not why you changed your mind and joined the ride to Farleigh Castle, to save Ellen from falling into my clutches?'

'Of course not.'

'No? Then perhaps it was because you have developed a liking for my company.'

'How arrogant you are. And quite mistaken.'

'You did not stop me from kissing you, at the picnic. In fact, I think you enjoyed the experience.'

'Pray do not try to flirt with me, Mr Arrandale. You are wasting your time.'

'Am I? But you blush so adorably.'

His fingers touched her cheek and she jumped up as if she had been burned.

'Quite the contrary.' She took a deep breath. It was time to nip in the bud any pretensions the man might have. 'I think I should tell you, Mr Arrandale, that your reputation is well known to me. Before you came to Bath Lady Hune delighted in recounting your scandalous intrigues. You may be her nephew, she may be very fond of you, but from what the dowager has told me I do not think you are a fit and proper acquaintance for Ellen.'

He had risen too and was looking down at her, a faint crease in his brow.

'That is the word with no bark on it.' He paused a moment, as if weighing his words. 'Lady Phyllida, I did not come to Bath with the intention of pursuing any…er…*scandalous intrigues.*'

'But you had not then seen my beautiful stepdaughter.'

'Madam, I—'

Phyllida drew herself up as tall as possible, but even so her eyes were only level with his mouth. It was a disadvantage, to have to look up to him, but where Ellen was concerned she must be strong.

'Mr Arrandale, I am well aware of the temptation Ellen must be to you, and others of your ilk. She is rich and she is pretty, but she is to be presented at Court next year and *I have no intention* of allowing anything or anyone to interfere with my plans, do you understand me?'

She forced herself to meet and hold his gaze,

hoping he would see how determined she was. To her consternation the lines deepened around his eyes and a disturbing glint appeared in their blue depths.

'I might almost take that as a challenge, Lady Phyllida.'

A tiny spark of anger flared. Her chin lifted a fraction higher.

'You may take it any way you wish, Mr Arrandale. I am not afraid of you.'

Richard stared at the slender woman standing before him. Egad, how had he ever thought her mousy? Her honey-brown hair highlighted the creamy perfection of her skin and anger had deepened the colour of her eyes to a rich sea-green. They positively sparkled in the candlelight. With that stubborn tilt to her head she was quite captivating. He admired her spirit, but did she really think she could prevent him, if he wished to seduce Ellen Tatham? A tiny voice in his head urged caution, he should walk away and leave her alone, but for the life of him he could not ignore this woman. When he had seen her sitting alone and forlorn in the antechamber he had stopped to tease her, wanting only to put her sadness to flight. Now she had thrown down the gauntlet and the desire to pick it up proved irresistible.

He could not help responding but he grinned to show he was only teasing her.

'Let battle commence, then, my lady.'

Phyllida stared at him. Did he think she was funning? Perhaps a young girl's reputation meant nothing to him, but if he or any other man were to compromise Ellen her life would be ruined. With a final, scorching look and a toss of her head Phyllida turned and walked quickly back to the ballroom. If he wanted battle then she was ready. She would defend Ellen with her life, if necessary!

Dawn was breaking by the time Richard returned to Royal Crescent, where a sleepy servant let him in. He collected his bedroom candle and made his way slowly and unsteadily up the stairs.

He had just gained the landing when he heard his name.

'Is that you, Richard?' His great-aunt stood in her doorway, a shadow against the lighted room behind her. 'I cannot sleep, my boy. Would you join me for a glass of Madeira?'

He had had a surfeit of the wine already but he could not refuse Sophia's request. With a murmured assent he followed her back into the room, blinking in the light. It was an antechamber to the

dowager's bedroom and he frowned when he saw
the decanter and glasses standing on a side table.

'Have you been waiting up for me?'

'Devil a bit,' she retorted crudely. 'Can you not
see I am in my cap and nightgown? When you
get to my age you will realise that sleep does not
come so readily. You may pour us both a glass
of wine and then sit down. Where have you been
tonight?'

'Oh, here and there.' He settled back in his
chair. 'I stopped off at Burton's. Playing hazard.'

'And did you win?'

He grinned. 'Of course.'

'Good. And were you at the Assembly Rooms
earlier?'

'I looked in.'

'I believe Miss Tatham is attracting a great
deal of attention.'

He was on his guard now.

'Is it any wonder? She is a diamond.'

'She is also a babe,' Sophia retorted. 'Not yet
eighteen.' She held up her empty glass. Richard
eased himself out of his chair and went to the side
table to collect the decanter. She continued. 'Rumour has it that there is a wager to see who can
be first to seduce the heiress.'

'Where in blazes did you hear that?'

'I have my sources,' she replied darkly. 'Are
you aware of the wager?'

'I am.'

As he stood over her, refilling her glass, she said sharply, 'Are you a party to it? Are you making a play for Miss Tatham?'

He did not answer immediately, returning the decanter to its tray and settling down again in his chair before saying lightly, 'I would be a fool not to do so. She is very beautiful, besides being worth a considerable fortune.'

His great-aunt snorted. 'A schoolroom miss who would bore you within a month.'

'She would be better off married to me than to many of the fellows who are chasing her!' He let his breath go in a long sigh and sat forward, rubbing his temples. 'I was at Burton's when the idea was suggested. I went along with it—'

'Of course. When have you ever refused a wager?' She gave a rueful smile. 'You are an Arrandale, after all.'

'I had intended—that is, I thought I might make a push to secure Ellen Tatham for myself. After all, her fortune would prove very useful. Now…' His breath hissed out. 'I have had plenty of affairs, Sophia, you know that, and I've enjoyed them, but I have never yet met any woman I wanted to marry.' He shook his head. 'Pursuing an heiress, seducing an innocent—I have never been in that line. If you want the truth, I don't think I have the heart for it.'

'You relieve my mind.' He heard the rustle of a silk dressing gown as the dowager sat forward in her chair. 'Richard, I have known you all your life. I know you were sent down in disgrace from Oxford. I followed your career in town, all the scandals, the affairs, but I have never believed that was the man you were meant to be.'

He laughed. It was a harsh, humourless sound, even to his own ears.

'I am an Arrandale, madam. Scandal is our destiny. Look at my brother. And your own grand-daughter, for that matter!'

'Perhaps it is too late for Wolfgang, and I admit Cassandra's elopement was foolish, yet it was her choice and she must live with it. But you—Richard, there is much goodness in you, it is merely that you have not discovered it yet.' When he lifted his head to look at her she smiled. 'You think at five-and-twenty you know everything there is to know but trust me, I am older and wiser than you and I say you are not a rake.'

He spread his hands. 'Then what am I?'

The question hung in the air, answered only by the soft tick of the ormolu clock on the man-telshelf. Richard gave a shrug and passed one hand across his eyes.

He said wearily, 'I think I am more drunk than I realised. I beg your pardon, Sophia.'

'No matter. It is not the first time I have seen

a man in his cups. Go to bed, Richard, but first help me out of this chair.'

He asked, as he pulled her to her feet, 'Shall I ring for your maid?'

'Lord, no, I have only to throw off my wrap and blow out the candle. I am not so infirm that I cannot do that for myself.'

He kissed her cheek. 'Goodnight, then, Sophia.'

'Sleep well, my boy.' She clung to his hands, her fingers thin as claws. 'In the morning things might seem clearer.'

Her words came back to him the following morning as he lay in bed, hands clasped behind his head, gazing up at the intricately carved tester above him. The night's sleep had confirmed his thoughts, that he was damned uncomfortable hunting a schoolgirl, even if she was an heiress.

He shifted restlessly. Why had he made that foolish remark to Lady Phyllida? He should have realised she was serious, and would think that he was, too. Blast it, he had no wish to fight with her, but she roused in him feelings he had never known before. Feelings that confused him. More than that, they frightened him. He was no longer in control when he was with her, he acted in ways he could not explain and he was very much afraid that it was only a matter of time before he did something they would both regret. What that might be his mind shied away from, and he turned his thoughts once more to the wager.

Richard had committed many sins in his career but he had never deliberately set out to hurt anyone but himself. And his name. He had besmirched that with scandal, but any good that was left to the ancient name of Arrandale had been destroyed when Wolf fled the country. But Richard would not seduce a chit merely for a wager. He would leave that to those whose conscience was less troubled. His own conscience reared up uncomfortably, telling him he could not abandon Phyllida and Ellen to their fate but he beat it down again ruthlessly. He was more a knave than a knight in shining armour, even though Phyllida made him feel like one. Ellen Tatham was none of his concern and Lady Phyllida had shown herself more than capable of defending her ward. After all, it was only until Michaelmas. Three more weeks. And Sophia was in much better spirits now. If she could do without him he would quit Bath, and leave Lady Phyllida and Miss Tatham to their fate.

Having made his decision, Richard rang for Fritt and dressed quickly, hurrying downstairs to join Sophia in the breakfast room.

She said, without looking up from buttering a

freshly baked muffin, 'I expected Fritt to bring your apologies this morning. How's your head?'

'Aching damnably.'

'It serves you right. Drinking dubious brandy at that gaming hell, then coming home and keeping me up to all hours and consuming nearly a bottle of my best Madeira.'

Despite the headache Richard grinned.

'You do not appear to be suffering from the night's revels, ma'am.'

'No, I am very well this morning. In fact I think I shall forgo my visit to the hot baths and take myself shopping later in Milsom Street instead.'

'Your spirits are clearly restored, Sophia. I am very glad of it, for I think it is time I left Bath.'

That did make Sophia look up.

'Oh, might one ask why you should suddenly decide to leave me?'

'It is not you, Sophia, but you know it was never my intention to remain here indefinitely.'

'And what about that outrageous wager concerning Ellen Tatham?'

He frowned. 'I told you last night I have no wish to be involved in that.'

'But you *are* involved, Richard.'

He shook his head, which set off a thudding pain inside his skull. He said irritably, 'I shall forfeit my stake, but I want nothing more to do with that damned affair.'

Sophia did not reply, but he knew she would not let the matter rest there. In the ensuing silence he addressed his plate of cold meats. The food and a couple of cups of scalding coffee were beginning to take effect and he began to feel more hopeful. He would convince Sophia that she did not need him and he could be at Brookthorn Manor by the morning.

'So you would leave Ellen Tatham to the mercy of the fortune hunters.'

'She is none of my concern.'

'And Lady Phyllida?'

Let battle commence.

How he regretted those words!

'She is perfectly capable of protecting her own.'

'Is she? Do you really think she can keep her stepdaughter safe from the rogues and libertines who are pursuing her? I do not.'

He put up his hands.

'Even if that is not the case she would not accept my help. She thinks me the villain of the piece. No, ma'am, it is better if I leave Bath.'

'You promised to stay until I was better.'

'You *are* better, Sophia.'

'I do not think so.'

'There is work to be done at Brookthorn. You

are always telling me I should not neglect my estate.'

'Brookthorn Manor has been neglected for many years. It will wait a little longer for you.'

'Sophia—'

'Dr Whingate will tell you I am not yet fully recovered.'

'Whingate will say whatever you tell him—'

Sophia dropped her knife with a clatter.

'Must I beg you to stay with me?' she burst out, a slight tremor in her voice that he had never heard before. Immediately he capitulated.

'No, of course not,' he said quietly. 'I shall remain, if that is your wish.'

He thought he saw a flash of triumph in her eyes but it was gone before he could be sure.

'Thank you, Richard.' She sat back. 'And you will do your best to protect the heiress?'

'Now, Sophia—'

'I know, she is nothing to you, but she reminds me of Cassandra, and I would not like any harm to come to her.'

Richard stared at his great-aunt. She had never asked anything of him before, save his company. How could he refuse? The image of Lady Phyllida rose in his mind, indignant, outraged. It would take all his skill to lay her ruffled feathers. A *frisson* of pleasurable anticipation ran through him at the thought of it, but there was alarm, too. Instinct warned him against tangling with Lady Phyllida.

'Very well,' he said at last. 'I will remain in Bath until that sawbones of yours tells me you are well enough to survive without me. And I will do my best to foil any attempts to seduce the heiress, but it won't be easy. Ellen Tatham is as headstrong and spirited as Cassandra, and Lady Phyllida regards me with suspicion.'

She smiled at that.

'A challenge for you, then, my boy. At least you won't be bored!'

Chapter Eight

For Ellen and Phyllida the round of parties, dances and outings continued unabated. Invitations poured in and it was difficult to keep up with them all, but at least Phyllida knew that with so many social engagements Ellen had little time for secret trysts or meetings, even if she were tempted to agree to them. Phyllida was gratified that Ellen was in such demand and the most pleasing aspect of it all was that Ellen's head did not appear to be turned by all the attention. She was as happy to visit the library or the Pump Room with Phyllida as to dance the night away.

Following her confrontation with Richard Arrandale, Phyllida was at pains to keep an even closer eye on her stepdaughter, but although Ellen's suitors were as attentive as ever, Mr Arrandale was not one of them and it was a full week before they met again. Lady Wakefield had arranged a riding party to see the monument on

Lansdown but Phyllida's sister was due to arrive in Charles Street on the same day. Phyllida had planned to allow Ellen to ride out under Lady Wakefield's aegis and with Parfett in attendance, knowing that if all else failed the groom was more than capable of quelling the high spirits of a girl he had known from the cradle. However, on the morning of the ride a carefully worded message arrived from Lady Wakefield to say that she had sprained her wrist and that the party would now be chaperoned by her married daughter, who was staying in Laura Place for a few weeks. The message was couched in the friendliest terms, which raised no suspicion in Ellen's mind, when it was read out to her at the breakfast table, but Phyllida knew immediately what must be done.

'I shall come with you.'

'But what about Aunt Hapton? I thought you wished to stay and make sure everything was ready for her?'

'I am sure I can leave that to Mrs Hirst. Besides, Olivia is not due until dinner time, and we shall be back well before then. Now, if you have finished your breakfast, Ellen, perhaps you would send word to Parfett to bring both our horses to the door.'

'I will indeed. I am so glad you will be able to come with us, Philly, Parfett is always much more strict with me when you are not there!'

* * *

The party was to congregate in Laura Place, and when Phyllida and Ellen arrived, Julia and Adrian were already mounted and talking to Penelope Desborough. As the young people greeted one another Phyllida moved closer to speak to Lady Wakefield, who was standing at her door.

'How is your wrist, ma'am?'

'Very well, if I do not use it.' The lady stepped on to the pavement. 'A very silly thing. I was playing battledore and shuttlecock with my grandchildren when I slipped and fell.' She looked towards the house, where Phyllida could see two young boys standing in the window. 'There they are, Charles and Edwin, delightful boys, but so lively. They really wanted to come with you but Grace, my daughter, thought that at seven and eight years old they were too young.'

'Perhaps next time.' Phyllida smiled and waved to the little figures.

'I admit I was hoping you would join the ride.' Lady Wakefield dropped her voice a little. 'Grace is the kindest soul but she is far too complaisant to keep a close eye on the younger members of the party.'

'I would not have done so if your son was the only gentleman in attendance, but knowing that was not the case…'

She let the words hang and Lady Wakefield gave her an understanding smile.

'I know how anxious you are to keep Ellen safe, Lady Phyllida. I had hoped to keep it a very private riding party and was not pleased when Adrian told me Mr Arrandale was coming, but then, when Grace met Mr Tesford at the Italian concert last night and invited him to join us, I was most put out! However, it cannot be helped, and to forbid either of the gentlemen to come along would only make them more fascinating to the girls, do you not agree?'

'I am afraid you are right, ma'am.' She glanced around. 'Perhaps they will not come.'

That hope was immediately dashed when Lady Wakefield declared that she could see the gentlemen approaching now.

'Well, you need have no fear,' Phyllida told her. 'I will be vigilant on behalf of the girls.'

'I am sure you will and I am grateful, for I fear Grace will be little help to you on that front. Now, let me present her to you.'

Grace Stapleton was a cheerful young matron a few years older than Phyllida and with a restless manner. She was constantly looking about her and when the two gentlemen arrived she immediately turned her horse and moved off to greet them. Phyllida let her go and afforded the men no

more than a distant nod as the little party set off
through the busy streets. She positioned herself
close to the three girls, ready to head off any gentleman who tried to talk to them but her caution
proved unnecessary. A glance ahead showed her
that Mr Tesford was riding with Grace Stapleton
while Richard had engaged Adrian Wakefield in
conversation. She relaxed, satisfied that for the
moment there was no danger.

The open heights of Lansdown were soon
reached and with the monument in sight they all
cantered across the springy turf towards it. They
agreed to leave their horses at a small stand of
trees within sight of the monument and by the
time Phyllida rode up with the Ellen, Julia and
Penelope, the others had dismounted. Two of the
gentlemen were already making their way towards the girls and Phyllida quickly requested
the grooms to help the young ladies to dismount.
Mr Tesford stopped when he saw Parfett run to
Ellen's side, but Richard Arrandale strode on and
Phyllida warily watched his approach.

He put a hand on her bridle.

'Since your groom is engaged, perhaps you
will allow me to help you down.'

She was prepared for Sultan to throw up his
head and protest at the strange hand on the reins
but instead he stood quietly, unusually obedient.

Traitor.

'Well, my lady?'

Richard was already reaching up to her. There was no choice, and just as she had imagined doing in a dozen restless dreams, Phyllida slid down into his waiting arms. They tightened fractionally and she wondered if he could feel the frenzied thud of her heart as she was pressed against his chest. How she would love to give in to the temptation to stay there, to close her eyes and rest her head on his shoulder, which was at such a convenient height for a tall lady. If only he had been a gentleman and not a rake. Disappointment seared and she addressed him sharply.

'Thank you sir, I am perfectly able to stand.'

'Of course.'

He let her go and she stepped away from him, concentrating on shaking out her skirts so that he might not see the heat in her cheeks. She did not look up until her groom approached.

'We'll keep the horses here, m'lady, under the trees, until you're all ready to leave.' Parfett took Sultan's reins from her and led the horse away, leaving Phyllida with only Richard Arrandale for company.

'The others are heading for the monument. Will you allow me to escort you?'

She ignored his outstretched arm and set off, saying as he fell into step beside her, 'At least while you are here I need not fear that you are seducing my stepdaughter.'

'I would be very unwise to attempt it here.'

The amusement in his voice struck her on the raw.

'You would be unwise to attempt it anywhere!'

'I think you are right, ma'am.' Her suspicious glance swept over him and he continued. 'Would you believe me if I said I had no intention of seducing Miss Tatham?'

'No, Mr Arrandale, I would not.'

Richard sighed. What else could he expect, when he had teased her so at their last encounter?

'Lady Phyllida, I swear, on my honour, that I have no improper intentions towards your stepdaughter.'

'You *have* no honour.'

'Does it not occur to you that there may be other men who may be a danger to your stepdaughter?'

She waved a hand.

'I am aware of the dangers. I will protect her from them all.'

She spoke with confidence and he admired her spirit, but he was suddenly afraid for her, too.

'Is there no male relative who can help you to look after Ellen?'

She frowned, surprised by his question.

'There are uncles and cousins enough. As

you will discover, should you attempt to compromise her.'

'Confound it, woman, I have no intention of compromising her!'

'Oh?' She stopped and turned to look at him. 'What has caused this change of heart? A week since you were only too ready to do battle with me.'

Richard looked down at the defiant figure before him. She was so slender a puff of wind might blow her away, yet here she stood, toe to toe with him. He felt the smile tugging at his mouth. She was at least talking to him. He would be honest.

'You,' he said simply. 'You made me change my mind. I do not want to fight with you, Phyllida.'

Her eyes widened and darkened as she understood his soft words. He saw the varying emotions played out across her countenance, the flash of understanding, then desire, quickly followed by fear and indignation. He was sorry when she began to walk on, keeping her gaze steadfastly ahead. He set off beside her, tempering his long stride to match hers.

'You will not turn me up sweet with your practised arts, Mr Arrandale.'

'I thought we had already agreed I could never do that. But perhaps I should take inspiration from Sir Bevil.'

'I beg your pardon?'

He nodded towards the monument, soaring up into the sky and topped by its proud griffin.

'Sir Bevil Grenville. He was a Royalist commander who fought his way up here and defeated the Parliamentarians, who were holding the high ground. Incredible odds, but he succeeded in opening the way for a Royalist march upon London.'

'Really?' she asked, diverted. 'I knew the monument was something to do with the Civil War but I did not know its significance—there was a battle on this very spot?'

'Yes.' They had reached the monument and he followed her as she walked close to the railings that surrounded it. 'It was erected nearly a century ago by his grandson to commemorate the battle. The griffin on the top holds the Grenville coat of arms.'

'How fascinating.'

He shook his head, pleased but bemused at the sudden change from frosty ice maiden to eager student. She was quite enchanting. Phyllida turned to him, her former animosity forgotten, at least temporarily.

'And what happened to Sir Bevil?'

'Sir Bevil?'

He looked into her eyes and felt something shift, deep inside.

'Yes,' she said. 'What happened to him?'

Richard struggled to think.

'Poleaxed.' Was he talking of Sir Bevil Grenville, or himself? Something had changed within him, but for good or ill Richard did not yet know. He forced his mind back to Sir Bevil. 'He was slain as his men gained the high ground.'

She considered the monument for a moment.

'So the poor man never lived to see his success,' she said slowly. 'And in the end it did not make any difference to the outcome of the war.' She turned back to him and the twinkle in her eyes deepened. 'Courageous, I grant you, but it is not inspiration you should gain from here, sir. Rather, you should take a warning not to attempt the impossible.'

Phyllida walked away, head held high. She was unable to suppress her smile and a delicious feeling of elation. The gentleman had certainly not been the victor of *that* encounter. Perhaps Richard Arrandale was not such a threat, after all.

At least, not to Ellen.

The rest of the party were on the far side of the monument and Phyllida walked around to join them. Adrian Wakefield and Grace were trying to read the poems carved into the stone while the three young ladies were strolling arm in arm with Mr Tesford beside them. When he saw Phyllida approaching he gave a slight bow and moved away. She looked at the girls, her brows raised.

'Have I interrupted something?'

'Not at all,' replied Ellen with feeling. 'He is the most tedious character, always trying to separate us. Thank goodness you came and scowled at him.'

'I did not scowl,' Phyllida protested.

'No, no, of course not,' agreed Penelope. 'But you did look a little serious, and the fact that he retreated so quickly confirms Ellen's suspicion that he is up to no good.'

'Really?' replied Phyllida, startled. 'Has he said or done anything untoward?'

Ellen shook her head.

'Oh, no, he is always very polite, but he does prowl around, watching us.'

'Watching *you*, Ellen,' Julia corrected her. She turned to Phyllida, saying with a giggle, 'Ellen thinks he is trying to make up to her, ma'am. Because of her fortune. And it is true, he threw out the broadest hints for Grace to invite him today. He told her he had always had the liveliest curiosity to see Sir Bevil's monument yet he has scarcely looked at it.'

'I have no doubt Mr Arrandale did much the same with your brother,' Phyllida responded.

'He would not need to do so,' put in Ellen.

'Adrian is friends with Mr Arrandale and he knows that his mama likes him, too, in spite of his wicked reputation. Lady Wakefield says Mr Arrandale has been a model of propriety while he has been in Bath. And I have always found him most entertaining.'

Phyllida was startled by Ellen's fierce defence of Richard and she replied swiftly, 'I believe that is the way with most rakes. They are universally charming and it behoves ladies—young and old!—to beware of them.'

The girls stared at her and Phyllida wondered if she had been wise to respond quite so sternly, then Ellen gave a little trill of laughter.

'Goodness, Philly, that is the nearest you have ever come to lecturing me.' She reached out her free hand. 'Come along, *Stepmama*, if you are so worried for our virtue you had best stay with us until it is time to ride back.'

Before Phyllida could remonstrate with Ellen for her sauciness Grace Stapleton came up, hanging on her brother's arm.

'Did someone mention going back? I think it is time we did. There is a cold wind blowing and the monument's exposed position means we feel the full force of it.'

'Then if everyone has seen enough, let us return to the horses, by all means,' said Phyllida, wondering, not for the first time, if she was indeed up to the task of taking care of her stepdaughter.

As the little party made their way back to the copse where the grooms were waiting with the horses, Arnold Tesford fell in beside Richard.

'I saw you trying to butter up the widow, Arrandale. You won't succeed. I have tried but she is having none of it. She keeps a close eye on the heiress, too.'

'Are you surprised?'

'No, but I thought the chit might be ripe for a lark. Young women are very keen on secret meetings, that sort of thing. They think it romantic.'

'Perhaps it is your methods that are at fault,' drawled Richard.

'Oh? Have you had more success?'

'None at all, but then, I have decided to withdraw from the lists.'

Tesford subjected him to another searching glance then, having satisfied himself that Richard was sincere, he nodded moodily.

'Aye, thinking of doing so myself. Not that she ain't a little beauty, but she eludes my every attempt to get close. I don't see that I'll ever get her into my bed.' He was silent for a moment. 'I suppose I could try abducting her.'

Richard's blood ran cold, not only for Ellen

Tatham but for the effect such an action would have on Phyllida. He feigned indifference.

'I doubt if she'd go quietly, she looks like a little spitfire. And even if you compromised her I wouldn't put it past the family to hush it up and forbid the banns.'

'Perhaps, but remember the wager. I should still be ten thousand pounds better off.'

'If you lived to collect it.'

Tesford stopped, his brows raised in surprise, and Richard felt compelled to explain.

'It's true that the widow is the girl's sole guardian, but that doesn't mean she is friendless.'

'You mean there is someone who would call me out?'

'Oh, yes,' said Richard grimly. 'And he's a crack shot, too.'

'The devil!' Tesford went very pale. 'I wonder if the others know that?'

'I have no idea,' said Richard, as they began to walk on again. 'If I were you I'd warn 'em.'

Now what had possessed him to say such a thing? According to Lady Phyllida, Ellen Tatham had plenty of male relations, but he had no idea if any of them would be prepared to fight for her honour. Still, if the thought kept vermin such as Tesford from attempting an assault upon the girl he could not regret it.

* * *

Phyllida used the ride back to Bath to think over all Richard had said and done. He had assured her he had no interest in Ellen, and his behaviour today had gone some way to confirm it, but she could not be sure. She had so little experience of men. Of life. She wanted to believe him, she *would* believe him, although she would not trust him, not just yet. She would give him the opportunity to prove himself. That, she thought, was a sensible solution, and one that made her feel just a little happier. When they reached the streets of Bath and the party broke up to go their separate ways, Julia asked shyly if Ellen might be allowed to join them at Laura Place for dinner. Ellen spoke up before Phyllida had time to reply.

'That is very kind of you, Julia, but I really must go home. My Aunt Hapton is arriving today. She is Phyllida's only sister and I should like to be there to greet her. But we shall all meet up again at the Denhams at the end of the week, will we not?'

'Was that not the most wonderful ride out, Philly?' declared Ellen as she rode back to Charles Street with Phyllida. 'So much more interesting when there is a goal to be reached, although I think on balance I preferred the ruins at Farleigh, did not you?'

She chattered on, and when they had left their horses with Parfett and made their way into the house she even went so far as to throw her arms about Phyllida and hug her ruthlessly.

'I am so glad Mrs Ackroyd could no longer keep me in Kent. I thought at first that Bath would be the most boring place, full of invalids and old people, but I am having a most enjoyable time. And Penelope and Julia are quite delightful, so I am not missing my school friends very much at all.'

Phyllida returned her embrace, her heart swelling with pleasure and no little relief. She felt she had made the right choice after all.

'I am very pleased to hear you say so,' she said. 'Now, I think we should go upstairs and change. We must be positively windblown and if your aunt catches us looking like this we shall both be in trouble!'

They had only just come downstairs again when Lady Olivia was announced. She sailed into the drawing room, full of energy and with an apology tripping from her tongue.

'I have bad news, I am afraid, I can only stay three nights and then must away to London. Hapton is already there, poor lamb, trying to rally the opposition to this disastrous peace that Addington has brokered and he needs me. There are dinners to arrange.'

This was said so much in the manner of a soldier anticipating battle that Phyllida was obliged to smile.

'Oh, well, that is a disappointment but at least we have you for a few days.'

She invited her sister to sit down upon the sofa beside her. Lady Olivia was some four years older than Phyllida and had always been described as the prettier of the two sisters. She was now considered a handsome woman. Since her marriage to Lord Hapton ten years ago she had provided her doting husband with a quiverful of children, including three lusty boys. She ruled her household with a loving tyranny, and supported her husband's political aspirations. She would happily have taken the newly widowed Phyllida under her wing, if her younger sister had permitted it, but Phyllida was no longer the shy and biddable girl who had left the Earl of Swanleigh's household six years ago. Marriage to the kindly baronet had given her the confidence to take control of her own life and she had no wish to give up her independence. However, that did not stop Olivia from expressing her opinions.

When Ellen retired after dinner, leaving the sisters to enjoy a little private conversation, her first act was to take Phyllida by the shoulders and turn her towards the light.

'Hmm, widowhood suits you, Phyllida, you are positively blooming.'

'Olivia!'

She shrugged off her sister's laughing protest and made herself comfortable on a sofa.

'It is true, you look even better than when Tatham was alive.'

'Be careful what you say, Sister,' Phyllida warned her, 'I was very fond of my husband.'

'And so you should have been. He looked after you exceedingly well and you blossomed under his care. You lost the careworn, anxious look you had as a girl. That of someone about to be reprimanded.'

'With good reason,' put in Phyllida, a touch of bitterness entering her voice. 'Nothing I did ever pleased Mama and Papa. Save for marrying Tatham, and even then they made it very plain how fortunate I was to find anyone to offer for me.'

'Yes, well, your lack of looks did not matter to Sir Evelyn. He wanted a good bloodline and I must say he was always very generous, considering you never produced the son he wanted.'

Phyllida flinched at her sister's bluntness, but she could not deny it. Sir Evelyn had married her for an heir, but when their union failed to bear fruit he had accepted the situation with grace, behaving with more forbearance than Phyllida's parents, who considered her failure to conceive a personal slight upon their family and continued to rebuke her for her undutiful behaviour until their deaths some four years ago, when a sudden chill carried them off within weeks of each other.

'No,' continued Olivia, blithely oblivious of her sister's sombre thoughts. 'You are looking very well. Of course, you are tall and your figure shows to advantage in these high-waisted fashions.'

The unaccustomed wistful note in her sister's voice was not lost on Phyllida, who said quickly, 'As the mother of a large family, Olivia, it is no wonder if your figure is not so, er, willowy as it was.'

'That is true. And speaking of children brings me to another thing I meant to say to you, Phyllida. It has taken me only a few hours in Ellen's company to realise that she has lost none of her liveliness! From everything I heard at dinner she is leading you a merry dance, with parties and outings every day.'

'And I am enjoying it immensely,' replied Phyllida, with perfect sincerity. 'I have never been so busy, nor felt so happy. You have said yourself I am looking very well.'

Lady Olivia shook her head, saying ominously, 'She will run you ragged, mark my words.'

'No, no. Ellen is certainly spirited, but she means no harm.'

'But?' Olivia prompted her. 'I can tell from your voice that something is worrying you.'

Phyllida sighed.

'I had not expected her to be so, so *courted*.' She paused, her brow furrowed as she sought to explain. 'I know she is an heiress, but gentlemen are positively falling over themselves to befriend her, and not all of them unmarried, which is not at all what I expected.'

'Men are always susceptible to a pretty face, married or not.'

'And Ellen is undoubtedly very pretty.' Phyllida sighed again. 'I wonder, sometimes…however, Ellen is very good. Her head does not appear to be turned one jot by all the attention she receives. But I confess I had not thought Bath would be so full of dangers. She must be accompanied everywhere.'

'I thought you had brought her maid with you.'

'Matlock? Yes, she is here and I do, often, send her out with Ellen.'

'But you prefer to be with her yourself, is that it? So you have exchanged looking after a husband for caring for his daughter. You should pack her off to her uncle. Tatham would have her, would he not?'

'Yes, but Walter and Bridget are so, so…'

'Stuffy?' suggested Olivia. 'Outmoded? Boring?'

Phyllida laughed. '*Yes*! They would put Ellen in the schoolroom with their own children and that dragon of a governess until her come-out next year, which would be disastrous. I am sure she would run away. No, I am her mama—'

'Her stepmama.'

'Very well, her stepmama, but it is my duty to look after her.'

Olivia snorted. 'You are not old enough to be anyone's mama.'

'I am four-and-twenty.'

'Yes, and you should be enjoying your freedom now that Tatham is dead. A rich widow is a very attractive prospect for a man, you know. Well, there is no point in being coy, Philly,' she continued, when Phyllida made a quiet protest. 'Tatham only married you to get an heir.'

'And I failed him miserably.'

'That is not your fault,' said Olivia robustly. 'Sir Evelyn's health was poor when he married you and you must admit he behaved very handsomely to you. I have no doubt you would find yourself a dozen suitors if you did not have Ellen constantly by your side. I cannot lie to you,

Phyllida, she does rather put you in the shade,' said Olivia, crushingly frank. 'If you would but send her to her relatives you could have a very pleasant life.'

'But how could I do that to her? She has never liked her Tatham relatives and having lost her father how could I turn her off?'

'Easily. She is not you, Phyllida, she is far more robust and could survive a few months with Walter and Bridget, I am sure. And although I am very fond of Ellen I must say that she is very forward. The sooner she is married off the better.'

'No, not at seventeen,' said Phyllida quickly. 'It is far too young. Why, even Papa—'

She broke off but Olivia finished for her, saying in her blunt fashion, 'Papa waited until you were eighteen before he married you to a man old enough to be your father. But you are not Ellen, that school she attended has made her far more independent than is proper for a gel. I have never been in favour of educating young women but I know her father was adamant about it. No, at eighteen you were far too young to be married, and far too innocent. But then, that is what Tatham wanted, a young bride he could keep to himself, no hint of scandal.'

Phyllida could not deny it. Sir Evelyn had looked after her very well, making it plain to any young buck and even to the married men of his acquaintance that any attempt to dally with his young bride would not be tolerated.

'You have no idea how to keep the rakes at bay,' Olivia told her.

Phyllida put up her chin.

'I am learning,' she said quietly.

Olivia pursed her lips.

'Yes, well, I shall come out and about with you while I am here and see for myself just how well you go on. It is a pity that Hapton needs me with him next week or I would remain in Bath with you. But if Addington can be made to see that the peace will not hold then I may be able to come back here very soon.'

After that dire warning no more was said on the subject and the two ladies soon retired to their beds, the one with her head full of plans to bring down the government, the other hoping for nothing more than to get through the next few days without mishap.

Lady Olivia might stigmatise Bath as a slow, unfashionable place, but she was not unknown amongst its residents. When they visited the Pump Room the following morning it seemed to Phyllida that her sister was acquainted with almost everyone present, and of the remainder she knew some relative and thus claimed a connection. Consequently, their progress around the room was very slow. Ellen had already gone off to talk to Penelope Desborough, and as Olivia showed a propensity to take over every conversation, Phyllida found herself with little to do. She was happy to stand back and watch, thinking with an inward smile that with her talent for remembering everyone's name and family connections, her sister was the ideal political hostess.

'My dear, I can see that you are very well regarded in Bath,' murmured Olivia, as they moved on from the latest introductions.

'I am glad to have earned your approval, Sister,' Phyllida replied drily. 'I—'

'But that does *not* meet with my approval!' Olivia interrupted her, staring fixedly across the room.

Following her gaze, Phyllida observed that Richard Arrandale was now part of a small group gathered about Ellen and the Desboroughs. Olivia gripped her arm and began to propel her through the crowds.

'I do not know what brought Arrandale to Bath but he is not the sort of man to be allowed anywhere *near* Ellen. His reputation is most unsavoury.'

'I know all about his reputation,' retorted Phyllida, bridling, 'but I assure you he—'

'Oh.' Olivia's pace slackened as they drew nearer and the whole group came into view. 'So he is here with Lady Hune. I suppose in that case you are obliged to acknowledge the connection.'

There was no time for Phyllida to reply. Mrs Desborough had spotted her and was even now smiling and making room for them to come up. More introductions followed. Olivia might not approve of Mr Richard Arrandale but there was no sign of it in her greeting, and if, in the course of their brief conversation, she gave the impression that Miss Tatham was under her especial protection and would not be allowed to fall into the clutches of a known womaniser, it was done so subtly that no one could take offence.

Phyllida glanced surreptitiously at Ellen, hoping she would not resent her aunt's interference and was relieved to see that she and Penelope Desborough had their heads together and were paying no heed to anyone else. When Olivia claimed Lady Hune's attention Richard had moved to stand beside Phyllida.

'I am impressed,' he murmured. 'I have never been warned off in such an elegant manner before.'

She fought down the urge to apologise.

'Your reputation precedes you, sir. You cannot blame my sister for disliking the acquaintance.'

'I do not blame her. I am impressed by her eloquence.'

'But it is unnecessary, is it not?' She raised her

eyes to his face. 'You have already assured me you have no interest in Ellen.'

The smile in his eyes deepened, drawing her in and rousing the now familiar excitement within her.

'No,' he said softly. 'I have no interest in Ellen.'

For one heart-stopping moment Phyllida thought she might faint. It was as if, suddenly, there was nothing solid beneath her feet. She felt giddy, lightheaded as she gazed up into those blue eyes and read her fate.

'Phyllida, my dear, we should get on. We need to get back for Ellen's Italian lesson.'

Olivia's hand was on her arm, the ground was firm again and she tore her eyes away from Richard's smiling face, trying to muster her thoughts into some sensible, coherent order.

'Yes, of course.' Her vague smile encompassed them all, she did not think she was capable of saying anything more. She put her hand out to Ellen who was looking at her with an arrested look on her face. 'My dear?'

At her gentle prompting Ellen started and with a murmured apology she hurried to join her stepmama and Lady Olivia as they made their way out of the Pump Room.

Phyllida was lost in her own thoughts as they made their way back to Charles Street, but Olivia

and Ellen were happily talking and her silence
went unnoticed. Her head was full of Richard
Arrandale, the few words he had spoken, the look
in his eyes that had sent her spirits into such disorder. Had she misunderstood him? How could
she believe that he might truly be interested in
her? It was too incredible, too much of a fairytale.

'And what do you think of Mr Arrandale?'

Ellen's enquiry brought Phyllida crashing back
to reality and it was with inordinate relief that
she realised the question was posed to her sister.

'A wastrel.' Olivia did not mince her words.
'He is a gamester and a shocking flirt.'

'Well, I like him,' replied Ellen, equally blunt.

'That is neither here nor there,' retorted
Olivia. 'It is common knowledge that he has
squandered his own fortune and may well have
his eye on yours. Your stepmama would do well
to keep you away from such characters.'

'But I will have to meet *such characters* as
you call them when I come out next year, so it
is as well that I am prepared, do you not think?'

There was no arguing with Ellen's simple logic
and Phyllida, seeing her sister for once at a loss
for words, burst out laughing.

Phyllida was genuinely sorry when Olivia's
short stay in Charles Street drew to a close. It
was very pleasant to have her company when they

went shopping or enjoyed a walk in Sydney Gardens and she also shared in the task of chaperoning Ellen about Bath. Even on the final morning Olivia insisted upon escorting Ellen to her dancing class.

'Let me do this one last thing for you, Phyllida. It will give me an opportunity to say goodbye to Ellen. I believe Matlock is to escort her to Laura Place with Julia Wakefield afterwards, so we can enjoy a little time together before I set off for London.'

'But surely you would prefer to spend the morning resting,' Phyllida protested. 'Or perhaps you might even wish to set off a little earlier.'

'Why should I need to rest when I will spend the better part of the day sitting in a chaise? And as for leaving earlier, I have bespoke a room at the Castle in Marlborough and have no wish to arrive there much before dinnertime, so my morning is free.'

With that she collected Ellen and went out, leaving Phyllida to spend a couple of hours in the morning room, catching up on overdue correspondence.

Phyllida had just finished the last of her letters and was placing it on a side table when her sister returned.

'Do take a seat, Olivia. I asked Hirst to bring in refreshments just as soon as you returned—' She stopped when she saw the look upon her sister's face. 'My dear, whatever is the matter?'

'I think it is you who had better sit down,' said Olivia, grimly. 'I have just heard the most appalling news.'

The butler's entrance brought a temporary halt to their conversation. Phyllida went to sit in a chair next to her sister and they waited impatiently until Hirst had served them both with a glass of wine and placed a plate of little cakes on the table before them. As soon as he had withdrawn Phyllida put down her glass and turned to her sister.

'Pray, now, tell me what has upset you so.'

Olivia did not reply immediately. She took a sip of her wine, but one foot was tapping impatiently, a sure sign that she was seriously troubled.

'I have heard the most disturbing report, Sister. After I left Ellen at her dance class I thought I might purchase some marzipan as a little gift for Hapton—he has such a sweet tooth—and thus I went to the confectioners in Milsom Street. There I met with Lady Heston—not a particular friend of yours, I know. She is considered a little *fast*, I believe, but we were at school together, and it is never wise to cut a connection. As Hapton always says, one never knows when someone may prove useful.'

'Yes, yes, but what has this to say to anything?' asked Phyllida, bemused.

Olivia's countenance grew darker.

'Lady Heston has a…a gentleman friend. I shall put it no stronger than that, although I have my suspicions.'

'Olivia, will you please get to the point?'

'The point is, dear Sister, that there is a wager between certain gentlemen in Bath, as to which one of them will be the first to seduce Ellen! And there is a prize of ten thousand pounds for the winner.'

Chapter Nine

'Ten thousand!'

'You may well stare,' said Olivia. 'I was truly shocked when I heard of it. Not that I should have been surprised, when I saw the likes of Richard Arrandale and Sir Charles Urmston in Bath.'

'I do not believe Mr Arrandale is a part of it.'

'Then you are a fool. His family is renowned for their outrageous behaviour.'

Phyllida wrapped her arms across her chest. She suddenly felt very cold. Had he lied to her? She could not believe it. Surely the look she had seen in his eyes had been genuine. But she could not think of that now. She must fix her mind upon the bigger problem.

She said, 'It certainly explains why so many gentlemen have been attentive to Ellen.'

'Like bees around a honeypot.' Olivia nodded. 'I think you would be wise to remove Ellen from Bath immediately.'

'Do you think I should tell her?'

'By no means. I do not believe in telling children more than necessary.'

Phyllida was tempted to reply that Ellen was not a child, but Olivia's experience of the world was so much greater than her own. Surely she must know best.

'Seduction implies that Ellen would be willing, does it not?' she said thoughtfully. 'My stepdaughter is spirited, but I do not believe she has any romantic inclinations. Indeed, she has told me as much.'

'But with such a sum at stake, the inducement for any man to attempt to win her is very high, and by fair means or foul,' said Olivia. 'What are you going to do?'

Phyllida considered.

'I think we should remain in Bath,' she said slowly. 'At least here we are well known, and Ellen is accustomed to being accompanied everywhere. If we removed to Tatham Park it would be much more difficult to keep an eye on her, for she is so used to going out alone there and it would irk her beyond bearing to be shadowed. And if I insisted upon it, she might even begin to slip off on her own.'

'You have allowed that girl far too much freedom, Phyllida. We would never have disobeyed our parents in such a manner.'

'*I* certainly would not have done so, but I recall several occasions when you went off alone to meet a beau.'

'Yes, well never mind that now,' said Olivia, hastily. 'Besides, there was no financial incentive for any man to seduce *me*.'

Silence fell. At length Phyllida turned anxious eyes upon her sister.

'It seems too fantastical. Are you sure it is true?'

Olivia sighed. 'Lady Heston was always prone to exaggeration when she was at school,' she admitted. 'That may not have changed, but I do not think she would have concocted the whole story for my benefit.'

'If there is the slightest chance that such a wager exists then I must be on my guard.'

'But you will not remove from Bath?'

'No, I think not, although I shall hire another manservant to go about with us.'

Lady Hune had only recently suggested it. Did she, too, suspect Ellen needed extra protection, possibly from her own great-nephew? Phyllida shook her head. 'I have seen no sign that Ellen favours any one of her suitors above the others, so I do not fear an elopement. But there is no saying that if I were to take Ellen away some of these, these *persons* might follow us with a view to staging an abduction. That would be very much more difficult in Bath, where we are surrounded by friends.'

'That is very true.' Olivia struck her hands together and uttered a little cry of frustration. 'Oh, I am tempted to write to Hapton and tell him I must stay here with you. I really do not see how you will cope with this on your own.'

Phyllida put up her chin. 'I will cope. I am not the shy little girl you once knew, Olivia, and where Ellen is concerned I can be a positive lioness, I assure you.'

Despite her brave words Phyllida could not rest and once Olivia had departed she fetched her shawl and told Matty she would meet Ellen from her dancing lesson and accompany her and Miss Wakefield to Laura Place. The walk gave her time to consider what Olivia had told her and she decided to take Lady Wakefield into her confidence.

'Are you sure it can be true?' asked that lady, when Phyllida had explained everything. 'Is it from a reliable source?'

'My sister had it from Lady Heston, ma'am.'

'Well, I do not like to doubt the lady's veracity but I find it hard to believe such a thing would happen in Bath.'

'Nevertheless I cannot ignore it,' said Phyllida.

'No, of course not.' Lady Wakefield thought

for a moment, a tiny crease furrowing her brow. 'It would explain the inordinate amount of interest that some creatures are taking in your stepdaughter. Mr Tesford, for example. And George Cromby. One cannot cut their acquaintance, of course, without solid proof, but I have never liked either man very much.'

'And then there is Sir Charles Urmston, and Mr Arrandale.'

Phyllida held her breath while Lady Wakefield considered the two names, only letting it go when the lady shook her head.

'I cannot think they would be party to such an outrage, but neither of them has a spotless reputation and how do we know what any gentleman is up to at these clubs and gambling hells? Even Wakefield has been known to visit them.' She caught herself up and added hastily, 'Not that I mean he would ever be involved in anything as reprehensible as this, I assure you! Hmm. Have you mentioned it to Ellen? No? Well, I think you are wise. It could damage her confidence.'

That made Phyllida smile, despite her concerns.

'I have no fears for Ellen's *confidence*, ma'am. It is more likely to make her angry, and to wish to punish those concerned.'

'Nevertheless it would do Ellen's reputation no good at all if it got out. I think we would be advised to keep this between ourselves, if we can. You may be sure that I shall take good care of Ellen whenever she is with Julia, and will send my own maid with her in the carriage when I send her home to you this evening.'

Thus reassured, Phyllida left Ellen in Lady Wakefield's care and went back to Charles Street via the registry office, where she set about finding another footman to add to her household.

The next evening was the Denhams' ball. Phyllida was tempted not to go, but what good would that do? If she was to prevent Ellen from attending parties in Bath she might as well remove from the city. A number of nosegays were delivered during the morning, from the tasteful to the absurd and Phyllida found Ellen in the morning room with them all spread out on the table. Normally she would have been amused by her stepdaughter's popularity, but Olivia's revelation prevented her feeling anything but anxiety.

'Goodness,' she said, forcing herself to speak lightly. 'Are you deciding which gentleman to favour?'

'Well, some of them are far too big to pin to my gown,' replied Ellen, surveying the array with a slight frown. 'And I have no wish to raise false hopes.'

'No, indeed,' replied Phyllida solemnly.

'There is a very pretty arrangement from Sir Charles Urmston and—oh, this is not for me at all.' Ellen picked up a small spray of white rosebuds. 'This one is for you, Philly. It is from Mr Arrandale.'

'Indeed?' She felt herself colouring under the speculation in Ellen's eyes. 'How, how ridiculous.'

But how gloriously flattering. And heartening. Surely Richard would not be showing her quite such attention if his target was Ellen. Dare she believe what her heart was telling her?

'I do not think it is ridiculous at all, Philly. Why should he not send you flowers?'

'Because I am far too old for such things. I cannot wear them, of course, but they are so pretty I shall put them in a vase.'

Taking the nosegay from Ellen she left the room, glad of the excuse to get away from Ellen's bright, enquiring gaze. No man had ever given her flowers before, not even her husband. When she had mentioned it, on the eve of their wedding, Sir Evelyn had laughed and said that once they were at Tatham she could have as many flowers as she desired, all she had to do was order the gardener to send them indoors. Suddenly, she was quite looking forward to the evening. Phyllida had planned to wear her lilac gown with the white overdress. It would mark her out as Ellen's chaperon and preclude her from dancing, but at the last moment she decided instead to put on the peach silk. She had worn it before, but unlike the lilac it had no demi-train, and she would therefore be free to dance.

If anyone should ask her.

The Denhams owned a large property on the outskirts of Bath, but this did not prevent the city's residents from making the journey, for Lady Denham's parties were renowned. Phyllida had offered to take up the Desboroughs, since they kept no carriage in Bath and by the time they arrived at Denham House the dancing was already in progress. A large ballroom had been built at the back of the house with glass doors leading directly on to the gardens, which Ellen had heard would be decorated for the occasion with hundreds of coloured lamps.

Ellen and Penelope went off to find Julia Wakefield while Phyllida took her place with the matrons. There was no doubt the three young ladies made an entrancing picture, Ellen's golden curls showing to advantage against the darker heads of her friends and Phyllida watched the gentlemen beginning to gravitate towards the little group. Ellen was wearing none of the flowers so hopefully sent to her but she needed nothing to augment her sparkling looks as she stepped on to the dance floor with Mr Naismith. Phyllida's eyes roved over the assembly. Sir Charles Urmston was present, as was Arnold Tesford and Henry Fullingham. George Cromby was dancing with his wife, so she hoped he would not be paying Ellen undue attention that evening. She wondered which of the gentlemen were party to the wager.

If indeed such a wager existed. Here, amongst so many friends and acquaintances it seemed too fantastical to believe. After all, Olivia had heard it from only one source, and Lady Wakefield was inclined to dismiss it as mere conjecture. Perhaps it was all gossip. She prayed that might be the case. A sudden flurry of excitement ran through the room and she glanced towards the door, standing on tiptoe to see above the crowd. The Dowager Marchioness of Hune had arrived, escorted by Richard Arrandale. Phyllida's heart skipped a beat when she saw his tall, elegant figure with the black coat stretched across his broad shoulders. His light-brown hair was brushed back and gleamed almost golden in the candlelight. She turned away, trying to ignore the fluttering in her stomach as she tried to concentrate on what Lady Wakefield was saying to her.

Richard could not remember the last time he had felt such anticipation when attending a party. For once he was not seeking out the most dashing matrons with whom to while away the evening. Instead his eyes were roaming the crowd, looking for the willowy figure of Lady Phyllida Tatham. He soon saw her on the far side of the room, standing with Lady Wakefield and Mrs Desborough. Sophia tapped his arm.

'There is a free chair beside Colonel and Mrs Ongar, I shall sit there and you can go off and enjoy yourself.'

He did not argue, and after delivering her to her seat and exchanging a few polite words with the colonel and his lady, Richard made his way across the room to Phyllida. She had her back to him and he had no idea if she was wearing his roses. They would not look amiss against the muted shade of her gown which was the colour of a ripe peach. Then she turned towards him, as if aware of his approach and he saw the low-cut bodice was unadorned. His smile did not falter, but his spirits plummeted like lead, only to rise again when he observed the shy smile of welcome in her eyes.

Lady Wakefield claimed his attention and he spent precious moments talking with her until he could invite Phyllida to stand up with him, but at last he was leading her out. Her hand on his arm and the hectic flush on her cheeks stirred the blood and made his heart pound. She used no arts to attract him yet she moved him far more than any of the ripe beauties he had known. He wanted to sweep her into his arms and carry her away. Perhaps there was a summer house in the gardens where he could whisper endearments to her and steal a kiss, or even more. Deuce take it, he was acting like a moonstruck schoolboy.

'You are laughing, sir. Not at me, I hope.'

Her soft voice interrupted his thoughts. The musicians were striking up but there was still time to talk before the movement of the dance separated them.

'No, ma'am, at myself, for being conceited enough to think you would wear my flowers.' They crossed, turned, but she did not reply and he said anxiously, 'Did they offend you?'

That brought her eyes up to his. The soft glow in them made his heart swell.

'Offend? No, no. But I did not think it right to...' She paused, her cherry lips firmly closed, as if reluctant to speak. She said, just before the dance parted them again, 'I have them in water. On my dressing table.'

The idea of his flowers in such an intimate setting sent his imagination rioting and he almost missed his step. Phyllida moved away and they circled other dancers before coming back together. The dance obliged him to take her hand and pull her close, which suited him perfectly.

'So you will think of me when you go to bed tonight.'

Colour flooded her cheeks and he felt the hot burn of desire in his blood. They separated again. It was a penance to smile at his next partner, to keep in time when he wanted to rush through the dance until he was beside Phyllida once more. When at last he did get back to her she was very composed and her eyes warned him to go carefully. He smiled. It should be as she wished. He would court her as he had never courted a woman before.

Phyllida's heart was singing. She had never enjoyed a country dance more, never known a partner to regard her with just such a look as Richard was bestowing upon her. When he asked her to remain for the next dance her hesitation was brief. A quick glance showed her that Ellen was joining another of the sets so she could relax her duties as chaperon for a little longer and give herself up to the exquisite pleasure of dancing with the partner of her choice. Every look, every touch inflamed her and kept her heart fluttering like a captive bird. If he had taken her in his arms there, on the dance floor, she thought she might well have surrendered to him and thought the world well lost.

'Now *you* are laughing,' he murmured when at last the music ended. 'May I share your amusement?'

'No you may not,' she replied, blushing and smiling at the same time.

'Perhaps I can persuade you—no, I can see Wakefield bearing down upon us, and if I am not mistaken he means to steal you away from me.' He squeezed her fingers briefly. 'Until later, Lady Phyllida.'

She felt a momentary regret when he released her hand and turned to acknowledge Lord Wakefield's cheerful greeting.

'Come along, Arrandale, time for you to give way and allow the rest of us to dance with your charming partner.' He bowed. 'Ma'am, if you would do me the honour?'

'With pleasure, my lord.'

Exhilarated and giddy as a schoolgirl, Phyllida slipped her hand on to Lord Wakefield's arm. Richard Arrandale should see that he was not the only man she would dance with that evening.

Richard watched her walk away, noting the sway of her hips beneath the folds of her silken skirts. His eyes moved up to the creamy skin of her shoulders and the slender column of her neck, kissed by a few honey-coloured curls that had escaped from her swept-up hair. By Jove, how he wanted her, and soon! The garden beckoned him with the promise of the night air to cool his heated thoughts and he made his way towards the open doors. He did not rush, pausing for a word here, a smile there, but he would not be turned from his goal. A few ladies tried in vain to catch his eye and secure him as a partner but he ignored them all and soon gained the terrace. One or two couples were visible in the shadows but he paid them little heed as he ran lightly down the shallow steps into the garden, lit not only by the rising moon but myriad coloured lamps strung beneath and between the trees. The grounds were extensive and he headed away from the immediate lawn, looking for a pavilion or orangery, somewhere he might take Phyllida. He had no doubt he would be able to persuade her to walk outside with him, the glow in her eyes had told him she felt the attraction between them. He wanted—needed— to hold her, to kiss her, to discover if she felt the same overwhelming desire that consumed him. And if she did he would take her in his arms and kiss those soft, inviting lips, feel her body melt against his own—

This pleasant reverie was interrupted when he heard a rustling in the shrubbery. Some couple was taking advantage of the seclusion, no doubt. He would not disturb them.

'Let go of me. Stop it!'

The angry whisper ended in a gasp. Richard stopped. The lady was clearly not willing. He shrugged, it was none of his business, yet he could not move on. There was something familiar about the female's voice. He turned and stepped between the bushes. There, before him, was Ellen Tatham, struggling in the grasp of Henry Fullingham.

'*Brava*, ma'am, you dance very well, it is a pleasure to watch you.'

Lady Wakefield's praise made Phyllida's smile grow even wider as Lord Wakefield carried her back to where his wife was standing. He was puffing from his exertion and she could not help comparing him to Richard, who had danced so effortlessly.

'I quite agree,' said Lady Hune, coming up. 'I am very pleased to see you enjoying yourself, Lady Phyllida.'

'Thank you, ma'am.' Phyllida made her curtsy to the dowager marchioness. 'And may I say how pleased I am to see *you* here tonight? You have kept too much to yourself recently.'

The old lady inclined her head.

'After the scandal of Cassandra's elopement I did not wish to go out, but my scapegrace nephew is determined that I should not dwindle into a recluse.'

Scapegrace. Phyllida smiled. The dowager was referring to Richard, but the term was clearly used with affection. She was beginning to believe he might not be quite so bad, after all.

'He is quite right, ma'am,' declared Lady Wakefield. 'One must get out, and not only to parties such as this. I am a great believer in fresh air.'

'Perhaps Lady Hune would like to join one of your little excursions, my dear,' suggested Lord Wakefield. He beamed at the dowager. 'I know you no longer ride, ma'am, but there is no reason why we should not take an open carriage. Julia is already pestering her mother to arrange another jaunt while the weather holds.' He chuckled. 'My daughter has a taste for the Gothic, and Miss Tatham is quite as bad. They were in raptures over Farleigh Castle.'

'Really?' Lady Hune turned to Phyllida. 'And do you accompany your stepdaughter on these jaunts?'

'Why, yes, ma'am, and I have to confess I enjoy them just as much as the young people.'

'I understand the druidical monuments are quite the rage now,' remarked Lady Hune.

'Indeed they are.' Lady Wakefield nodded. 'Julia has been pressing me to arrange a ride to see the standing stones at Avebury, but I have told her it is quite out of the question. It is too far to ride there and back in a day.'

'What is too far?' asked Julia, coming up at

that moment and tucking her hand into her father's arm.

'We are trying to arrange another outing, my love,' said Lord Wakefield, smiling fondly at her.

'Oh, yes, please! And we should go soon, before the season starts and the weather begins to turn.'

'What would you think to Stonehenge?' asked Lady Hune.

'Stonehenge?' cried Julia, 'Oh, how I would love to go there! There is a picture of it in one of Papa's books and I am mad to see it for myself.'

Lady Wakefield shook her head.

'Out of the question, my love. Why, it must be all of sixty miles there and back.'

'If I might offer a suggestion.' Lady Hune waited until all eyes in the group were turned upon her. 'I have a house nearby, at Shrewton, where we might all spend a night or two. That would give you a full day to explore the druidical stones. It is large enough to accommodate everyone, including you, Lady Phyllida. You and your stepdaughter must join us.'

Julia clapped her hands. 'Oh, yes, do say we can go, Papa!'

'Well, well, that is very generous, Lady Hune.' Lord Wakefield beamed, clearly delighted.

'And what of you, Phyllida?' Lady Hune put

a hand on her arm. 'I shall not take a refusal from you.'

Phyllida beamed at her.

'I have no intention of refusing, ma'am.'

She dare not ask if Richard would be accompanying them, but she thought it very likely, and the idea lifted her spirits even higher.

Lady Hune nodded, satisfied.

'Very well, I shall send word to have the house put in readiness. Miss Wakefield is quite right, of course. We should make the outing before the Bath season begins. Shall we say the week after next, the last week in September?'

There was a murmur of assent. Phyllida found herself once more under the dowager's scrutiny and she nodded.

'Ellen and I have no commitments to detain us in Bath that week, my lady.'

'Then it is agreed,' declared the dowager. 'We shall go to Stonehenge.'

'Thank you, ma'am,' said Lord Wakefield. 'What a treat that will be for our young ladies.'

Phyllida was unable to suppress a smile. A journey of pleasure, made with friends, would be a treat indeed, not only for Ellen but herself, too, especially if Richard Arrandale was one of the party. She glanced around, hoping she might see him in the crowd. She wanted to stand on tiptoe and search the room for him. More than that, she wanted to find him and spend the rest of the evening at his side. It could not be, of course, however much she desired Richard's company it would be a dreadful example to set before Ellen. She glanced at the press of dancers, wondering if she should seek out her stepdaughter but then she decided against it. Ellen would not quit the ballroom while the music was playing, she was sure of it, so Phyllida felt at liberty to think of her own concerns.

Richard hesitated. Despite his promise to Sophia he had signed his name to the wager, and even though he had decided not to take part, interrupting Henry Fullingham would be considered bad form. But, dash it all, he could not stand by and let the chit be ravished.

Even as the thoughts raced through his head Fullingham gave a yelp of pain and jumped away from Ellen.

'Why, you little—'

'Having trouble, Henry?' Richard's drawling voice stopped the fellow as he was about to advance once more upon Miss Tatham.

'Nothing to concern you, Arrandale.'

'Now there I beg to differ.' Richard kept his tone cheerful. 'Clearly the lady has had enough of your company.'

'Yes, I have,' declared Ellen. 'Go away, Mr Fullingham, now.'

Fullingham was undecided and angry at the interruption. Even in the darkness Richard could see his hands clenching into fists and he said softly, 'Pray do not even consider it, Henry. I should hate to have to mill you down, especially in front of a lady.'

For a tense moment he thought the fellow would not heed him, then with a curt nod he lounged away, leaving Richard alone with Ellen Tatham. He spoke quickly to reassure her.

'No need to worry about me, Miss Tatham. I have no designs upon you.'

'No, I didn't think you had,' she said unexpectedly. 'Thank you for coming to my aid, sir.'

'You are very welcome. We had best get you back to the ballroom.' He followed her through the gap in the bushes and they set off together towards the house.

'I suppose you think I am very foolish, to put myself in such a situation.'

'I admit I was surprised at you, Miss Tatham.'

'It was just that I was being pursued around the ballroom by Mr Tesford, and when Mr Fullingham suggested we step out on to the terrace I thought it would not do any harm, and in any case I was very warm. Then he took my fan— playfully, you see—but he dropped it over the balcony, and we had to go and retrieve it.' She gave a little huff of exasperation. 'I see now that it was all a ruse to get me away from everyone, and I never thought I should fall for such a thing—'

'Do not upset yourself over it, my dear. You are not the first to make such a mistake and you will not be the last.'

'It was very fortunate that you should come along when you did.' She glanced up at him. 'Can I count you my friend, Mr Arrandale?'

'Why, yes, I suppose so.'

'Good. Then I shall call you Richard and you may call me Ellen.'

'I do not think that is appropriate,' he replied, startled. 'I doubt if Lady Phyllida would approve.'

'I do not see why she should object. You are Lady Hune's great-nephew, after all, and I know Philly likes you.'

Richard stopped.

'Miss Tatham,' he said gravely, 'my reputation is such that Lady Phyllida might not consider me a suitable friend for you.'

'Oh, stuff. Most of it is nothing but gossip, I am sure.'

'I regret that it is not merely gossip. Most of it is all too true.'

'You mean you really are a dangerous rake?'

The awe in her voice made him laugh in spite of himself.

'I *was*,' he told her, adding lightly, 'I have decided to reform.'

'I knew it,' she said triumphantly. She slipped her arm through his and gave him a little tug. 'Come along. We must get back to the ballroom before we are missed.'

Richard was thankful that there was no one in sight as they made their way along the lamp-strewn path to the house, where the sounds of the orchestra could be clearly heard from the open windows. When they reached the steps leading to the terrace Ellen stopped.

'I must look terrible, having been, been *mauled* by that man.'

'You have escaped remarkably lightly,' he said, looking her over critically. 'Your hair is no more untidy than it would be from energetic dancing.'

She put her hands on her shoulders.

'But he grabbed at my gown and I think the tie at the back is undone.'

Richard was sufficiently experienced to know she was not being coquettish, but what surprised him was that he felt nothing but a mild exasperation with the chit as she tried to reach around herself.

'Here, let me.'

He turned her about and quickly began to fasten the ribbons. Egad, he must be growing old, he felt positively avuncular.

* * *

Phyllida's head was pounding. She was constantly being drawn into conversation when all she wanted to do was think of Richard Arrandale. He caused such a tumult of new and exciting emotions within her that she felt quite confused by it all. She must take care, of course. She still had Ellen to look after and must do nothing that would reflect badly upon her, but surely there could be no harm in allowing Richard to call. To be her friend. The thought was comforting. She had not realised how alone she felt. And he was so well acquainted with the world, he might even be persuaded to advise her, where Ellen was concerned. No, no, she must not assume too much. It was all speculation, he had said nothing to warrant this glow of happiness she felt, but it had been implied in his every look.

With a smile and a murmured, 'Excuse me...' Phyllida moved away from her friends. The music was loud and merry, the noise in the room growing quite raucous, and she wished there was some empty room where she could be alone for a little while and collect her thoughts. Impossible, of course, but there was the garden. She had glimpsed the coloured lamps through the windows, they winked and beckoned to her, inviting her to slip outside. She would do so, just for a few moments.

She stepped out through the nearest window, closing her eyes as the cool air caressed her cheek. Sheer bliss after the stuffy heat of the ballroom. She would not go too far, merely take a short stroll around the lawn. A set of shallow steps led down from the centre of the terrace and it took her but a moment to reach them.

It took her even less time to see who was standing at the bottom of the steps, and to destroy all her happiness.

Chapter Ten

Phyllida took in the scene in an instant. Ellen, her cheeks flushed, hair tousled and Richard standing behind her, fastening her gown. There could be no mistaking what had been going on. While she had been wrapped in a euphoric dream, the rake had been ravishing her stepdaughter.

'How dare you?'

The words were inadequate, but they had an effect.

'Philly!' Ellen looked up guiltily, but Phyllida's eyes were fixed on Richard.

'Go inside, Ellen.'

'Philly, it is not as it seems—'

Phyllida cut her off.

'Do as I say, if you please. Immediately.'

If anything was needed to fuel Phyllida's rage it was the look Ellen cast up at Richard, as if needing his approval before she would leave. He gave a little nod and Ellen hurried away into the ballroom. Pain sliced into Phyllida like a dagger. Was the girl already under his spell?

'I know it is not an original line, but it is not as it seems.' Richard was coming up the steps towards her. 'I found Miss Tatham in the gardens, fending off an admirer and I brought her back.'

'You expect me to believe that?'

'As a matter of fact I do. Phyllida—'

She stepped back quickly as he reached for her.

'I am not that gullible.' She almost spat out the words as her frail, barely acknowledged hopes shattered and pierced her heart.

He shrugged, feigning indifference but she saw by the tightening of his mouth that he was angry.

'It is the truth and Miss Tatham will confirm it.' He continued, observing her hesitation. 'You are very ready to jump to the wrong conclusion, Phyllida. I thought you knew me better than that.'

'I know you for a charming snake,' she flashed. 'I have no doubt that you, too, are a party to this wager, this vile plan to deflower my stepdaughter.'

She watched him carefully, hoping he knew nothing of the wager, that he would disclaim any involvement. Instead she saw the damning understanding in his eyes. The disappointment only fuelled her anger and she wanted to hurt him, as she was hurting.

'But of course you are. What else would one expect of an Arrandale?'

His hands clenched. He gave her one last angry look from narrowed eyes and strode past her into the ballroom.

Phyllida pressed one hand to her mouth, as if to force back the tears. Deep breaths, one, then another. And again. She must go back indoors as calm and serene as she had come out. At least she must appear so. It had all been a lie. Every look, every smile he had bestowed upon her, had been designed to gain her trust, to allow him to get closer to Ellen.

And what did you expect? You were never interesting enough to attract a suitor when you came out, why should that change now, when you do not even have youth on your side?

She could almost hear Olivia saying the words in her blunt, matter-of-fact manner. What a fool she had been! Another steadying breath, a moment to gather her courage and she stepped through the long windows into the light, noise and stifling heat of the ballroom. Ellen was hovering close by and immediately pounced upon her.

'Philly, I am very sorry,' she said contritely. 'It was very foolish of me, I know, and it will not happen again.' She touched Phyllida's arm. 'Did Mr Arrandale tell you what happened?'

'We will not discuss it now, if you please.' The music had stopped but the crowded room rang with laughter and bustling movement. Phyllida looked around her, thankful that there was no one near enough to hear them. Ellen caught her arm.

'Have you fallen out with him? You should not, you know, he was most gallant.'

'I have said we will not discuss it.'

'But we must.' Ellen drew her further into the empty corner. 'Mr Naismith was following me around like a lost puppy, and Mr Tesford was also shadowing me in the most tiresome fashion, so I stepped outside with Henry Fullingham, only *he* proved to be a toad, until Mr Arrandale rescued me from him—'

Phyllida stopped her.

'Do you mean *all* these gentlemen were importuning you?'

'Not Richard.' She added, observing Phyllida's look of shock, 'He is my friend, we are on first-name terms.'

'Oh, no, you are not!' Phyllida drew herself up. 'Ellen, this has gone far enough. I cannot condone your behaviour this evening. It was most improper of you to go off alone into the gardens. I should not have to tell you that. And if you do not mind me then I shall...I shall pack you off to your Uncle Tatham.'

'You would not!'

'Believe me, I *would*. It is for your own safety.'

Phyllida met Ellen's reproachful glance steadily. This was too serious for cajolery, the girl must realise that she was deadly serious. After a moment Ellen sighed.

'I beg your pardon, Philly. Are you very cross with me?'

Phyllida was not immune to the beseeching look in those blue eyes. She said more gently, 'You are very young, Ellen, a mistake now could ruin your whole life. I have to do all I can to avoid that.'

'But it was not your fault. Richard said—'

'*Mr Arrandale*, if you please, Ellen. He is a dangerous character and I have no wish to hear what he said to you. Neither do I wish you to speak to him again this evening.'

For a moment Phyllida thought Ellen would refuse to obey her, but something in her face made the girl pause.

'Very well,' said Ellen at last. 'If that is your wish, but you are very wrong about him, Phyllida. He really did rescue me from Mr Fullingham. If he had not been there I fear it would have been more than my gown that was undone.'

'Ellen!'

'Well, Philly, it does not do to be mealy-mouthed about these things.' Ellen looked past her. 'Oh, Julia and Penelope are waving to me.

May I go to them? Please, Philly, I promise I shall be as good as gold for the rest of the evening.'

Phyllida frowned.

'I should take you straight home,' she said severely.

'Oh, please do not do that, Philly. If you drag me away like a naughty schoolgirl that really would set tongues wagging. I have learned a valuable lesson this evening, I promise you. Let me show you that I can be a model of decorum and respectability.'

Fighting down the desire to insist they leave immediately Phyllida nodded and Ellen went off to join her friends. She was right, if they left so precipitately there would be questions and conjecture, and who knew what gossip might arise. Besides, Phyllida had brought the Desboroughs with her and she could not abandon them. She closed her eyes and rubbed her temples, fearing the next few hours would feel interminable.

'Lady Phyllida, are you unwell?'

She heard the soft voice, warm with concern, and her eyes flew open.

'Lady Denham, I beg your pardon. I have a slight headache, that is all.'

She tried to smile, to alleviate the anxious look upon her hostess's face.

'Ah, 'tis a migraine, I have no doubt. I suffer from them myself.'

'No, no, merely the heat, and the noise. I shall be well again immediately.'

'You will recover more quickly if you have a little peace.' Lady Denham took her arm and led her from the ballroom. 'There, that little door in the corner. It is my own little room and you may sit there quietly, if you wish.' She laughed when Phyllida hesitated. 'You are thinking someone might already be in there? No, you will be quite safe. The room is locked and the key is behind the very ugly vase you see on the console table over there.'

'You are very kind, but I cannot leave Ellen—'

'I will keep watch on Miss Tatham while you are gone, I know how you worry about her.'

Her hostess's kindness almost overset Phyllida. She murmured gratefully, 'Just ten minutes, then.'

Lady Denham patted Phyllida's shoulder. 'As long as you wish, my dear.'

Phyllida let herself into the little room. Candles burned in two of the wall sconces, not enough for sewing or reading, perhaps, but sufficient for Phyllida to make her way to one of the padded armchairs and sink down. The noise from the crowd was muted and she leaned back and closed her eyes. Really, when had she grown so old that parties such as this exhausted her? Honesty compelled her to admit her exhaustion had little to do with the party and everything to do with Ellen and Richard Arrandale. He knew about the wager, he had not denied that, but both he and Ellen denied that he had been flirting with her. Phyllida sighed. Ellen was a minx but she was not deceitful and if Richard had truly rescued her from one of her beaux then she should be grateful for it.

There was a sudden rush of noise. Someone had entered the room. Phyllida opened her eyes and sat up.

'I saw you come in. I thought you might be ill.'

Richard turned to close the door behind him. It was only partly true. He wanted to talk to her. For once in his life he had been acting honourably and he wanted her to believe it. He *needed* her to believe it.

'I am not ill, so you may return to the party and leave me in peace. But you will stay away from my stepdaughter.'

'Blast it, Phyllida, why can you not understand that I am not trying to harm Ellen?'

With a cry of frustration she flew out of the chair.

'Then just what are you trying to do?'

'Damn it all, woman, I am doing my best to protect her!'

He pressed his lips together to prevent a further outburst. He was a man noted for his sang-froid, what was it about Phyllida that made his even temper desert him? She was facing him across the room and even in the dim light he saw her eyes were shadowed with pain. He wanted very much to go to her, take her in his arms and kiss away that troubled look.

Richard opened his mouth to speak but she put up her hand to silence him. She came towards him, her hands clasped across her stomach and when she addressed him the words were slow and delivered with an obvious effort.

'Mr Arrandale, as Ellen's guardian it behoves me to ask you what your intentions are towards my stepdaughter. You say you wish to protect her. Can…can it be that you, that you are *in love* with her?'

Oh, lord.

Richard looked into those soft eyes raised so anxiously to his and the truth hit him like a runaway horse. He was not in love with Ellen. In fact, he had no interest in the girl at all, except that she was Phyllida's stepdaughter and if Phyllida's happiness depended upon Ellen, then his did, too. It was so simple. He was in love with Phyllida Tatham.

The revelation shocked him, robbed him of speech for just a moment too long.

'Of course not.' Phyllida drew back, her lip

curling. 'You mean only to amuse yourself, do you not?'

'No! Phyllida, I—'

'You have no permission to use my name!' She cut across him, her eyes flashing. 'You can have nothing more to say to me, or to Ellen.' She drew herself up, shoulders back, almost quivering with fury. 'I shall give orders that you are not to be admitted to my house. We will of course be obliged to meet, since we have some mutual acquaintances in Bath, but believe me, sir, I should prefer to have nothing more to do with you.'

The disdain in her tone lashed him and he retorted without thinking.

'And what of Ellen, will you forbid her to speak to me?'

'No. That would be foolish in the extreme. It would merely push her into imagining herself as a latter-day Juliet.'

'Always so damned reasonable!'

'Yes, I am. I shall be watching you, Mr Arrandale. You shall not play fast and loose with my stepdaughter.' She glared at him. 'If you had any vestige of honour in you at all you would leave Bath now that I have found you out.'

'Found me out?' He shook his head, thinking of Urmston and Tesford and Fullingham. 'Madam, you have it all wrong.'

'Have I?' she said furiously. 'Can you deny

you signed up to the despicable plan to ruin my stepdaughter? That you took advantage of my friendship with Lady Hune to effect an introduction with us?'

'We were already acquainted.'

'One dance at Almack's,' she said contemptuously. 'And even that you did not remember.'

'No, not at first, perhaps.' Even as the words left his lips Richard cursed himself for a fool. He saw the flicker of pain in her eyes, brief but unmistakable, then she raised her hand and pointed one shaking finger towards the door.

'Get out. Now.'

The words were quiet and all the more effective for it. Richard's brain was reeling. He knew he was not thinking properly. There was nothing he could say or do to retrieve the situation. In silence he made a stiff little bow, turned on his heel and left.

Phyllida glanced at the clock. She had been in this room for more than the ten minutes she had promised herself. She must get back. She must find Ellen and take her home. A laughing group of merrymakers surged past as she slipped back into the ballroom and she had to flatten herself against the wall to avoid being crushed. Once they had moved on she looked around the room. Lady Wakefield and the dowager had found seats at the far side and Phyllida began to move towards them, wondering how best to explain to Lady Hune that she and Ellen could not go to Stonehenge. By the time she reached the ladies she had realised it was impossible to do so, when only moments ago she had accepted the invitation so eagerly. The dowager would insist on a reason for this sudden change of mind and Phyllida had no answer, without disclosing Ellen's folly and Richard Arrandale's dastardly behaviour to his great-aunt.

Ellen's explanation of events came back to her. Was she perhaps maligning Richard unfairly? Had he behaved honourably on this occasion? It could not be. Everything she knew about the man said he was a rake and he was not wealthy enough to refuse the chance to win ten thousand pounds. She had to face the fact that his behaviour towards her, and towards Ellen, was calculated to win their trust. But it was all a sham.

As if she had conjured it, the restless, shifting throng parted briefly and she saw Richard on the far side of the room. He was standing beside a voluptuous brunette, bending close to murmur something that made her laugh and rap him playfully on the knuckles with her fan. Quickly Phyllida turned away, her fears confirmed. Richard Arrandale was no gentleman, and the only interests he had at heart were his own.

* * *

'You are very quiet.'

In the blackness of the carriage Richard felt the tap of Lady Hune's ebony stick against his leg.

'Forgive me, Sophia, I must be fatigued.'

'From flirting so outrageously.'

'That would be it.'

He forced himself to smile, even though he knew she could not see him. He had had to do something for the rest of the infernal evening, after Phyllida had ripped up at him and left his spirits flayed and sore. Lady Heston had been throwing out lures to him all evening. It was a comfort to his bruised self-esteem that someone appreciated him. His great-aunt's voice interrupted his thoughts.

'Do you wish me to drop you off in Union Street, at that hell you frequent?'

'Not tonight.'

He had no interest in gambling. He wished to heaven he had never gone to Burton's. Even more he wished he had refused to get involved in that damnable wager.

'You have not asked about that little matter we discussed,' she said. 'It is all arranged. We go to Shrewton Lodge a week on Monday. The Wakefields, Mr and Mrs Desborough and their daughter, and of course Lady Phyllida and Miss Tatham.'

He turned his head to look at her, but Sophia's face was no more than a pale blur in the darkness.

'Are you sure? When was it agreed?'

'Before you fell out with Phyllida. Do not deny it, I saw you studiously ignoring one another for the last hour. Would you like to tell me what it was about?'

'I was trying to be a gentleman, for once.' He rubbed a hand across his eyes. 'My actions were misconstrued. I think I may have ruined your plans, Sophia. I doubt Lady Phyllida will come to Shrewton now.'

For a while there was silence in the carriage, the only sound the rhythmic clop of the horses' hoofs and the creak of wood and leather. Then he heard Sophia's soft, determined voice.

'She'll come.'

There was little time for private speech once the Desboroughs had been set down at their door, so when they reached Charles Street Phyllida sent Ellen up to bed. She waited until Matlock had gone downstairs before following Ellen to her room.

'Are you come to scold me, Philly?' Ellen eyed her nervously. 'I pray you won't. I was about to blow out my candle, I am too tired even to read tonight.'

'No, I have not come to scold you.' Phyllida

perched herself on the edge of the bed. 'I have been thinking that perhaps we should remove from Bath.'

'Oh, pray do not do so on my account, Philly!'

'I thought we might spend a few weeks at Worthing. The weather is so warm, do you not think we would be much more comfortable by the sea?'

'I would prefer to remain here, with all my new friends.' Ellen reached out and caught her hand. 'Please don't take me away,' she begged. 'I have promised to be good. And indeed, I *have* behaved myself since I have been with you. I have not once slipped out of the house alone, or exchanged love letters with anyone, or persuaded any gentleman to sing outside my window—'

'Did you do so at Mrs Ackroyd's?' asked Phyllida, momentarily diverted.

'Oh, yes, several times. It was mostly the very young men, you see, when they had been too *pushing*, but sometimes the older gentlemen could be just as silly, trying to entice me away from my friends to flirt with them, or even to enter their carriage! If I thought they needed a lesson I would tell them how partial I was to hearing a love song outside my window at night. My room was at the back of the house, but Cook slept just above and when they came serenading she would tear into them and threaten to throw the contents of her chamber pot over them if they did not desist.'

Phyllida smothered a laugh.

'I am relieved you have not been playing such tricks here!'

'Oh, no, I have been trying to be so good, and I thought I was succeeding very well, until I allowed myself to fall for Mr Fullingham's silly ruse this evening. But that will not happen again, Philly, and I quite see that I must behave with even greater circumspection in future. I promise you I mean to do whatever you wish, Philly. You may positively hedge me about with guards and chaperons and I shall not utter one word of complaint.'

'That is very good of you, my love, but I am coming to realise that Bath is more fraught with danger for a young lady than I had ever envisaged.'

'What, because a gentleman tried to make love to me?' Ellen laughed at that. 'I have already explained that it was entirely my own fault and I have learned from it.'

'But I think I should remove you to somewhere less dangerous.'

Ellen shook her head.

'Darling Philly, I am as safe in Bath as anywhere—indeed, if you were ever to read *The Monk* you would believe that no one is safe, even in a nunnery! No, to be serious, Mrs Ackroyd always says that most young ladies, even heiresses, are perfectly safe if only they remain on their guard. She says it is their own foolish hearts that so often let them down, but you know I have no interest in any of the gentlemen I have seen in Bath. Indeed, it is a very sad fact that I have never yet found any gentleman who has made me want to throw my cap over the windmill.' A loud sigh filled the darkness. 'I fear I am going to be very hard to please.'

'I am glad to hear it,' replied Phyllida seriously. How was she to make Ellen understand? She tried again. 'I am concerned for your safety, my love. There are—there appear to be—gentlemen in Bath with an eye to your fortune.'

'But that will always be so, will it not? I am an heiress.'

'Yes, but these are unscrupulous men who, who would stop at nothing.'

Ellen's eyes sparkled.

'You mean they would seduce me? Well, I have already told you I shall not allow that, so short of laying hands upon me and performing a physical abduction I am in no danger at all, am I?'

'Perhaps not, but—'

'And another thing,' said Ellen, triumphantly. 'If we were to go to Worthing, or Brighton, or anywhere, I might meet the gentleman of my dreams who will sweep me off my feet and I will not be able to help myself. So we will be much safer if we remain in Bath, won't we?'

Phyllida retired, momentarily defeated and too exhausted to argue further. When she left Ellen's room she found Matlock on the landing, a pile of clean sheets in her arms.

The maid said in her abrupt way, 'Miss Ellen's right, my lady.' When Phyllida raised her brows she continued, by way of explanation. 'The doors in this house being so ill fitting, I couldn't help overhearing, and if you want my opinion we'd be best keeping Miss Ellen here, where there's a whole army of folks to look out for her, not only myself and Parfett but also the servants from Lady Wakefield's household and others that I've got to know around the town. There isn't one of 'em wouldn't hesitate to come forward if they thought Miss Ellen were in any trouble.'

'Thank you, Matty, that is a comforting thought.'

'Aye, well, I know you're worried about her, my lady. Miss Ellen's always been one to land on her feet, but she can be hot to handle when she's un-happy. I'd rather have her behaving herself here in Bath than misbehaving somewhere else.'

'I believe you are right. Perhaps we would be wise to stay here, where we already have such good and trusted friends.' Phyllida stretched a tired smile. 'Goodnight, Matty. Ellen is lucky to have you to look after her.'

She moved on, but not before she heard the old retainer mutter as she walked away.

'If you asks me, it ain't Miss Ellen who needs looking after.'

Ellen arrived at the breakfast table the following morning in high good humour. Phyllida had risen from her bed feeling dull and listless and it was an effort even to respond to Ellen's cheerful greeting. The girl was clearly full of energy, and as soon as Hirst had retired and they were alone, Ellen launched into speech, explaining again what had happened in the garden. Knowing it would take more effort to stem the flow than to allow Ellen to talk herself out, Phyllida kept silent.

'So you see, Philly,' said Ellen at last, 'Ri—Mr Arrandale is completely blameless in the whole affair.'

No. He is playing his own game.

Phyllida knew it would be useless to say as much to Ellen.

'Perhaps,' she conceded. 'However, there is no doubt that what happened to you last night could have been very serious. You must understand, Ellen, that a scandal now could ruin your chances of a successful come-out.'

'I do understand, Philly, and I promise I shall

be more careful in future.' She put her elbows on the table and rested her chin on her hands. 'It is very unfair, don't you think, that we must behave with such propriety at all times while a man may flirt and behave in the most outrageous fashion and no one will think any the worse of him.'

'That is not quite true. A man may gain a bad reputation, which will make it prudent for respectable people to approach him with caution.'

'You are thinking of Mr Arrandale,' said Ellen. 'He has been very wild, I know, but that is all in the past.' She beamed at Phyllida. 'He is reformed now. He told me so.'

Hollow laughter echoed in Phyllida's head.

That is just what a rake *would* say.

Richard was relieved, if a little surprised, that rumours of the wager were not more widespread. The appearance of another footman in the Tatham household did not go unnoticed with the gentlemen who frequented Burton's gaming hell in Union Street, and dampened the spirits of at least two of those who had signed up for the wager.

Richard had joined them at the card table, and the conversation naturally turned to the heiress.

'The chit is damnably elusive,' grumbled Tesford. 'She won't make any effort to give her protectors the slip.'

Sir Charles Urmston drained his glass and

called for another bottle before inspecting his hand.

'I must say she seems immune to the charms of every gentleman,' he murmured, hesitating over his discard. 'She flirts most deliciously, but cannot be tempted into anything remotely clandestine.'

Richard listened in silence. A glance at Henry Fullingham showed that he was scowling, but he said nothing of his unsuccessful attempt to seduce Ellen in the Denhams' garden.

'And now there's a new footman following her everywhere,' observed Tesford, staring moodily into his glass. 'Big, burly fellow who looks very handy with his fists. I am minded to withdraw.'

'So, too, am I,' agreed Fullingham.

'And lose your thousand pounds without a fight?' Urmston's brows rose a little and both men flushed angrily.

'What have you in mind, to snatch the chit off the street?' retorted Fullingham.

'It's a possibility,' murmured Sir Charles.

'Not for me,' remarked George Cromby, shaking his head. 'A little dalliance with a willing gel is one thing, but abduction—it would be bound to get out and I have my family to consider. Think of the scandal.'

Tesford flicked a sneering look at Richard.

'Scandal has never worried Arrandale, but he

has already given up. Told me so himself,' he added, when a murmur of surprise ran around the table.

'He was bamming you, Arnold.' Sir Charles Urmston laughed softly. 'Putting you off the scent to give himself the advantage. Ain't that so, Arrandale?'

Richard did not deny it, but Arnold Tesford gave a short laugh.

'Well, he hasn't done very well so far. His attempts to get the widow on his side have failed dismally, from what I saw at the Denhams'. Tore you off a strip, didn't she, and barred you from calling—my man was drinking with one of the Denhams' footmen in the Running Horse t'other night and the fellow said he, er, overheard it.'

'Really?' murmured Urmston. 'You must be losing your touch, Arrandale.'

Richard smiled, outwardly unmoved by the laughter around the table, but as he made his way back to Royal Crescent he thought morosely that perhaps Sir Charles wasn't so far off the mark.

He awoke the following day to a leaden sky that promised rain, and after a hasty breakfast he announced to Sophia that he would accompany her to the Pump Room.

'This is an honour,' Sophia remarked as they rattled off around the Crescent in her ancient carriage. 'Are you going to drink a cup of the famous waters?'

He smiled a little at that.

'Not quite.'

'Well, perhaps you should try it. You have been quite out of sorts these past few days. You have an umbrella, too.' Her keen eyes searched his face. 'Do I take it you do not mean to return with me?'

'That very much depends.'

'Upon what?'

He grinned. 'Upon whether I find a more attractive prospect.'

'You are fobbing me off. Very well, if you do not wish to tell me your plans so be it. I shall ask you instead about Arrandale. There was a letter for you, was there not, from the steward?'

'Why, yes, he tells me the repairs to the roof are now finished.'

'It is a bad business,' declared Sophia, shaking her head. 'You should not be using your own money to maintain your brother's house.'

'If I did not it would fall into ruin and the staff would have to be turned off. That I will not allow. Why, most of them were there when I was a boy, they are like my family. You know very well that since Father's death the entailed property has been in the hands of the lawyers, and they won't budge without instruction from my brother.' He paused, fighting back his frustration. 'It would be easier if I could manage Arrandale properly, sell some of the land or the timber to raise the funds to maintain the place, but that rascally lawyer of my father's insists that nothing can be done without Wolf's authority.'

'It is almost ten years since your brother fled the country, Richard, and you have heard nothing from him. He may well be dead by now. You could claim the inheritance.'

'No. I would never do that. Not while there is a chance Wolf is alive.'

'So you continue to pour your own money into Arrandale. Money you can ill afford.'

Richard could not deny it. He was trying to achieve the impossible, using the meagre income from Brookthorn to support a much larger estate.

'You are a fool, Richard,' Sophia continued in her sharp, direct way. 'It cannot go on, my boy. And do not look to gambling to restore your fortunes.'

'I do not. Neither do I look to the heiress.'

'Miss Tatham? I never thought you did.' She added, in the casual voice he had come to mistrust, 'I think Lady Phyllida is more your style.'

Richard was about to agree when Sophia continued.

'You could do worse, my boy. Tatham provided well for both his ladies.'

'Really?' Richard frowned. 'There is nothing

in her style to suggest it. I thought all the money had been settled on Miss Tatham.'

'Not at all. Phyllida is a very wealthy widow.'

She could not have delivered a more severe blow. He shrugged and replied carelessly, 'Then that is another reason she would never entertain my suit. She would think I was interested only in her fortune.'

Sophia gave a very unladylike snort.

'Sometimes, Richard, for a man with your reputation for pleasing women, you understand very little about them.'

Chapter Eleven

Having decided that they would stay in Bath, despite the dangers, Phyllida was determined that life would go on as normal. Or as normal is it could be. Ellen cheerfully accepted that she must always be accompanied when she went out, and when Phyllida could not go with her she was to take either Matlock or the new footman she had engaged, a brawny Irishman named Patrick who came with glowing references from a respectable family, well known to Lady Wakefield.

'It relieves my mind greatly to know that you can vouch for the family,' Phyllida told her when they met at the Pump Room a few days later. 'I am grown so suspicious of everyone these days.'

'That is not such a bad thing.' Lady Wakefield gave her an understanding smile. 'Are you regretting taking on the responsibility? It must be quite onerous, to have sole charge of your stepdaughter.'

'I know it, ma'am, and I have considered moving Ellen out of Bath.' Phyllida lowered her voice. 'My housekeeper intercepted a note only yesterday. It suggested an assignation and when I told Ellen of it she was quite unsurprised, but she *did* tell me that she had no intention of meeting any gentleman in such a clandestine manner. I am very thankful for it, but I fear if she were to be confined at Tatham, or even worse in the schoolroom with her young cousins, as my brother-in-law has suggested, who knows what her rebellious spirit might cause her to do?'

'Very true. Better that you keep her here, under your eye.'

'That is what I think, ma'am.' Phyllida laughed suddenly. 'And I am becoming most adept at chaperoning! When Sir Charles Urmston *happened upon* us in Milsom Street and invited us to step into the confectioners and try the latest batch of Naples Diavolini I gave him no opportunity to converse privately with Ellen and kept up such a flow of inane chatter while we sampled the delicious chocolate drops that by the end of it I was quite exhausted. And yesterday, when Mr Tesford intercepted us in Sydney Gardens I took up my place between him and Ellen. I am always determinedly cheerful, but any gentlemen, be he potential suitor or would-be seducer, must be shown that I am not to be distracted from my role as chaperon.'

'Good for you,' declared Lady Wakefield approvingly. 'Although, you need not worry over her today. Once she and Julia have finished their dancing class this morning they will return to Laura Place under the watchful eye of Julia's maid. Graveney is very much like your Matlock, she is very protective of her charges. She shall also accompany Ellen in the carriage, when I send her back to you after dinner.'

'Thank you, I know I need not worry about Ellen for the whole day.'

'What will you do with yourself?'

Phyllida laughed. 'I hardly know.'

But in truth she knew only too well. She would busy herself with her accounts and with her household duties, tasks that would occupy her mind, because if she turned to her painting, her books or strolling in Sydney Gardens, then the nagging ache that had been with her since the Denhams' party would intensify and her thoughts would again be filled with Richard Arrandale.

Phyllida had spent the days and nights following the Denhams' party going over the events of the evening and trying to understand Richard's behaviour. Her head told her the man was a rake and that any chivalrous action would be designed to ingratiate himself with Ellen, but her heart did not want to believe it. Ellen was convinced that he was reformed and Phyllida had to admit that in these matters Ellen appeared to be wise beyond her years. Lady Wakefield, too, believed Richard Arrandale to be a reformed character. Even after Phyllida had confided to her all that had occurred on that night she had no hesitation in defending him, or in concluding that he must be truly fond of Ellen. Could she have been wrong? Phyllida wondered. Could Richard really be the honourable man her heart wanted him to be? The trouble was, she thought sadly, if that was so, then she had insulted him most grievously.

Resolving not to waste her free time in fruitless speculation Phyllida took her leave of Lady Wakefield. The clouds that had been gathering all morning had descended even lower and as she reached the Pump Room doorway the first fat spots of rain began to fall.

'Lady Phyllida.'

She tensed as she heard that familiar voice at her shoulder.

'We have nothing to say to one another, Mr Arrandale.'

'Are you going to Charles Street? That is on my way, allow me to escort you.'

'No, thank you,' she responded icily. 'I am perfectly capable of walking alone.'

'But it is raining and you have no umbrella.

And I do.' Phyllida knew it was a mistake to look at him but she could not help herself. The corners of his mouth had curved upwards and he was smiling at her in a way that broke through all her resolve. He held out his arm. 'Shall we?'

As if they had a will of their own her fingers slid on to his sleeve. In her own defence, Phyllida told herself that if she refused him he was quite capable of walking behind her all the way to Charles Street.

They stepped out of the Pump Room. Phyllida was obliged to keep close to his side to avoid the rain, which was now falling steadily.

She told him, 'If you expect me to thank you for your gallant behaviour the other evening you will be disappointed.' When he made no reply the guilt that was worming away inside her became unbearable. 'But I do beg your pardon, for what I said to you that night.'

'You admit, then, that I meant no harm to Miss Tatham?'

'She has assured me that was the case.'

The words came out stiffly, but Richard was heartened by them, until she added, 'At least on that occasion,'

He smothered an exclamation.

'Lady Phyllida, there are other, far more dangerous men seeking to undo your stepdaughter.'

'I am aware she is the subject of a wicked gamble, Mr Arrandale, but whether the other participants are more dangerous than you is questionable.'

'You are an innocent, Lady Phyllida. You do not know what these men are capable of.'

'Just because I have lived retired does not mean I am not aware of what men are like.'

'From gossip and discreet whispers!'

'And from novels,' she flashed, stopping to look up at him. 'I have read *Clarissa*.'

'What, *all* of it?'

She put up her chin. 'Yes.'

A grin tugged at his mouth.

'By George, your marriage must have been extremely dull if you had so much time to read.'

Her eyes flashed. Richard laughed. She had withdrawn her hand but he caught it and tucked it on to his arm again, saying as they began to walk on, 'Forgive me for that last remark, ma'am. Will you concede it is a fair trade with the insult you flung at me at the Denhams' party?'

'I shall concede nothing,' she replied with icy dignity but did not pull away. It was progress, of a sort.

They strolled on and Richard exerted himself to draw her out, talking to her of books and art and the theatre. Inwardly he was smiling, thinking how well their steps matched, how similar were their tastes.

How conveniently tall she was, so he would only have to drop his head a little to reach those full red lips. He glanced down at her profile with its straight little nose and determined chin. She was frowning a little as she considered the question he had asked her about the new Theatre Royal in Drury Lane.

'I think it is the fact that it is so large,' she was saying. 'The audience is too distant. Too…'

She looked up at him at that moment, her lips remaining pursed around the word long after the sound had faded. He watched the colour rise in her cheeks, saw her eyes darken as she recognised the attraction between them. Then her head snapped back, she gazed ahead of her and presented her profile to him once more.

'You were saying?' he prompted.

'I seem to have forgotten it. But it is no matter, for we are in Charles Street now. I am home.'

'Yes.' He found himself wishing they had another mile to walk, just for the pleasure of her company. He gave a little bow.

'Then I shall take my leave of you, until next week. Our visit to Shrewton.'

Phyllida drew a deep breath. The decision she had been putting off for so long was now clear.

'We shall not be going,' she said. 'I shall write

to Lady Hune today to inform her that Ellen and I will not be able to join her party.'

'May I ask why you have changed your mind?'

'I might have misconstrued your actions at the Denhams', Mr Arrandale, but that does not alter the fact that you are party to a vile conspiracy against Ellen and where she is concerned I dare not trust you.'

Richard's brows rose fractionally, but he said nothing, merely inclined his head and walked away. She watched him go. He had not tried to change her mind, he had not argued, merely accepted her news. She should be glad, for she would have had to resist his persuasions and although she knew she was doing the right thing, it would have been hard. She must keep away from Richard Arrandale, for her own sake as much as Ellen's. How could she allow herself to become fond of a man she would not let near her stepdaughter?

She hurried indoors and went directly to her writing desk. She must write now to Lady Hune and when Ellen returned that evening, she must face the even more difficult task of breaking the news to her.

The note to Lady Hune received a reply by return, inviting, nay, commanding Phyllida to call upon her that very afternoon. Phyllida toyed with the idea of declining, but only for a moment. She had planned to spend the time writing to Olivia but since she had no good news to convey the task was no more welcome than taking tea with the dowager marchioness. She therefore changed her gown and made her way to Royal Crescent.

'Your letter came as no surprise,' said Lady Hune, as soon as they were alone. She poured tea into a cup and handed it to Phyllida. 'My nephew told me to expect it.'

'In truth, ma'am, I should have sent it days ago. I beg your pardon, and hope it will not affect your arrangements overmuch.'

'I take it your reason is that Richard will be one of the party?'

'Yes.' Phyllida saw no reason to prevaricate.

'I suppose it is useless for me to tell you that, despite his reputation, Richard has no designs upon Miss Tatham?'

Phyllida shook her head. She wanted to believe it, part of her *did* believe it, but she no longer trusted her own judgement. How could she, when she knew now that she was in love with Richard Arrandale?

'My mind is made up, Lady Hune. It is best if Ellen and I do not go to Shrewton Lodge.'

'I hope you will forgive me, my dear, but I disagree.'

Phyllida blinked. 'Ma'am?'

'I know of the wager concerning your step-daughter.'

'And do you know also that your nephew is a party to it?'

Phyllida was unable to keep the bitterness out of her voice.

'Yes. He was foolish to agree to it, but men were ever thus. He assures me now that he has no intention of following it through.'

'He is hardly likely to tell you anything else, ma'am.'

To her surprise Lady Hune smiled.

'He is a rascal, Phyllida, I know, but in this instance I think he is sincere.' She paused for a moment. 'He is not a bad man, my dear. I believe I know him as well as anyone and I assure you he had no wicked intentions to ruin your step-daughter.'

Phyllida gave a tiny shake of the head. The marchioness was undoubtedly biased.

Lady Hune continued. 'Even if I am wrong, have you considered? The terms of the bet are for one of these so-called gentlemen to seduce Ellen before Michaelmas.'

Phyllida looked up.

'I did not know that,' she said slowly. 'So it will all come to naught once the twenty-ninth is past?'

'Yes, when we are at Shrewton. It was this knowledge that persuaded me to arrange the visit for next week. Think, my dear. You will have Lady Wakefield and myself to help keep an eye on Ellen with you, plus her maid, whom Richard tells me is quite fearsome.'

Phyllida did not notice her last words. She was thinking that even if Richard was planning mischief, she would have only one rake to look out for, rather than several. She looked up to find Lady Hune smiling at her.

'So, Phyllida, will you reconsider?'

'Well, what did she say?'

Richard asked the question as soon as he entered his great-aunt's drawing room, shortly before the dinner hour.

Sophia nodded. 'She and Miss Tatham are coming to Shrewton.'

Richard let out a sigh of relief, his breath a soft hiss in the quiet room.

'Then we will be able to keep Miss Tatham out of harm's way for the last few days of the wager.'

'You truly think the danger is that great?'

'With ten thousand pounds at stake?' He handed Sophia a glass. 'Men have committed murder for less.' He threw himself down on the sofa. 'I cannot tell you how hard it has been, keeping the wolves at bay.' A wry grin twisted his mouth. 'I never thought turning respectable could be so exhausting.'

'It is good practice for when you become a father.'

The grin disappeared. 'Please, Sophia, spare me that.'

'Why should I? You will want an heir, and Phyllida Tatham is a young woman. '

He scowled. 'I mislike your jest, madam.'

'No jest, Richard. I have seen the way she looks at you.'

'You are mistaken,' he said bleakly. 'She thinks me beyond hope.'

'Then you must show her otherwise.'

'Perhaps, once Michaelmas is passed she might be persuaded to overlook my reputation.'

'A reputation you have done nothing to refute. The face you show the world is that of a devil-may-care rakehellion, but it is very far from the truth. Who knows, save I, that the better part of your income goes into the upkeep of your brother's house rather than being lost at the gaming tables? And how long is it since you kept a mistress?'

'Faith, my lady, you profess to be very well informed of my affairs!'

'I have my sources. I know full well that very few of those ladies seen hanging on your arm in London find their way into your bed. In my time I have seen many magicians play their tricks, all smoke and mirrors. You have been the same, my boy, hiding behind your reputation as a rake.'

'And why should I do that?'

'Why? To show the world you are equally as bad as your brother. To draw society's disapproval away from Wolfgang and on to yourself.'

He stared at Sophia. She was right, of course. His father had always decreed Richard was no better than his brother and he had done his best to confirm that view. At first it had been boyish pranks, a way to gain his parents' attention, but this had changed after Wolf disappeared. Richard had adored his brother and when he could not defend him he had tried to outdo him in excess. Never murder, if one excluded the duels, but by the time he reached his majority Richard had been notorious for his drinking, his wenching and his deadly ability with pistol and swords.

Had it made him happy? No. There had been a savage satisfaction in being considered the worst of the Arrandales but not happiness, or contentment. That was something he had glimpsed, briefly, here in Bath, but it could never be within his grasp. He pushed aside the thought and raked his fingers through his hair, turning his thoughts back to his brother.

'I cannot believe Wolf is a murderer.'

'Nor I, but unless and until he returns we will not know the truth. One thing I do know, my boy: sacrificing yourself will not help him.'

Richard knew it, but he shied away from discussing it further. He looked around, seeking some other subject to distract his great-aunt. His eyes alighted upon a folded paper on the table at Sophia's elbow.

'I beg your pardon, did I interrupt you reading your letter?'

'It is from Cassandra.' She picked up the letter and handed it to him. 'She is in Paris. She seems happy.'

A shadow crossed her face, she suddenly looked older, more frail and Richard cursed his absent cousin. He opened the letter and quickly scanned it. Cassie addressed her grandmother with love and affection, but no sign of remorse.

'She is a minx to make you suffer like this.'

'The young do not realise the pain they cause.'

He kept his eyes on the sloping writing as he asked casually, 'And have my escapades grieved you, Sophia?'

'Naturally.' She reached out and caught his free hand. 'But I have hopes that that is about to change.'

He squeezed her fingers, touched by her belief in him.

'I shall try not to let you down, love.'

'What a beautiful day for driving to Shrewton.'

Ellen's cheery remark lightened Phyllida's spirits as they left the house. It was a true autumn morning, crisp and bright with a clear blue sky and a slight mist just lifting from the hills. Three carriages were drawn up, Phyllida was to join Lady Sophia in the first, Ellen would travel with Julia and her parents in the second while Matlock rode in the third vehicle with Lady Hune's maid, her butler and Richard's man, Fritt. Mr Adrian Wakefield, they learned, had cried off from the visit, having been invited to join a party of friends in Leicestershire.

Richard, Phyllida noted, was accompanying them on horseback. At first she was relieved that the gentleman would not be riding in one of the carriages, but as they drew out of Bath and the road widened she changed her mind, for he spent the majority of the day riding beside their carriage, directly in her view. He looked lean and athletic astride the black hunter, straight-backed, his strong legs encased in buckskin and leather. The familiar ache was almost a pain. He was so handsome, everything a young girl would dream of in a hero. If she thought of him thus, how much more susceptible was Ellen? Phyllida closed her eyes, but although she could block him from her sight she could not block him from her mind. She might keep Ellen safe from his machinations now, but what if he should follow them to London when Ellen made her come-out next year? She had promised Ellen she should not be forced into marriage, that she should have the husband of her choice. But what if, *what if* she chose Richard? Phyllida could think of no one more desirable. No one less suitable. But at that point a terrible doubt shook her. Was it jealousy that made her think him the wrong man for Ellen?

Hot tears threatened. They prickled at her eyelids and filled her throat. She would argue against the match, of course, but if Ellen really loved him and Richard proved faithful, she knew she would not stand in their way.

'My dear, is anything the matter?'

Lady Hune's concerned enquiry made Phyllida fight back her unhappiness.

'Nothing, ma'am. I assure you.'

'You looked so sad.'

Phyllida forced a smile. 'I was merely thinking what I shall do once Ellen is married. She is so beautiful I do not expect her to remain single for long after her presentation.'

'Really?' observed Lady Hune. 'She tells me she is in no hurry to take a husband.'

'She has said as much to me, but that may change, when she falls in love. And when she is married she will no longer need me.' She added thoughtfully, 'I think, if the peace holds, I shall go abroad. I have always wanted to travel.'

'You might marry again.'

'No!' The word came out swift and sharp.

Phyllida gave Sophia an apologetic glance. 'No,' she repeated, softly this time. 'I have no thoughts of marriage. Not any more.'

Sophia's smile was sceptical and Phyllida turned her eyes again to the window, resolutely staring at the passing landscape rather than the tall rider cantering just ahead of them.

Shrewton Lodge was an old manor set within its own park. The house itself was built of golden stone from Ham Hill and had been much altered, until it was a sprawling mass of gabled wings and tall chimneys.

'It is very beautiful,' declared Phyllida as they bowled along the curling carriageway towards the north front of the house.

'Do you think so?' Lady Hune leaned forward to get a better view. 'It has a certain charm, I suppose. I have spent many happy times here over the years.' She sat back. 'But it is a tiresome mix of styles, with several staircases and labyrinthine corridors. All dark panelling and uneven floors that cause the doors to swing open or shut of their own accord.'

'I am not deceived, ma'am, I can tell you like the house. It is a pity you do not make more use of it.'

The marchioness smiled at her. 'Ah, but when

you get to my age, Bath and its society is far more entertaining than the country.'

They pulled up before the arched entrance where liveried servants were waiting to greet them. Phyllida could only guess at the hard work that had gone into preparing the old house for their visit, but judging from the beaming faces of the staff they were very pleased to welcome their mistress. A diminutive figure ran out to take charge of Richard's horse and Phyllida recognised him as Collins, Richard's groom. She had not seen him on the journey and concluded that he had travelled down in advance. As she followed the others into the house it occurred to her that Lady Hune and her great-nephew had taken a great deal of trouble over this visit.

Once indoors, they found themselves in a large galleried hall, the heavy oak panelling decorated with ancient weapons and hunting trophies. Impatient of unpacking and too young to need a rest after their journey, Ellen and Julia begged to be allowed to explore. Receiving assent from Phyllida and Lady Wakefield, their hostess gave her permission, adding severely, 'But be warned, dinner will be early, and you must present yourselves in good time, washed and dressed as befits young ladies and not a couple of hoydens.'

'We will indeed, ma'am,' laughed Ellen. 'Thank you!'

'If there is one thing I envy young people, it is their energy,' murmured Sophia, smiling after them.

'If they had your wisdom it would make them truly formidable,' remarked Richard, holding out his arm to his aunt. 'Let me escort you to your room, ma'am.'

Phyllida watched them ascend the main staircase while she waited with Lord and Lady Wakefield for Mrs Hinton, the housekeeper, to come and show them to their rooms.

'There is something very attractive about a reformed rake, I think,' remarked Lady Wakefield, with something very like a sigh.

'I admit I was a little suspicious of him at first, but I have never seen anything of the libertine about him,' replied Lord Wakefield. 'I believe he spends a deal of time gambling at Burton's, but that is true of so many gentlemen. It seems to me his name has been tarnished by gossipmongers with nothing better to do.'

Phyllida said nothing. They had clearly fallen under his spell and without explaining her own encounters with Richard Arrandale it would be impossible to change their opinion of the man. For herself, if he was reformed let him prove it.

* * *

In Phyllida's opinion, the rooms allocated to her and Ellen could not have been better. All the guest rooms were reached by a long shadowy corridor on the opposite side of the galleried hall to the family's apartments. The rooms were connected by a dressing room that included a bed for Matlock, who would be acting as maid to them both during their short stay. The windows looked over the drive rather than the prettier formal gardens of the south front but Phyllida did not mind that. They were as far away from Richard Arrandale as possible, and that was all that was required.

Dinner was an ordeal. Really, thought Phyllida, it was very kind of Sophia to place Richard beside her and keep him away from Ellen, but the marchioness did not realise how unsettling she found his proximity. He behaved with perfect propriety but she was painfully aware of him, his thigh, encased in the tight knee breeches, just inches from her own. She was conscious of every look, every word he bestowed upon her.

'You are not hungry?' he asked, his voice low and concerned as he watched her push her food around the plate.

'Y-yes, of course. It is all quite delicious.'

* * *

Richard felt a warm smile spreading inside him as he watched the hectic flush mantle her cheek. She might deny it but she felt the attraction just as much as he. If they were not in company he would kiss her, here and now. Instead he tempted her appetite with succulent slices of chicken and a little of the fricassee of mushrooms. She was wearing lilac, as if to remind everyone that she was a widow, yet the lacy white overdress shimmered in the late afternoon sunlight, giving her an ephemeral grace. Like an angel. He found it difficult to drag his eyes away from her, to respond when anyone else spoke to him. He wanted to dine with her alone, to kiss her while her lips tasted of the honey and Rhenish cream she was currently enjoying, before savouring every inch of her body as he slowly removed the fine silk that clung to each delicious curve.

He shifted on his seat, his body hot and aroused by the very thought of it. Enough. If she suspected his thoughts she would shy away from him like a frightened colt. She might be a widow, but she was so delightfully innocent.

All too soon the ladies withdrew and Richard was left alone with Lord Wakefield to enjoy their brandy. He had never found it so hard to converse, to contain his impatience to see Phyllida again, but thankfully Sophia had given him an excuse not to linger. She was clearly fatigued by the journey and had announced that she would retire immediately after dinner, but she ordered Richard to show their guests the gardens before the sun went down. He therefore allowed Lord Wakefield no more than one glass of brandy before he escorted him to the drawing room.

The ladies were gathered around the pianoforte, where Phyllida was playing a lively sonata. Richard started towards the little group but he was intercepted by Ellen Tatham.

'Richard, I must speak to you privately.'

He glanced quickly at Phyllida. She was engrossed in her music but he would not risk her thinking he was behaving with any impropriety, so he moved to the window, in full view of the others but where they would not be overheard.

'Well, Miss Tatham, what is so urgent?'

'Did you know that I am the subject of a...a wager?'

'How on earth did you learn of that?'

'I have my sources.'

He laughed. 'That sounds so much like my great-aunt! Very well, yes, I do know of it, but you are not to let it worry you.'

'Oh, no, of course not. When I was at school the gentlemen in the town were often making such bets. And it is much better for one to be aware of these things, do you not agree? Does Philly know of it? Is that why she has been so concerned for my safety these past weeks?'

He paused a beat before replying.

'It is, and you must behave yourself, and not cause her any more anxiety than she already suffers on your behalf.'

'You are very fond of my stepmama, I think.'

Richard did not attempt to deny it. He said slowly, 'She is very wary of me and will not accept my help to protect you, but be assured, Miss Tatham, I have taken my own measures to keep you safe.'

'Really?' Her eyes widened. 'Have you set another man to spy on me?' When his brows snapped together she continued blithely. 'I know very well that it was you who persuaded Patrick's last employers to send him to us.'

'The devil you do!'

'He let it slip when he was accompanying me to my dancing lesson one day, but you need not worry, I warned Patrick that he is not to speak of it to anyone else.'

'Miss Tatham, you are a minx.'

'Thank you. And if you have set people to watch me, then I am very grateful for it. I just wish I might tell Philly, for I know she worries a great deal about me.'

'No! Ellen, I forbid you to tell Lady Phyllida anything about this.'

'I will not say a word, if you do not want me to, even though I know it is for her sake that you are going to all this trouble for me.'

With another seraphic smile she wandered away, leaving Richard wondering who else knew of his feelings for Lady Phyllida.

Chapter Twelve

'Your great-aunt misled us, Mr Arrandale,' remarked Lady Wakefield as they strolled along the wide paths edged with trimmed box. 'I was expecting a house in holland covers and romantically overgrown gardens.'

'My aunt enjoys her comfort,' he replied. 'She sent an army of servants ahead of her to ensure everything was in order.'

'But not the gardens,' put in Phyllida, looking about her with approval. 'There are no signs of recent cutting or weeding here, everything is in excellent order.'

'The gardener has been here since he was a boy and his father before him. One cannot put a garden under holland covers, Lady Phyllida.'

He was smiling and for the life of her Phyllida could not help but respond. A cry distracted them. Ellen and Julia had run on ahead and now they were calling and beckoning to the others to catch up. The girls disappeared around the house and as Phyllida turned the corner she realised what had excited them. A large statue of Neptune surrounded by dolphins dominated the south-facing gardens and from its centre a large fountain of water frothed high into the air before it tumbled back into the surrounding pond.

'Oh, it is quite delightful,' exclaimed Lady Wakefield. 'But, girls, be careful. You do not want to wet your gowns.'

'Too late, I fear,' laughed Phyllida, watching as the girls sat on the low wall surrounding the fountain, trailing their hands in the water. Lord Wakefield chuckled.

'They look like a couple of water nymphs.' He shot a glance at Richard. 'You will not tell me Lady Hune keeps the fountain playing when she is not here.'

'No, sir, she sent instructions that it should be cleaned and set working for the duration of our visit. What do you think of it, Lady Phyllida?'

'It is enchanting.' She smiled, putting her hands together and pressing her forefingers to her mouth as she watched the water rise up from the central column, cascading back into the pool below, droplets of water sparkling like diamonds in the setting sun.

'Good. I am glad you like it.'

There was something in his voice, a note of

quiet satisfaction that made her look at him and she felt a light, fluttering excitement deep inside, a delicious sense of anticipation.

Stop it, Phyllida.

'Come along, girls,' Lady Wakefield called out. 'Come away from the water now. We must see the rest of the gardens before the sun goes down.'

Phyllida stepped up beside Lady Wakefield as they moved on to the west front of the house with its terraced lawns giving views of the extensive park and woods beyond.

'The trees are already beginning to turn,' said Richard. 'In a few weeks more they will be a blaze of red and gold.'

'That must be a magnificent sight,' observed Lord Wakefield.

Phyllida stared at the trees but she knew Richard's eyes were upon her.

'Yes. I wish you could see it.'

He is speaking directly to me.

The tug of attraction between them was so strong it was like a physical thread, pulling them together. A sudden, wild joy rose inside Phyllida as she thought of what he might mean, but she quickly stifled it. She dare not allow herself to think such things were possible, not until he had proved himself, until she could trust him.

And that might take a very long time.

* * *

The next day was dominated by their visit to Stonehenge. By the time they set off the rising sun had burnt off the morning mist and they rode in two open carriages, the better to enjoy the excellent views the journey afforded. Julia and Ellen took along their sketchbooks, determined to capture the magnificent druidical monument on paper, for who knew when they might have another chance? Phyllida had seen pictures of the site, but still their first view of the huge stones rearing up on the flat plain made her catch her breath.

The dry weather meant they could drive the carriages across the short turf and stop closer to the monument. As the party alighted a woman in rags came running up, offering to be their guide. They declined, but Phyllida saw Richard slip the woman a few coins before sending her on her way. The day was warm and the party was happy to roam amongst the stones, wondering at their size and speculating about their origin and purpose. After a lively discussion they all agreed to discount myths of giants and gods in favour of Mr Stukeley's book with its arguments for an ancient civilisation and Ellen and Julia wandered off to find a good spot for their sketching. The rest of the party broke up to stroll around as they wished.

Phyllida was happy to wander on her own

and when she saw Richard start towards her she quickly changed her own direction and moved away. She was still not ready to trust him, but whenever he was near her she dared not trust herself either. She had decided therefore that it would be best to avoid him. From the corner of her eye she saw him stop and turn back. It was what she had intended, but it did nothing for the heaviness that settled over her spirits as she continued to make her solitary progress. A few minutes later she stepped between two of the towering blocks and saw Sophia resting against one of the fallen stones.

'Are you quite well, Lady Hune?'

'I am a little tired,' the old lady admitted. 'But I would not spoil anyone's pleasure.'

'Let me give you my arm back to the carriage,' said Phyllida. 'We may sit there in comfort while we wait for the others.'

'Are you sure, my dear?'

'Perfectly. I have seen enough here and would like to view the whole edifice from a distance, which I can do perfectly well from the carriage.'

Satisfied, Sophia took Phyllida's arm and they began to stroll back towards the waiting vehicles.

'Did my nephew show you the grounds yesterday, Phyllida? What did you think of them?'

'Quite delightful, ma'am. I hope I shall have

the opportunity to explore the park a little to-morrow.'

'Feel free to wander where you choose, my dear.'

'Thank you. You said yesterday you had been happy there, was that with your husband, my lady?'

'Yes, we spent the summer months here when my son was born, and when I was widowed it became my home. Much more comfortable than the dower house at Hune. I brought Cassandra to Shrewton when her parents died and Hune's cousin inherited the marquessate. Richard, too, spent time at the Lodge with me. We were here when the scandal broke about his brother. I believe it has always felt like home to him. It was never part of the Hune estate, you see. It is mine to dispose of as I wish and it will be Richard's eventually. Cassandra's father provided very well for her, so she does not need it. Richard may use it as he will. He may even sell it, since he is foolish enough to spend every penny he has on keeping his brother's property in order.'

Phyllida looked at her, puzzled, and Lady Hune answered her silent question.

'Richard is convinced Wolfgang is still alive, but in his brother's absence he has no access to the Arrandale fortune and he uses his own money to repair and maintain Arrandale House.'

'Oh.' Phyllida bit her lip. 'I am ashamed to say I thought he frittered his money away,' she confessed. 'I thought he spent it on drinking and gambling and, and the like.'

'As does the rest of the world.' Lady Hune sighed. 'It has amused him for years to maintain his rakish reputation, but he is paying for it now, I think.'

Phyllida's head came up. 'But his reputation is not undeserved, ma'am.'

'He *was* very wild, I grant you, but his family and his world expected nothing else. His father was a rogue who showed little affection for his sons. He left them to grow up without the precepts of charity or honour. When Wolfgang's wife died in mysterious circumstances his father immediately shipped the boy off to France and by that very action he as good as admitted his guilt. Richard was a schoolboy at the time. He was adventurous, energetic but no more wayward than any other seventeen-year-old, yet he was considered by his father to be as dissolute as his brother.'

Phyllida was moved to exclaim, 'Oh, poor boy!'

'Poor boy indeed. He was expected to behave badly and he did so.'

'So badly that before he reached twenty he was notorious,' said Phyllida, thinking back to her one short Season.

Sophia gripped her arm, saying urgently, 'Show him a little charity, Phyllida. He was never as black as he was painted.'

They had reached the carriage and Phyllida made no reply as they settled themselves on the comfortable seat, but she reflected upon Sophia's words as she looked back towards the monument. She could see Richard standing behind the girls, admiring their sketches. Even as she watched Ellen looked up and laughed at something he had said, completely at ease with him.

How she would like to believe Lady Hune, but there was so much at stake and if she was wrong it would be Ellen's life that was ruined.

However, when the party arrived back at Shrewton Lodge at the end of the day Phyllida allowed Richard to hand her down from the carriage without hesitation. His grip on her fingers was firm and she looked up briefly to meet his eyes, a shy, tentative smile in her own.

Richard's spirits lifted as he followed Phyllida into the house. She was melting, just a little. She had every right to be cautious, but he hoped if all went well that by the time they returned to Bath they might be friends. He felt a wry grin growing inside him. It was an unusual term for Richard to use for a woman, but in Phyllida's case he knew he not only wanted her in his bed, but in his life, too.

Fritt was already filling his bath when Richard went up to his room, and he took particular pains over his dress that evening, laughing to himself as he thought Fritt must think him the veriest coxcomb, changing his coat three times before he was satisfied.

He tried to hide his disappointment when he found himself sitting at the other end of the table to Phyllida at dinner. It did not matter, he would bide his time. He did not wish to rush her. When he and Lord Wakefield joined the ladies after dinner they found Phyllida and Lady Wakefield playing at cards with Julia while Ellen and Sophia were deep in conversation on the far side of the room. He followed Lord Wakefield across to watch the card players.

'Lady Hune and Miss Tatham have had their heads together since we came in,' chuckled Lady Wakefield as they approached.

'I think Miss Tatham reminds my great-aunt of Lady Cassandra,' said Richard.

'Ah, yes, her granddaughter,' murmured Lady Wakefield. 'Poor child.'

Julia looked up. 'Why poor, Mama? She married the man she loves and Lady Hune says she is now happily settled in Paris.'

Lady Wakefield shook her head. 'He stole her

away from her family, and may yet turn out to be an unscrupulous rogue.'

'And there are many such men in society,' added Phyllida. 'Even in Bath.'

Richard met her eyes without flinching.

'I agree wholeheartedly, my lady.'

Phyllida quickly returned her attention to the cards. Was he trying to convince her he was not one of them? She did not yet believe he had re-formed, even if he had convinced Lady Wakefield and Lady Hune.

The evening passed very quietly which was due, everyone agreed, to a combination of the day's exertions and the unseasonably warm weather. The long windows from the drawing room were thrown wide but the evening air was sultry, though there was little cloud and a bright moon was sailing serenely across the night sky.

But Phyllida did not feel at all serene. She was on edge, nervous. She could not relax. Richard's eyes were on her, she sensed that he was watching her every move. It was unsettling, and strangely arousing. Her lips and her breasts felt full, ripe as the berries they had picked together so recently. When the tea tray was brought in and she carried his cup to him the merest touch of their fingers heated her blood. She turned away quickly but her spine tingled with anticipation.

* * *

Ellen and Julia were yawning and as soon as they retired she followed them, glad to be away from Richard's unnerving presence, but she could not forget him. He dominated her thoughts. She went to bed and tried to read, but the flickering candle made the print dance before her eyes and instead of words she saw his face, felt those blue eyes boring into her. Even when she blew out the flame and settled down his image haunted her, achingly handsome in the dark evening coat that clung to his lithe figure and his smile that she found so hard to resist. She pushed the thoughts from her mind at last and drifted to sleep, only to dream of Sir Evelyn, her late husband. They were in the marital bed and she was listening to his breathing, knowing he was not sleeping. But then it was not her kindly husband beside her but Richard. He was turning, reaching for her, wanting her. Her hands clenched on her nightgown and she dragged it up, arching her body, ready to give herself to him.

Phyllida sat up, gasping. She felt hot, dizzy with the tumult of emotions swirling inside. Heavens how she wanted him, so much that he invaded her very dreams. She sank back, willing herself to be calm.

It was then that she heard a noise, the faint click of a door closing and the whisper of hasty footsteps past her room. Quickly she slipped out of bed and threw on her wrap.

'Matty?'

Quietly she opened the connecting door, but the soft regular breathing from the bed told her that the maid was sleeping. She crossed the dressing room and went into Ellen's chamber. A square of moonlit sky at the window offered sufficient light for Phyllida to see that the room was empty.

Alarm shook her. She hurtled out into the corridor, just in time to see a tantalising glimpse of billowing skirts disappearing around the corner. She followed, but when she reached the gallery she could see no one. Something caught her eye and she strained her eyes to peer across to the opposite landing where she thought she saw a figure, a shape, dim and ghostly, fading into the black-shadowed void of the passage. Picking up her skirts, she dashed around the landing and into that far corridor. Above the thundering of her heart she heard a stifled giggle but when she turned the corner the corridor was empty. Phyllida was alone. She bit her lip and looked at the doors. One of these rooms was Richard's, Sophia had told her so, hoping its distance from the guest chambers would reassure her.

Silently Phyllida moved forward, straining her ears to listen. Nothing. Then she noticed the faint line of light beneath the second door. Someone was not asleep. She crept towards the door, a board creaked within the room and then she heard the faint but unmistakable sound of girlish laughter. Ellen's laughter.

She had prayed she was wrong but now rage, dismay and hurt consumed Phyllida. In a fury she grasped the door handle and stormed into the room.

'Ellen, you will leave here this min—'

Her words trailed away. A single candle burned beside the bed, which was empty. Richard was standing by the open window, but there was no sign of Ellen. The door swung shut behind Phyllida but she barely noticed, for her eyes were fixed on Richard.

He was exactly as she would expect a rake to look, his hair a little wild, dark and gleaming in the candlelight, coat and waistcoat removed, his unrestrained shirt flowing in full and sumptuous folds over his powerful torso and unbuttoned to display the dark shadow of hair on his chest. The width of his shoulders and upper body was enhanced by the tight breeches that encased his thighs. He looked tall, powerful, masculine. Irresistible. No wonder Ellen had fallen in love with him.

Phyllida marched forward and looked all around the bed, expecting to find the girl hiding in the shadows on the floor.

'Where is she?' she demanded angrily. 'Where is Ellen?'

'She is not in here.'

Phyllida glared at him. 'Do not lie to me, I heard her—'

He reached out and caught her arm, pulling her closer. At the same time she heard another stifled giggle.

'There,' he ground out, turning her towards the window. 'There is your precious stepdaughter.'

Phyllida stared. Moonlight flooded the gardens and illuminated two pale figures. Julia and Ellen were dancing in the fountain. Richard's hands tightened on her shoulders.

'If you had walked on a little further you would have seen that there are backstairs at the end of this passage, leading to a garden door.'

'Oh. I thought…I thought…'

'I know exactly what you thought,' he flashed, his words harsh and bitter, 'The very worst of me!'

The shock of relief had not quenched Phyllida's outrage. It surged up, relentless, like fat on a fire, fuelled even more by her own feelings of guilt and remorse. The cool, reasonable façade she had kept up for so long shattered and she turned upon Richard like a wildcat.

'And why not? Have you not given me reason to think the worst of you? "Let battle commence", you said.'

'And have I not shown you since then that I did not mean it?'

She gave a savage laugh. 'A few weeks of good behaviour!'

Impatiently he dragged her away from the window and she found herself pinned against the heavily carved bedpost.

'Hush! Do you want to draw their attention to us? Remember where you are, madam!'

She remembered.

She was in Richard Arrandale's bedroom, something she had dreamed of, wished for, but had thought could never happen. But he had *not* enticed Ellen there and the hot blue fire sparking in his eyes was not only anger, but passion, too. And desire. She saw it, recognised it and felt it stir her already heated blood. He wanted her. She had put her hands against his chest to steady herself. Now she slid them upwards, wound them around his neck as she reached up and kissed him. There was no reasoning, just an overwhelming need to taste him, to blot out the aching loneliness that was life without him.

His response was immediate. He crushed her to him and returned her kiss savagely. She parted her lips, giving him back kiss for kiss, revelling in the hot, sensuous tangling of her tongue with

his. He drew back a little and she nipped his lip.
He groaned against her mouth, sending her diz-
zied senses flying still higher. His hands moved
to her shoulders and he pushed at their silk covering. Quickly she shrugged it off and the wrap
fell to the floor with a whisper. Richard's mouth
shifted away from her lips to kiss her jaw, moving on to the tender spot beneath her chin and
then down towards her breast, leaving a burning
trail in its wake.

The ribbon ties of her nightrail snapped easily
beneath his fingers and he cupped one breast in
his hand. Phyllida gasped as his thumb circled the
hard nub, but the pleasure only increased when
his mouth covered its twin. Her head went back
and she moaned softly. Her heart was thundering,
making it hard to breathe, but just as she thought
she might swoon Richard gathered her up, swept
her into his arms and laid her gently on the bed.

She cupped his face, feeling the rough stub-
ble against her palms. He kissed her, his hands
fumbling with the fastening of his breeches. His
urgency excited her. During her marriage the cou-
plings with her husband had been slow, measured
and unexciting. Now she felt a breathless, frantic need to have Richard's skin press against her
own. She sat up and clutched at his shirt, drag-
ging it up and over his head. She paused to gaze
in wonder at his naked chest, the muscled con-

tours shadowed and exaggerated by the single candle's flame. Richard moved away from her to shed his breeches and stockings and impatiently she threw off her nightrail.

Richard stood beside the bed, looking down at Phyllida. She had fallen back against the covers, her creamy breasts rising and falling with every ragged breath. Her naked body lay open and inviting, her eyes dark, molten with desire. He was aroused, taut as a wire and his jaw clenched when she reached out and ran her fingers over his erection. By sheer force of will he held off from throwing himself upon her and sating his lust there and then. He wanted to satisfy the yearning he sensed in her. To bind her to him for ever. He stretched himself beside her, cradled her cheek as he moved closer for another long, lingering kiss. Her body arched against him as he ran his fingers down her side, dipping into the valley of her waist, caressing the swell of her hips, revelling in the silky smoothness of her skin.

Fierce exultation ran through Phyllida. She felt glorious, all-powerful, her body thrummed with wild anticipation. His fingers were moving with slow deliberation over her body and she trembled as they edged towards her core. Then, even as his tongue flickered between her parted lips she felt his fingers slip inside her. Instantly her body reacted, arching, clenching. She felt as if she was flying, soaring high and free. She broke away from his kiss, moaning. The pleasure was almost unbearable, but those gentle fingers continued their inexorable rhythm. Her body was no longer hers to command, it moved against his hand. Her skin tingled, heat flooded her in a shimmering wave yet still he did not stop. The surge that had been mounting inside her suddenly broke. She bucked, cried out. Richard stifled her scream with his mouth and at the same time he moved over her and she felt the ultimate triumph as he entered her, matching her bucking rhythm as he drove her to the edge of oblivion and beyond.

Phyllida opened her eyes. It was still dark but she heard the crow of a cockerel, so dawn must be approaching. The birth of a new day, and she felt reborn, too. She had shared such pleasure with Richard as had only been hinted at in her marriage bed. It was all so new and exciting. Frightening. She needed to think. Silently she slipped from the bed.

Richard stirred and his hand reached out, only to find the bed beside him was empty and cold. He opened his eyes to the grey light of the breaking dawn. Phyllida was standing by the open window, slightly to one side, in the shadows, where she could look out without being seen. Desire surged through him at the sight of her. She had put on her wrap but it did little to disguise the curve of her body, the firm breasts, tiny waist and those long, long legs that had wrapped around him as he drove into her, pleasuring her, he hoped, as much as himself. His body began to stir again and he shifted restlessly. She turned then, as if aware that he was awake, but instead of the serene smile he expected her face was pale, the eyes solemn.

'What is it?' He sat up. 'What is wrong?'

To his relief the shadowed look fled.

'Nothing. That is, Ellen—'

'You need not worry about Ellen. She is safe enough. As soon as I saw her and Julia Wakefield in the gardens last night I sent word to Sophia's dresser. Duffy will have scolded them back indoors when she thought it was time. She is quite used to doing so, you know. She often had to chase after Lady Cassandra.'

Phyllida's smile was a little forced.

'I fear I have not acted as befits a chaperon.'

'You are too young to be a chaperon. I have always thought so.' He put out his hand. 'Come back to bed.'

'I should go.' But she was moving towards him.

'Not yet.' He pulled her on to the bed beside him, wrapping his arms around her. She melted against him, raising her face for his kiss and returning it with a passion. He murmured against her hair, 'It is still early, no one is yet abroad.'

She laughed, a soft, throaty sound that made his heart race, but she struggled in his arms and immediately he let her go.

'The servants will be rising soon and I dare not risk being seen. Think of the scandal.'

He cared nothing for that, but he knew it mattered very much to her.

'Very well,' he said. 'Leave me, if you must.'

She nodded but as she moved away from him he caught her hand, pressing a kiss into the palm. Looking up, he saw the glow in her eyes, the shy smile that curved her lips but still she disengaged herself and glided away from him. He propped himself on one elbow and watched as she slipped out of the door, closing it almost silently behind her.

Richard rolled onto his back and put his hands behind his head, smiling. She had felt so good in his arms, so right. He could not wait to have her there again, to awake that smouldering desire and make her cry out for him once more, but he would not rush her. The trust she had in him was fragile and he must take care not to break it. The feeling of well-being intensified: he could afford to be patient, they had the rest of their lives to enjoy each other. Richard blinked, realising that it was not a brief affair that he envisaged, but a lifelong commitment. Marriage.

It was a shock, but he suddenly knew that he wanted to abandon his wayward life, to forgo the bustle of London and spend more time at Brookthorn, looking after his property. A shaky laugh escaped him.

'By God you are ready to settle down.'

But only if Phyllida was beside him, only if he could wake up every morning to find her in his bed, her hair spread over the pillow in wild abandon and those greeny-grey eyes dark with desire. With love. He needed her to love him as he loved her.

Richard turned and pulled the bedcovers over him, but it was not the cold of the morning air that made him shiver, it was the tiniest whisper of doubt that Phyllida might not accept his proposal. She was no lightskirt, no wanton woman, and their lovemaking last night would have meant a great deal to her, but he could not forget the shadow he had seen in her eyes. She was a woman of principle, and it was just possible that his reputation was too much for her. The thought that he might lose her, even now, chilled him to the bone. He contemplated going after her immediately, asking her now if she would marry him, but already there were faint sounds from below. The house was stirring. He must wait, do the thing properly with no breath of scandal.

He heard a faint scratching at the door and his heart leaped when he thought Phyllida had returned, but the sudden elation evaporated quickly enough as he heard his valet's soft voice asking if he was awake.

'Come in, Fritt.'

'I beg your pardon for disturbing you so early, sir, but Collins has sent word, asking if you could go to the stables.' Immediately Richard was on the alert and he was reaching for his clothes as the valet continued. 'They have apprehended an intruder in the grounds, sir.'

Richard made his way to the stable block, turning without hesitation towards the buildings furthest from the house, where no horses had been kept for many years. Inside he found Collins and two of the men he had hired to patrol the grounds. They were standing watch over a man dressed in rough country garb. He was seated on a stool, his hands bound behind his back.

'Found this fellow prowling in the gardens,' the groom explained. 'He tried telling us he worked on the estate, but we'd made ourselves acquainted with all her ladyship's people soon as we got here, so we knew that weren't the case.'

Richard stared hard at the man.

'Well, who are you and what are you doing here?'

When his question elicited nothing more than a vicious glare Richard shrugged. 'Very well. Collins, take him to the magistrate, and take along a brace of pheasant.'

'I ain't no poacher!'

The groom grunted with satisfaction. 'Then if you don't want to hang you'd better tell us what you was doing prowling around the gardens, my lad.'

The fellow licked his lips and looked nervously from the groom to Richard.

'I ain't done nothing wrong.'

'You are Sir Charles Urmston's man, are you not?' barked Richard.

'What if I am?'

'And what were you doing in the grounds?' Richard's eyes narrowed. 'Would you prefer to take your chances with the magistrate? If you are lucky you may get off with transportation—'

'Sir Charles brought me here.'

The reply was swift, and once he started talking the words came tumbling out.

'We followed you from Bath. He's been dropping me off at the edge of the park each morning. He said I was to look out for a yellow-haired chit. He'd pointed her out to me in Bath, so's I'd know who she was. Sir Charles couldn't come into the grounds himself, you might have recognised him, but he said if anyone saw me I was to say I was one of the dowager's tenants.'

'And what were you to do when you found the lady?'

'I was to take her to him. He's waiting in his carriage on the Salisbury Road.'

Richard strode out across the park, making directly for the point where the main road to Salisbury ran close to the palings. He was relieved Urmston had not set his servant to prowl the grounds during the night. He might well have evaded Richard's guards and come across the girls playing in the fountain, and if Ellen had been snatched away in the dark it would have been almost impossible to find her. His mouth tightened as he thought of Phyllida's distress if that had happened. Well, today was Michaelmas. If he could keep the girl safe until midnight then the damned wager would be over.

Not that that would be the end of it. Ellen Tatham was still an heiress and a beautiful one at that. He had no doubt she would be pursued by any number of men and it would fall to her stepmother to look after her until she could be safely married off. A rueful grin tugged at his mouth. It would seem he was not only prepared to take on a wife, but a full-grown daughter, too. Before he had come to Bath the idea would have appalled him, now he found himself looking forward to it.

His amusement died away as he neared the edge of the park. The trees and bushes grew thickly here, providing for the most part a dense barrier between the grounds and the road, but there was a definite track meandering through the bushes. No doubt this was the point used by the daily staff to make their way to and from the lodge. Soon he could see the highway, and a carriage drawn up at the roadside. Richard approached cautiously. A coachman and guard were sitting up on the box but a caped figure stood behind the carriage, pacing restlessly to and fro. Screened by the bushes, Richard moved along and stepped out into the road just as the man was at the furthest point from the carriage.

'What the—?'

'Good day to you, Sir Charles.'

Urmston's face registered surprise, anger and disappointment before he recollected himself.

'Arrandale. I, um…'

'You are waiting for your henchman to bring Ellen Tatham to you,' suggested Richard.

'How perceptive of you.' Urmston's thin lips curved into an unpleasant smile. 'I take it you have foiled my little plan.'

'I have. I suspected you might try something

like this. Your man is even now on his way to Salisbury in the soil cart. You may collect him from there.'

Urmston's face darkened.

'Devil take you, Arrandale, you have stolen the march on us all.'

'It would seem so,' replied Richard, unmoved.

'You have the heiress here all right and tight and mean to have her for yourself. Very clever, using Lady Hune to befriend the heiress and her stepmother.'

'It was certainly an advantage.'

'You are a cunning devil, Arrandale. I suppose you plan to seduce the wench under Lady Phyllida's nose. Or have you already done so?'

Richard's lip curled. Let him think what he liked, the truth would be out soon enough, but he could not resist one final twist of the knife.

'You shall hear all about it tomorrow when I return to Bath to collect my reward.' He grinned at the thought: not ten thousand pounds, but Phyllida's hand in marriage. Sir Charles was glaring at him, chewing his lip in frustration. Richard laughed. 'Admit yourself beaten, Urmston. Off you go to Salisbury to find your lackey, and leave me to enjoy my victory.'

Sir Charles stood for a moment, undecided, then with a final, vicious, 'Damn you Arrandale!'

he turned on his heel and strode to his carriage, barking orders to his coachman.

Richard watched the carriage drive off. Another hurdle overcome, but he would keep his men on the alert, just in case. It would not do to let down his guard now, not when everything was working out so well. Smiling, he turned to retrace his steps, only to find an outraged figure on the road behind him.

'Phyllida!'

Chapter Thirteen

'You—you *rogue*! You scoundrel.'

'Oh, lord, you were not meant to hear any of that.'

'Obviously not.' She was pale and shaking with anger. 'You have been making May game of me.'

'No!' Richard ran after her as she turned on her heel and almost ran back into the park grounds. 'Phyllida, listen to me.'

He touched her arm but she shook him off.

'I have listened to you far too much. Never again.'

'I have no intention of harming Ellen. You know that.'

She stopped and fixed him with a look of burning reproach.

'I know nothing of the kind. You and your... your *sort*, you will stop at nothing for your pleasures, I am well aware of that. I should never have trusted you, but I was weak, and as guilty as you last night.'

'Last night was not planned, but when you came to my room—how could any man resist you?'

Her chin went up. 'Easily.' Her voice trembled. 'I know I am no beauty, I have been told often that I was fortunate to find a husband, let alone such a good one as Sir Evelyn.'

'Stop it!' He caught her arms, frowning. 'You *are* beautiful. And desirable. I have wanted you for weeks now, you know that.'

She tore herself free.

'You want any woman who crosses your path,' she hissed. 'You are a *rake*. That is what they do. But you shall not have Ellen, not for your precious wager, not ever.'

'I do not want Ellen. Phyllida, it is you I want. I love you.' The words were out before he could stop them. So much for caution, for taking his time and earning her trust. He caught her hands and dropped to one knee, saying with a reckless laugh, 'My darling girl, will you marry me?'

Thus the practised rake made his first proposal of marriage. Even to his own ears it sounded awkward and insincere. Phyllida's cheeks, at first red, now turned white with rage.

'How dare you laugh at me?' She snatched her hands away.

'I am not laughing at you. I am very much in earnest. Blister it, I should be in a pickle if I went around proposing to ladies without meaning it. What if one of them accepted me?'

Richard jumped to his feet. Good God, what had happened to his wits? Where was his fabled charm? He was making a bad situation worse! Phyllida was staring at him as if he had run mad.

'You need not be anxious about it on this occasion,' she threw at him. 'Oh, *what* a fool I have been. How easy a conquest. From the start you have tried to win my approval. From the very first time you came to Charles Street, *pretending* to remember that we had danced together at Almack's. You knew it was very likely to have happened, since we were in town at the same time.'

'Yes, it was a lucky guess,' he admitted. 'But I recalled it later.'

You witless fool!

Richard cursed. It was as if he was standing outside his own body, watching himself do everything he could to turn Phyllida against him.

'Oh, I am sure you did.' Her scathing tone told him clearly she did not believe him. 'No doubt you remember every plain, tongue-tied débutante you have been obliged to stand up with.' She started towards the house again, saying bitterly, 'Oh, you were very clever, Mr Arrandale. You knew I was suspicious so you never overtly courted Ellen, instead you made a friend of her and pretended to be concerned for her safety.'

'I *am* concerned for it. I even sent extra men down here knowing that someone was likely to make a final bid to seduce her.'

'You were protecting your investment. No doubt it amused you to keep the wager going to the very last minute, to wait to make your move on Ellen until today, Michaelmas itself.' She stopped again, dashing away a tear. 'And when I presented myself in your room last night, you could not resist the opportunity to add the chaperon to your list of conquests.'

'There is no list!' he retorted. 'Phyllida, I have not looked at another woman since I came to Bath, only you.' He grabbed her shoulders. 'I will show you!'

He dragged her into his arms and kissed her. It was a savage, angry kiss and she stood perfectly still, like a rock against his onslaught. At last he let her go, his breathing ragged and laboured.

Her eyes blazed at him, darts of green fire that accentuated her deathly white face. Slowly she raised her hand and drew the back of it across her lips, as if to wipe away the taste of him.

'What does that show me, except that you are practised in the arts of the libertine.' She uttered the words with a slow, icy deliberation. 'I know

your true self now, Richard Arrandale, you shall
not beguile me again with your rakish charm.'

She turned on her heel and walked away from
him, rigid with fury, head held high, and Richard watched her go.

He had lost her.

As soon as she reached the house Phyllida went
in search of her hostess, to inform her that she
and Ellen were leaving.

Lady Hune was all concern.

'My dear, will you not wait until tomorrow,
then we may all travel back to Bath together.'

'I am very sorry, ma'am, but it is impossible.
We cannot stay.'

'Will you not tell me why you must go?' Her
sharp eyes were searching. 'It has something to
do with Richard, does it not?'

Phyllida fought with her conscience, but she
could not lie.

'Forgive me, I do not consider you responsible
for your great-nephew's actions, ma'am, I know
you hold him in esteem and think him misunderstood, but I do not—cannot—share your opinion
of him. He has deceived me most grievously. He
contrived this whole visit as an elaborate charade
to seduce Ellen.'

'And has he succeeded?'

'No.' Phyllida bit her lip. She could not bring

herself to admit her own weakness. 'But there is still time, if we remain here,' she continued. 'He knows now that I would forbid the banns, but even so, there is ten thousand pounds to be won just for…for ruining my stepdaughter. A man would have to be a saint to forgo such a sum.'

And Richard Arrandale had proved himself to be no saint.

For a long moment Sophia did not speak.

'I find it hard to believe that Richard has deceived me so completely,' she said at last. 'I cannot believe it.'

'I do not ask it of you, ma'am. Just as I would never ask you to choose between a friend—and I do count myself as your friend—and a family member. That is why Ellen and I must leave.'

'Have you told her yet?'

Phyllida sighed. 'No, but I must do so without delay. If you will be good enough to order the carriage, we will pack immediately.'

'Of course. I hope our acquaintance can continue, my dear. I value your friendship.'

'And I yours, Lady Hune, but I fear it will be difficult, while your great-nephew is in Bath.'

'I live in hope that it is all some misunderstanding.'

'Oh, my dear ma'am…' Phyllida tried to blink away the threatening tears '…you do not know how much I wish it could be!'

She left the room quickly and Sophia rang for her butler. She gave him precise instructions for the travelling carriage to be prepared for Lady Phyllida and asked him to send her great-nephew to her. Croft returned in a very few minutes with the news that Mr Arrandale was nowhere to be found.

'His man thinks he might be in the park, my lady,' Croft offered.

Sophia nodded. 'Very well, that will be all. Send Mr Arrandale to me as soon as he comes in.' She added, when the door had closed behind her servant, 'I do not know what he is about, but I fear he has made a mull of it.'

It was not to be expected that Ellen would submit quietly to the news that they were leaving, but Phyllida's clear distress kept her from protesting too much. They returned to Bath in one carriage, which meant that Matlock travelled with them, but even when the maid fell asleep Ellen forbore to press Phyllida for her reasons for leaving Shrewton so suddenly.

Phyllida was thankful for the respite. She knew it was time to tell Ellen the whole story of Richard's perfidious actions, and she was not looking forward to it. She tried to sleep in the carriage, but when she closed her eyes she could not stop the memory of that final kiss from intruding. It had taken every ounce of willpower for her to remain unmoved. Her body had screamed to respond and if he had not released her when he did she thought she might well have surrendered, even though she knew it was wrong, even though she knew he was making a fool of her. It was that knowledge that had given her the strength to walk away from him.

It was raining when they reached Bath and the chill dampness in the air announced that summer was finally over. Hirst was surprised to see them return a day early, but being an excellent servant he soon had the candles burning in the main rooms and a cheerful fire blazing in the drawing room. It was here, after dinner and sitting in the comfortably cushioned chairs flanking the hearth that Ellen finally demanded to know the truth and Phyllida told her everything. Well, nearly everything. She stopped short of revealing that she had spent the night in Richard's bed.

Ellen was remarkably unmoved.

'I knew about the wager,' she told Phyllida. 'I heard a rumour and Richard confirmed it to me, but you have it wrong, Philly. Richard was doing his best to protect me.'

'He was saving you for himself, Ellen.'

'I do not believe it for a moment. We are

friends, that is all, and he knows I have no intention of marrying for a long time yet.'

'It is part of his charm that he is so very…likeable,' said Phyllida, pleating the folds of her skirt between her fingers. 'He draws one in, puts one at ease. When you are with him it is as if you are the only person in the world who matters.'

Ellen looked at her closely.

'You are in love with him.'

'I am not!'

Phyllida's cheeks flamed, giving the lie to her words, and Ellen clapped her hands.

'Oh, by all that is famous, I knew it! How I shall tease Richard when I see him.'

'You will not see him. I forbid you to see or speak to Mr Arrandale again. And in fact, we shall not be in Bath much longer. We are going to Tatham Park.'

'But why? The wager is over, there can be no danger now, and the Bath season is about to begin.'

'The idea of coming here was to give you a taste of society. You have had that, even before the season, so we shall return to Tatham. It is only for the winter months. I am sure Bath in the dead of winter cannot be so very entertaining.'

'It will be more so than Tatham,' Ellen retorted. 'You said yourself you were bored to screaming point when you were there.'

'But that was because I was in deep mourning, and I was there alone. This time we shall have each other, and…and we will be able to dine with our friends there, and attend the local assemblies.'

She expected Ellen to point out that all her particular friends had moved away but instead she merely asked how soon they were leaving Bath.

'It is Friday tomorrow, a day or so to pack up…I think we can be away on Monday.'

'No!' Ellen flew out of her chair and dropped to her knees before Phyllida. 'There are preparations to be made, packing to be done. The house at Tatham will need to be opened and made ready for us.'

'That can all be done in a trice.'

'No, no—' Ellen shook her head vehemently '—we have friends here, we must take leave of them.'

'We may write notes to them. That can be done in a morning. If it were possible I would be away from here before Lady Hune's party returns—'

'That *would* set everyone gossiping. They are bound to discover we left Shrewton a day early and if we fly from Bath in such a hurried manner it will be assumed we have something to hide.'

Phyllida bit her lip. Ellen was right, and the most likely guess would be that Richard had seduced Ellen. Not that she cared a jot for Richard's reputation, of course, but Ellen's good name must not be questioned.

'There is also the sketching party,' Ellen continued, sensing victory. 'Lady Wakefield has invited me to go with them to Beechen Hill next week. On Wednesday, if the weather permits, and I would dearly like a sketch of Bath to remind me of my stay here.' She caught Phyllida's hands and squeezed them. 'Do say we may stay for that, Philly dearest. We would then have time to order some new winter gowns. And to take a proper leave of all our friends.'

Phyllida felt herself weakening. She was relieved by Ellen's acceptance of the situation. She had been braced for tears, even tantrums and even another full week in Bath was a small price to pay to reward her stepdaughter's co-operation.

'Very well, we will delay our departure until Thursday.' A sudden gust of wind sent the rain pattering against the window and she added, 'But if the sketching outing is postponed for inclement weather you must give up the idea. I shall not stay longer.'

'No, of course not, dearest Stepmama.'

Ellen jumped up, smiling. Her blue eyes were glowing as if they had been discussing a special treat rather than their imminent withdrawal to the country. Phyllida frowned, but before she could speak Ellen gave a yawn.

'Goodness, the journey has made me very tired. I think I shall go to bed.' She bent and hugged Phyllida. 'Goodnight, Philly, my love. Sleep well, and do not be too unhappy. Everything will work out for the best, you will see.'

Phyllida returned her embrace and wished her a goodnight, too exhausted to question Ellen's words or her behaviour.

The continuing dank, dismal weather of the next few days mirrored Phyllida's spirits as she made her preparations to leave Bath. She gave strict instructions that Mr Arrandale was on no account to be admitted, should he call at Charles Street. That he was still in Bath she learned from his great-aunt when they met in the Pump Room a few days later. Phyllida was determined not to mention his name, but Ellen was not so reticent.

'Yes, he is staying with me a little longer,' said Lady Hune, in response to Ellen's direct enquiry. 'Richard has given me his word he will remain until the doctor tells him I am well enough to live alone, and since my doctor is out of town he must kick his heels in Bath a few more days. There is nothing wrong with me,' she added quickly, observing Phyllida's look of concern. 'It is merely that the trip to Shrewton Lodge was more tiring than I anticipated.'

'I am so sorry you had to put yourself to such trouble for us all,' said Phyllida quickly.

'It was merely that I am unused to so much travelling in such a short time. The visit itself was delightful. I am only sorry you felt it necessary to leave so precipitately.'

'Yes, so was I,' put in Ellen. 'Especially when you and I were getting along so famously, ma'am.'

'Ellen!' Phyllida frowned at her stepdaughter's forthright speech.

'Do not scold her, Lady Phyllida, I enjoy Miss Tatham's company, she cheers me up.' The dowager's attention was claimed by another acquaintance and as Lady Wakefield arrived in the Pump Room at that moment, Phyllida carried Ellen off to talk to Julia. They had not met since Phyllida's departure from Shrewton and the girls soon had their heads together. Phyllida took the opportunity to inform Lady Wakefield of her plans to leave Bath.

'We shall be sorry to lose you, of course,' returned that lady. 'But I am not surprised, it is clear something has upset you.' She patted Phyllida's arm. 'Do not worry, my dear, I do not mean to pry, although I can guess that you have had some sort of falling out with Mr Arrandale.'

Phyllida could not prevent herself from saying bitterly, 'I am not convinced he is so innocent as everyone seems to believe.'

'Truly? I know he has a fearsome reputation, but he has been behaving himself in Bath.' A sudden inquisitorial gleam came into Lady Wakefield's eye. 'Or am I mistaken?'

Phyllida felt the betraying blush rising through her body. She said hastily, 'He was involved in the wager to seduce Ellen.'

'That is very bad, of course. I cannot understand why gentlemen must act so reprehensibly. It does make it very hard for those of us with daughters to look after. However, I believe he is regretting his rash behaviour, and we have certainly seen nothing of it. Indeed, Adrian informs me Mr Arrandale has turned over a new leaf.'

Phyllida shook her head. 'I do not believe in repentant rakes,' she muttered darkly.

'How soon do you intend to leave?' asked Lady Wakefield.

'Thursday at the earliest,' said Phyllida. 'Ellen persuaded me to allow her to stay for your sketching party to Beechen Hill on Wednesday.'

'Really? I do not recall setting a day for it, but no doubt the girls have arranged it between themselves.'

Lady Wakefield glanced up, smiling as an elderly matron came up to speak to her and Phyllida moved on. The Pump Room was crowded with her acquaintances and she would use this opportunity to take her leave of them. Ellen remained with Julia, but Phyllida was not concerned for her. Richard Arrandale was not in the Pump Room. In fact none of the gentlemen whose attentions to Ellen had been so marked were in evidence, which convinced Phyllida that they had all been party to that horrid wager. Thankfully Ellen did not appear worried to have lost the majority of her suitors and Phyllida was now happy for her to go off with her friends.

When it was time to leave Phyllida found her stepdaughter sitting beside the marchioness. They were deep in conversation but they broke off as she approached.

'Well, now,' she said, forcing a smile, 'what is this talk of bishops, Lady Hune? Is my step-daughter showing a healthy interest in religion?'

'I regret not,' replied Sophia. 'She has an *un-healthy* interest in special licences.'

'I wondered how easy it was to obtain one,' said Ellen. 'One of my friends at Mrs Ackroyd's Academy ran off and was married by special licence.' She laughed. 'Do not look so concerned, Philly, Lady Hune has explained that the marriage would still not be legal without a guardian's permission, if the bride is underage. I promise you I am not thinking of one for myself.'

'You should not be thinking of such things

at all,' retorted Phyllida. 'Lady Hune must be shocked by your conversation.'

'Not at all,' Sophia assured her. 'I find Ellen very entertaining. I shall miss you both when you have gone to Tatham Park.'

They took their leave, and Phyllida felt a pang of regret that her friendship with the marchioness must be suspended, at least for the present.

The mood around the gaming table was very cheerful, which was not surprising, Richard thought. None of them had won the wager to seduce the heiress, and the agreement they had drawn up now meant that each of them would be getting back the majority of his stake. Burton himself had brought the betting book and his cash box and was even now counting out the money and taking a small commission for himself.

Sir Charles Urmston's voice made it heard above the general conversation.

'So Arrandale, the widow outfoxed you in the end.'

Richard instructed a hovering waiter to attend to a guttering candle before replying, 'It would appear so.'

'Miss Ellen Tatham and her reputation are un-blemished and I hear the widow is taking her out of Bath at the end of the week.'

'Can you blame her?' declared George Cromby. 'Keeping an heiress out of harm's way must be an exhausting business. To be honest I am glad this damned affair is over. If my wife had got wind of it I should have been in the suds!'

'Nevertheless it grieves me to let a fortune go begging,' muttered Tesford. 'What say you, Urmston?'

'One should know when to admit defeat,' murmured Sir Charles. He shot a malevolent glance towards Richard. Neither man had spoken of their encounter at Shrewton but it was there, between them. It did not worry Richard. Urmston was a bully. He had a sharp tongue, but he was unlikely to cause any more damage.

'The gel is being presented next year,' said Cromby. 'You single gentlemen could go to London and try your luck there. It may prove easier in town.'

'I doubt it,' grumbled Fullingham. 'If Arrandale with all his famous charm couldn't win the chit in Bath I don't see any of us succeeding in London, where a host of more eligible suitors are likely to be pursuing her.'

'And the stepmother has proved herself a veritable dragon,' drawled Urmston. 'Surprising for one who looks so insignificant.'

It was all that Richard could do to stay in his seat, but if he leapt to Phyllida's defence that would only rouse conjecture. No, he thought as he made his way back to Royal Crescent in the early hours of the morning, he had done enough damage to Phyllida. Best that he should stay well away in future. At least he had the best part of his thousand pounds back. That would go some way to the repairs needed at Brookthorn. If only he could get back there, but Sophia insisted she was not yet well enough for him to leave her. Most likely she was lonely, he concluded, but although he sympathised he knew he could not remain much longer. Bath held too many painful memories for him.

The following morning he tried to persuade his great-aunt again that she could do without him, only to be met with the same story. The journey from Shrewton had taken its toll and she was not yet recovered.

'And Phyllida's decision to quit Bath has overset me,' she continued. 'Do you tell me that has nothing to do with you, Richard?'

'I shall not tell you anything,' he replied, shying away from even thinking about it.

'Have you tried talking to her?'

'Phyllida does not believe in reformed rakes.'

'By heaven, boy, then you must persuade her!'

He put up his hand as if to ward off a blow.

'Sophia, please, do not continue with this. It does not concern you.'

'You are my family, Richard, of course it concerns me.' She stared at him for a moment, until his implacable look convinced her he was not to be moved. She sighed. 'Very well, I will not tease you more with it. But perhaps you will do a little errand for me? I have a book from the circulating library in Milsom Street and wonder if you will return it for me?'

'With pleasure, ma'am, but do you not wish to come with me? It is a fine day for a stroll.'

'Thank you, Richard, but, no. I shall wait here for your return.'

Richard set off immediately, pondering upon his great-aunt's health. Whingate was currently in the country but as soon as the doctor returned he would ask him to call. It was unlike Sophia to be so lacking in energy. It did not take Richard long to reach the library and his task was soon completed. He was turning to leave when he heard someone call his name.

'Miss Tatham!'

She beckoned him towards the shelves where she was standing. She drew a book from the row before her and, pretending to peruse it, said quietly, 'I have been waiting for you.'

Richard kept his distance. He picked up a book.

'This is not wise, Ellen,' he said warily. 'We should not be seen together.'

'Oh, fiddle, I know you have no designs upon me.'

'That is not the point.'

'How long do you stay in Bath?'

'Another week, no more. As soon as Whingate pronounces my great-aunt fit I shall leave.'

'Where will you go?'

'I do not know, and if I did I should not tell you,' he responded bluntly.

She pouted but did not pursue the matter. Instead she said, 'I saw a man following me yesterday. Is he your creature?'

'Why, yes, although I doubt if there is a need for it now.'

'Oh, pray do not take him away just yet.'

His brows rose a little. That damned wager must have unsettled the girl more than he had realised.

'If you wish I will leave the men in place until you leave for Tatham Park.'

'Thank you. Phyllida would be overcome with grief if anything should happen to me.'

Richard barely noticed the blinding smile she gave him, his thoughts distracted by a stab of jealousy. Would Phyllida grieve if anything happened to him? He doubted it.

'I feel much safer knowing you are looking out

for me,' murmured Ellen. She looked around. 'You had best go. I sent Matty off on an errand but she will return any moment and I would not have Phyllida know we had been speaking together.'

He could not help himself.

'How is your stepmama?'

Ellen gave him a thoughtful look.

'She is in very low spirits.'

Her words twisted like a knife, but he forced himself to say cheerfully, 'No doubt she will revive once she is back at Tatham.'

'I think she is more like to go into a decline.'

He said quickly. 'Why do you say that?'

Ellen gave him an innocent look.

'Oh, I do not know, but she has been quite out of spirits since we returned from Shrewton. I wonder why that should be?'

'I have no idea, Miss Tatham.' He lifted his hat. 'Good day to you.'

He hoped Sophia's doctor would give him a good report of her health when he returned at the end of the week. He needed to get out of Bath, whether to lose himself in the distractions of London or immerse himself in the business of restoring Brookthorn he did not care, as long as it helped him to forget Phyllida Tatham.

Phyllida carefully folded another gown and laid it on top of the clothes already packed into the trunk. Tomorrow they would set off for Tatham Park and everything must be in readiness. Matlock had offered to do the packing for her, but Phyllida had instructed her to accompany Ellen to Laura Place to join Lady Wakefield's sketching party. The invitation had included Phyllida but she had used the excuse of their imminent departure to cry off.

In truth she had no spirits for company and she knew Ellen would be perfectly safe with Lady Wakefield, who had assured her that no gentlemen would be accompanying them. It had been impossible to refuse all the invitations that had come in over the past week but Phyllida had accepted only those where she could be certain she would not meet Richard. Her plan had worked, she had not seen him, but he was there, in her mind, ready to fill her thoughts as soon as she let down her guard.

He crept in now as she laid the peach silk in the trunk. It was the gown she had worn to the Denhams' party. How her spirits had soared when she had danced with Richard. Her heart had beat so heavily it had almost drowned out the music, especially when he had smiled at her and she had felt her own smile spreading until it felt as if her whole face was beaming with delight. With an impatient huff she turned away from the trunk. What a simpleton she was and how he must have laughed at his easy conquest. Even then, with ample evidence to the contrary, she had been prepared to believe he was a good man.

But no more. At Shrewton Lodge he had shown his true colours, he had seduced her and shown no remorse. Instead he had laughed at her. Going down on one knee he had ridiculed her with actions that brought back memories of their one dance at Almack's and her foolish daydream that she might reform him. She had felt quite sick then, much as she had done when she was a girl, sitting on the benches while the gentlemen passed her over in favour of those who were prettier, livelier, richer...

Angrily Phyllida dashed away a tear. She was no longer that shy innocent girl but a woman of independent means with a stepdaughter to consider. She had been foolish enough to fall in love with Richard Arrandale, but she would not let that break her. Life would go on and she would survive her mistake. Her hands slid protectively across her stomach. Whatever the consequence of giving into her passion, she would survive.

Through the open door voices floated up from the hall below. Matty had returned and was even now coming upstairs. Quickly Phyllida wiped her cheeks. No one must know her weakness, the constant aching loneliness that filled her waking moments. It would pass. Pray heaven it would pass quickly.

She heard Matty's firm tread on the landing and prepared to greet her, but when the maid appeared she was far too distressed to notice Phyllida's forced cheerfulness. She burst out wildly,

'Oh, my lady, I've lost Miss Ellen!'

Chapter Fourteen

'What do you mean, you have lost her?'

Phyllida stared at Matlock, whose usually severe countenance was wild and ravaged by tears.

'Miss Ellen said she wanted to buy a little present for Miss Julia so we stopped in Milsom Street on the way to Lady Wakefield's, to buy some ribbons. Miss Ellen asked me to wait outside. Well I thought nothing of that, for there was her parasol to hold, and her sketchpad and pencils, and the shop was very crowded. So I waited, and when she didn't come out after ever such a long time I went in, but she wasn't there. The assistant said she thought Miss Ellen might have left by the side door, the one that comes out into the passage. I went on to Laura Place, thinking somehow I had misunderstood her. But she wasn't there, my lady. She had never arrived.'

'Oh, good heavens!' Phyllida put her hands to her cheeks but Matlock hadn't finished.

'The family had already set off for Beechen Hill. Lady Wakefield's butler told me they had received a note from Miss Ellen crying off from the sketching party.' Matty sank down on to a chair and pulled out her handkerchief. She said, between noisy sobs, 'Oh, my lady, I do fear Miss Ellen has run away.'

'I do not believe it,' declared Phyllida, but in her heart there was already a numbing chill when she recalled the fierce hug Ellen had bestowed upon her before setting off that morning. She ran into Ellen's room and her heart shrank into a hard icy block when she saw the note propped against the trinket box on the dressing table. With trembling hands she picked it up.

'Oh, my lady, what does she say?'

Matlock's shaking voice came from the doorway.

'It would seem you are right, Matty, she has run away. Eloped,' Phyllida replied calmly, but inside she was burning up. How had she missed the signs? Ellen had shown no preference for any of the gentlemen who clustered about her. Who had stolen her heart? Phyllida knew that only the deepest passion would have persuaded Ellen to take such a rash step. She closed her eyes.

Please, please let it not be Richard....

'I beg your pardon, ma'am, but Mr Arrandale is below, and insists upon speaking to you.' The butler's voice was like the answer to her silent prayer. 'I am very sorry, my lady, but I couldn't keep him out, leastways not without an unseemly scuffle on the doorstep, so I've put him in the morning room. If you like, I could fetch Patrick and the scullery boy to try to eject him...'

'No. Thank you, Hirst, I will go down to him.'

Pulling herself together, Phyllida followed the butler to the morning room, where she found Richard pacing the floor. Almost before Hirst had closed the door upon them he spoke.

'Did you know Ellen was going out of town today?'

She shook her head.

'She was engaged to join the Wakefields for a sketching party to Beechen Hill. Her maid has just returned to say Ellen gave her the slip in Milsom Street.'

His brow darkened still further.

'My man tells me he saw Ellen climbing into a travelling carriage at the White Hart. The blinds were drawn down so he could not see who else was in the carriage, but there was a quantity of luggage on the roof.'

Phyllida swayed. She put a hand out and gripped a chair back.

'So it is true. She has eloped.'

'This is no time for weakness, madam,' he said roughly. 'I have sent runners to find out which road they are taking. My curricle is outside, if you will allow me to drive you, we should be able to catch up with them before nightfall.'

His brusque tone steadied her. She could send a message to the stables for her own carriage, but that would take half an hour at the very least, and by that time who knew where they might be?

'Of course,' she said. 'You are right. There is no time to lose. I will fetch my cloak and bonnet.'

'Good girl. I shall wait for you outside. I told my people where to find me, if there was any news.'

Phyllida ran back up the stairs. She must keep her mind upon the task of finding Ellen. Questions about why Richard should be going to so much trouble could wait.

Minutes later she was heading out of the door, tying her cloak strings as she went. Richard was standing beside his curricle, talking to a soberly dressed man in a plain brown frockcoat. With a nod he dismissed the man and turned to hand Phyllida into the curricle.

'They were taking the London Road,' he said shortly. 'We can ask after them at the turnpikes.' He added, after a brief hesitation, 'I have not brought Collins, I thought you would prefer that we should travel alone.'

'Yes, thank you. The fewer people who know of this the better.'

They set off at a cracking pace. Phyllida clung on to the side of the curricle at first, until she grew accustomed to the speed.

'Tell me,' she said then. 'Who was that man?'

'One of those I hired to keep watch over Ellen. I apologise, I know I had no right to do so, but I wanted only to keep her safe. You cannot know how much I regret I did not prevent that damnable wager from ever taking place.'

Her hand fluttered. She said shortly, 'All that matters now is that we find them.'

Phyllida's worries about losing track of their quarry soon eased. At every turnpike the keeper recalled seeing the travelling carriage occupied by a fashionably dressed gentleman and a beautiful young lady in a pale-blue walking dress.

'At least we can be confident they are not heading to Gretna,' remarked Richard, setting his team in motion again after quizzing the pike keeper at Bathford.

'Nor London,' said Phyllida as they set off towards Melksham.

'No.' He frowned. 'That surprised me, for they might be expected to hide in town for weeks, certainly until they could persuade someone to marry them.'

'Perhaps this…this gentleman, whoever he is, has no thoughts of m-marriage.'

'From what I know of your stepdaughter I would not expect her to settle for anything less,' he retorted. 'What exactly did she say in her letter?'

Phyllida clasped her hands together hard and tried to stop her voice from shaking. 'That the task of protecting her was too much to ask of me. That she w-wanted to relieve me of the burden. I s-suppose she thinks a husband is the answer.'

Richard gave a crack of laughter. 'Heaven help the husband!'

Phyllida racked her brains, trying to think back for any clue, any sign she had missed that would have told her what Ellen was planning. With a gasp she clutched at his arm. 'Richard! She was talking to your great-aunt about a special licence. That means they only have to hide out somewhere for a week!'

'They would still have to convince a priest that she is of age. And even then the marriage would be illegal.'

'But the damage will have been done.' Phyllida bit her lip. 'She will be ruined. Oh, who can have persuaded her to embark upon this outrageous scheme? I would like to think it is a young man who truly loves Ellen, but I very much fear it is someone who has designs upon her fortune.'

'Someone like me, perhaps?'

She said quietly, 'I no longer think you want Ellen for her fortune.' It was true. His concern for Ellen argued that he cared a great deal for her. Her hands were locked together so tightly it was almost painful. 'My biggest worry is that it might be Sir Charles Urmston.'

'Urmston left Bath yesterday morning,' he told her. 'Let me put your mind at rest on one point, Phyllida. Whoever it may be, if he does not make Ellen happy then he shall answer to me. She shall not be tied to him, even if I have to make her a widow to prevent it.'

So there it was. Even through her anxiety for Ellen she could feel her heart breaking.

They continued in silence, until they reached the village of Atford, where the road forked. Richard pulled up outside the church. Phyllida looked at the diverging roads and beat her fist upon her skirts in frustration.

'Which way now?'

There was an ancient sitting on the low wall of the church grounds and Richard hailed him. A few moments' conversation elicited the information that a travelling carriage, heavily laden and travelling at speed, had driven through the village a short while earlier, on the Devizes road. As they set off again Richard glanced across at Phyllida. Her face was pale and strained and he reached out to put one hand over hers.

'Don't worry, we are closing on them.'

He felt her tremble and she said in a low voice, 'After this, sir, I c-cannot doubt your devotion to Ellen. If…if we can save her from this folly, and if she wants you, Richard, then I shall not stand in your way.'

'If she—' He broke off, requiring both hands and his concentration to control the team as they approached a bend. Once they were on the straight he declared, 'Confound it, Phyllida, what are you saying? Ellen does not look upon me as anything more than a friend. And it is certainly not Ellen I want.'

'How can you say that, when you have spent the past month pursuing her?'

'I put my name to that preposterous wager, but it did not take me long to realise I had made a mistake.' He glanced down at her. 'You have no confidence in your own charms, Phyllida!'

She sat up straight, wondering if she dare believe what she was hearing. Could he truly love her? There was no time to consider that now. They were driving into Melksham and her eyes alighted upon a dusty travelling carriage standing before a large coaching inn.

'There they are!'

Richard drew up behind the carriage and almost before they had come to a stand Phyllida jumped down and ran inside.

'Where are the occupants of that coach?' she demanded of the landlord, who was emerging from the noisy taproom. If he was surprised to be addressed so abruptly he did not show it, merely waved his hand towards a door at the far end of the corridor.

'In there, ma'am. It's a private parlour.'

With Richard hard on her heels Phyllida burst into the room, only to stop so quickly that Richard all but cannoned into her. She felt his hand on her shoulder, but whether it was to stop himself from colliding with her, or as support for the scene before them, she did not know.

Ellen, a picture in pale blue, was standing by the window and sitting in an armchair beside her was Lady Hune.

'You see,' declared Ellen, smiling, 'I told you they would come.'

Obedient to the pressure of the hand on her shoulder, Phyllida moved into the room. She heard Richard close the door behind them.

'Perhaps one of you would be good enough to explain what the *devil* is going on here?' she demanded angrily.

Ellen moved towards the table at the centre of the room, waving her hands towards the food and drink that covered its surface.

'Do sit down and take some refreshment with us,' she said. 'We made sure you would be hungry after your journey. And we deliberately ordered that the coach should be left outside and not be brought into the yard, so you really couldn't miss us.'

'I think, Lady Phyllida, that we have been duped,' remarked Richard. He guided Phyllida to a chair and gently pushed her down. 'And very neatly, too.'

Ellen beamed at him.

'I knew if you saw me running away you would go to Philly.'

'Do you mean there is no elopement?' said Phyllida. 'But what of the fashionable gentleman seen at the turnpikes?'

'One of Lady Hune's footmen,' replied Ellen. 'It is surprising how easily people can be fooled by seeing a fashionable hat and coat upon a man.'

'And may I ask where you obtained this hat and coat?' asked Richard calmly.

He was sitting beside Phyllida at the table, holding her fingers in a sustaining grasp with one hand while with the other he filled two wine-glasses. She herself could think of nothing to say.

For the moment, relief at finding Ellen safe and well had replaced her anger.

'We borrowed those from your room,' explained the dowager. 'I am afraid I had to coerce your valet into agreeing to help us, but I do not think he was too reluctant, for you have been going around like a bear with a sore head for the past week.'

'And so will Fritt have a sore head, when I have finished with him,' he muttered. 'How *dare* he allow himself to be embroiled in your harebrained scheme, Sophia!'

'Oh, pray do not blame Lady Hune,' said Ellen quickly. 'This was all my idea. Ever since we returned from Shrewton Lodge I have been trying to hit upon a way to get the two of you together. I was very much afraid that Phyllida and I would go off to Tatham and you, Richard, would return to London and take up your rakish life again.'

'Ellen!'

'I beg your pardon for my plain speaking, Philly, but it is true, and Lady Hune agreed with me. As Mrs Ackroyd says, desperate times call for desperate measures, and I knew if you thought I had eloped you would both come after me. I did think of running off with Mr Tesford or Mr Fullingham, but when I suggested it to Lady Hune she thought that would not be wise.'

'After what happened with Fullingham in the

Denhams' garden I am very glad you didn't,' retorted Phyllida. A sip of the wine Richard had poured for her was having its effect and she was beginning to feel a little better.

'But then I was not prepared,' argued Ellen. 'This time I would have made sure I had my hatpin ready to use, if necessary. However, then Lady Hune suggested we should make it a sham elopement.'

'I fear we have shocked you, Lady Phyllida,' said Sophia, smiling a little.

'Nothing your family does could shock me,' retorted Phyllida bitterly. 'After all you are an Arrandale, ma'am, are you not?'

'I am, and proud of it. And I think Ellen will make a wonderful addition to the family—as Richard's stepdaughter, of course.'

Phyllida's breath caught in her throat. Richard was still holding one of her hands and she felt his fingers tighten.

'Lady Phyllida has not yet agreed to marry me.'

'But she will,' replied Lady Sophia. 'The two of you have been smelling of April and May for weeks. *I* think she could do better for herself, but if she wants to ally herself to an Arrandale you are amongst the best, Richard.'

He shook his head, saying unsteadily, 'Great-Aunt Sophia, your encomium almost unmans me.'

Phyllida's lips twitched as she met his eyes and saw the lurking laughter in his own.

'Damned with faint praise, I think.'

'Exactly.' He lifted her fingers and kissed them. 'So now you know what my family think of me, will you do me the honour of accepting my hand and my heart? Will you make an honest man of me?'

The world stood still, waiting for her answer. Phyllida knew Ellen and Sophia were holding their breath and she saw the hint of a shadow in Richard's smile, as if he too was uncertain. She smiled.

'Yes, I will accept your offer, Richard. Gladly, and with all my heart.'

A collective sigh went around the room. Phyllida kept her eyes on Richard's face, saw his smile deepen, the flash of fire in his eyes, the promise of desire that set her body tingling.

He pulled her close and kissed her lips. Sophia tutted and Ellen gave a little squeal of delight, but he ignored them both, murmuring for her alone, 'I will do my best to make sure you never have cause to regret it.'

'You may wish to use this.' Sophia's voice recalled them to their situation. She was holding up a paper. 'It is a special licence. The church and parson are waiting for you across the road. And we are not twenty miles from Shrewton.

Since I went to all the trouble to make the Lodge ready for visitors you might wish to use it for your honeymoon. You need not worry about Ellen, Phyllida. I shall take her back to Royal Crescent with me and send for her maid to join us—after she has packed up your trunk and sent it on to Shrewton, of course. So there is no hurry for you both to return.'

Richard gave a crack of laughter.

'You have worked it all out between you, have you not?'

'Of course,' said Ellen, twinkling. 'I said when I came to Bath that we might find Philly a husband, although I was very much afraid she would set her heart on one of the dull, worthy kind.'

Lady Hune laughed. 'There is nothing dull or worthy about Richard!' She pushed herself out of her seat. 'Now, shall we go to the church?'

The wedding passed off without incident. Lady Hune had had the forethought to bring a wedding ring, a heavy plain band that she explained had belonged to some distant ancestor and if the reverend gentleman who conducted the service had any reservations he was far too in awe of a dowager marchioness in his church to voice them. Sophia carried Ellen back to Bath immediately after the ceremony, leaving Richard and his new bride to make their way to Shrewton Lodge.

'Happy?' he asked Phyllida as they bowled out of the town in the afternoon sunshine.

'Yes, of course. But it has all happened so fast.'

'I beg your pardon,' he said quickly. 'I have rushed you, I should have waited until we could arrange a more fitting wedding.'

'No, no,' she assured him. 'I have had one wedding with all the pomp and ceremony, I do not wish for another.'

'Truly?' He reached for her hand.

'*Truly.*' She smiled, 'But are you happy, Richard?'

'Happier than I can say. It has all worked out so well, especially for Sophia. Ellen has helped her to overcome her sadness at Cassie's elopement, and you have fulfilled her wish that I should become a respectable married man.' He squeezed her fingers. 'And I mean to be very respectable, my love!'

Her smile could not be contained. 'Do you? Now that *will* be a challenge!'

He grinned. 'Witch!' Richard returned both hands to the reins as he said cheerfully, 'Ellen will live with us, of course. Sophia is already hinting that she will come to London to help with her come-out next year. I hope you will not object to that?'

'No, no, not in the least! Oh, dear, I fear I

should have thought of all these things before I married you.'

'How could you? When we set out this morning you had no idea that we were to be married. I hope you will not regret it, Phyllida. I shall do everything in my power to make you happy, I promise you.'

'I believe you will,' she murmured. She tucked her hand in his arm and rested her head on his shoulder. 'But life will be very different for you, too, my love.'

'I am looking forward to it,' he said. 'Marriage to you will go a long way to restoring my family's name.'

'I will help you to achieve that in any way I can.' She paused. 'What of Arrandale?'

'Until I have proof that Wolf is dead I must continue to maintain the house for his return. I am sorry to say it will limit my own funds, but we shall get by, with a little prudent management.'

'Of course we shall. And my money will help.'

'Ah, I had forgotten about that!'

'You do not sound very pleased.'

'I am not. Everyone will say I married you for your money.'

'Let them. You did not give it a thought, did you?'

'No, Sophia mentioned it, but—' Swearing under his breath, Richard brought the curricle to a halt and turned to face her. He grabbed her shoulders. 'Do you not realise that you have married me without making any provision, any settlement to protect yourself?'

'How could I?' she said, turning his earlier words back upon him. 'When I set out this morning I did not know we were to be married.' She smiled and put one hand up to his cheek. 'I am content, my love. It is a measure of how much I trust you.'

Her fingers slipped around his neck and she gently pulled his head down until their lips met in a deep, lingering kiss that only ended when a mail coach rattled past and they heard the catcalls and whistles from the passengers.

They broke apart, Richard cursing under his breath as Phyllida hid her face in his shoulder.

'I beg your pardon.' His arm tightened protectively about her. 'I am a devil to expose you to such ribaldry—'

'No, no.' She raised her head, her countenance alight with laughter. 'I am not at all upset, I assure you. Was it so very bad?'

He grinned at her. 'Quite scandalous, my love.'

As they set off again she said thoughtfully, 'Well, I think it is possibly the most outrageous thing I have ever done in my life, but I suppose I shall have to get used to it, now I am an Arrandale.'

'Not at all. I intend that we shall be the very model of respectability.'

'What, all the time?'

Greatly daring, she placed her hand on his thigh and her heart raced when she heard his growled response.

'That might be a little too much to expect.'

Laughing, she settled down beside him for the drive to Shrewton Lodge, where it was clear they were expected. The housekeeper was at the door to welcome them.

'We have no butler here, sir, Mr Croft having gone back to Bath with Lady Hune, but I think Hinton and I can manage.'

'I have no doubt of it,' replied Richard. 'You have always done a magnificent job in the past when I have come here to stay. You always spoil me.'

'Now give over, Master Richard,' protested Mrs Hinton, clearly pleased. 'We will do our best, as you well know. And I believe your groom and valet, and my lady's maid, will be joining you here before the day's out.'

'That is so,' agreed Richard. 'Which bedchamber have you prepared for us?'

'Lady Hune instructed that the Blue room should be prepared for you—'

'Then we shall go there directly and, er, rest.' He took Phyllida's hand and led her up the stairs.

'Richard we cannot disappear immediately!' hissed Phyllida, as soon as the housekeeper was out of earshot.

'Oh, yes, we can.' His grip on her hand tightened and he led her through the corridors to a large room that smelled of beeswax and lemons. 'The Hintons have clearly been busy here.'

Phyllida dropped her bonnet on a chair and moved towards the large canopied bed, running her hands over the hangings, rich blue silk embroidered with silver thread.

'It is quite beautiful.'

'No, *you* are beautiful.' Richard put his hands on her shoulders and turned her to face him. 'I saw it that very first time I danced with you at Almack's. I *do* remember it, I assure you.'

She shook her head.

'No, I was too shy and awkward.'

'At first, perhaps, but you were such a graceful dancer, and you have a goodness and sweetness of temper that give you an inner beauty.' He put his fingers under her chin and gently eased it up so she was obliged to meet his eyes. 'Since then you have gained in confidence. You now have elegance and poise, too. You are quite, quite perfect.'

He kissed her then, his blood stirring when she put her arms around his neck and returned his embrace, tangling her tongue with his own. He was aware of the change as her body pressed against him and she drove her hands through his hair, holding him to her. Impatience overcame them both, their kisses grew more heated and they began to scrabble at each other's clothes, tearing at buttons, strings and ribbons, shrugging off sleeves, shirts, gowns while continuing to share those frantic, excited kisses that set the body aflame.

At last they broke apart and Phyllida stared at Richard's naked torso, her mouth drying at the sight of the sculpted contours, the wide shoulders and narrowing waist, all she could see since the rest of his delicious body was still encased in buckskin breeches. She reached out for him, wanting to run her fingers through the dark smattering of hair that covered his chest but he caught her hand and spun her around.

'No,' he growled. 'Not until we have you out of those damned stays. '

She laughed then, a warm, guttural sound that was strange to her own ears. It sounded so...so confident, so powerful. She felt a slow vibration through her body as he pulled out the ribbons from the corset that confined her. He went slowly, drawing the ribbon out of each eyelet with infinite care, his fingers brushing against the fine linen shift beneath as he gradually released her from her cage of whalebone. Her skin tingled, she ached to be free, to turn and press herself against his body but he was intent on unlacing her completely. Unable to bear the wait, she gave a little sigh of exasperation.

'Can you not go any faster?'

'I could.' His mouth descended to her shoulder and he gave it a little nip. 'But there is no hurry.'

Her body told her differently, but she forced herself to keep still, felt the desire pooling in her belly, the growing ache between her thighs. She put back her head and moaned softly as he continued to unlace her while his mouth trailed a line of kisses down her neck. Then the stays were gone, but now his arms imprisoned her. His hands came around to cup her breasts, only the thin shift remained between their hot bodies. He pushed her forward slightly and she put out her hands to support herself on the bed.

'Stay there.'

Dazed, languorous with desire she remained there, staring at the patterned bedcover. She heard the soft scuffle as Richard shed his boots and buckskins and then he came close and removed her shift in one smooth movement. She almost swooned with excitement as she felt his naked body on her back, skin on skin. His hands came around her again, caressing her breasts, thumbs circling the dark peaks until they swelled and hardened while he pressed himself against her buttocks. He was kissing her neck, nipping and sucking, drawing from her soft moans of excitement. He moved one hand down, caressed her waist, smoothed over her hips and then his fingers slid between the soft curls at the apex of her thighs, seeking out her hot, aching core.

She gasped as her body responded.

'Richard—'

'Hush,' he murmured the word against her neck as he continued to kiss her, sending little darts of pleasure deep into her body.

'But I want to, to pleasure you, too.'

'And you shall, but this is for you. Trust me.'

I do!

She was leaning further over the bed while his fingers drove into her, teasing, drawing up the desire that flamed inside. It was rippling out from her core, she was no longer in control. Her hips pushed back towards him. Instinctively she was offering herself to him while all the time those tantalising fingers worked their magic. She felt herself opening, aching, and then as his fingers drew back he entered her, gently but inexorably filling her. She gave a joyful cry, then gasped as his fingers continued to play her, one hand circling and caressing her breast while the other stroked and teased to a frenzy the sensitive nub between her thighs.

She was crying out now, every measured thrust Richard made carrying her higher. She was flying, soaring. Unable to take him in her arms her body gripped him and they moved together in perfect harmony until the moment when his hands slid to her hips and he held her firm. She gave a tiny cry of triumph as he spent himself within her.

Exhausted, they crawled into the bed and Richard pulled the covers over them.

'Oh, I did not *know*...' she breathed as he took her into his arms. 'I would never have thought it could be so, so wonderful. Thank you.'

He laughed softy against her hair. 'It has never been like that for me before.' He sought her lips and kissed her. 'It must be because we are joined in love.'

'Is that it?' She cupped his cheek, gazing into the face that was now so dear to her. She felt sated, joyously happy and she could not help teasing him. 'Do you think you can be happy then, as a respectable, married man?'

His eyes narrowed.

'We may look respectable to the rest of the world, madam wife, but here in the bedchamber I think we will be quite scandalous!'

The look he gave her sent the desire curling up inside her once more and she shivered with delicious anticipation.

She said innocently, 'But I thought you had reformed, sir.'

With a growl he reached out and pulled her to him and Phyllida gave herself up to the pleasurable task of discovering just how wrong she was.

* * * * *

*This is the first story in
Sarah Mallory's brand new Regency quartet,*
THE INFAMOUS ARRANDALES.
*Look for further books in the series,
coming soon!*

MILLS & BOON®

Why not subscribe?

Never miss a title and save money too!

Here's what's available to you if you join the exclusive **Mills & Boon Book Club** today:

✦ *Titles up to a month ahead of the shops*
✦ *Amazing discounts*
✦ *Free P&P*
✦ *Earn Bonus Book points that can be redeemed against other titles and gifts*
✦ *Choose from monthly or pre-paid plans*

Still want more?

Well, if you join today we'll even give you
50% OFF your first parcel!

So visit **www.millsandboon.co.uk/subs**
or call Customer Relations on 020 8288 2888
to be a part of this exclusive Book Club!

SUBS_2014

MILLS & BOON®

HISTORICAL

AWAKEN THE ROMANCE OF THE PAST
